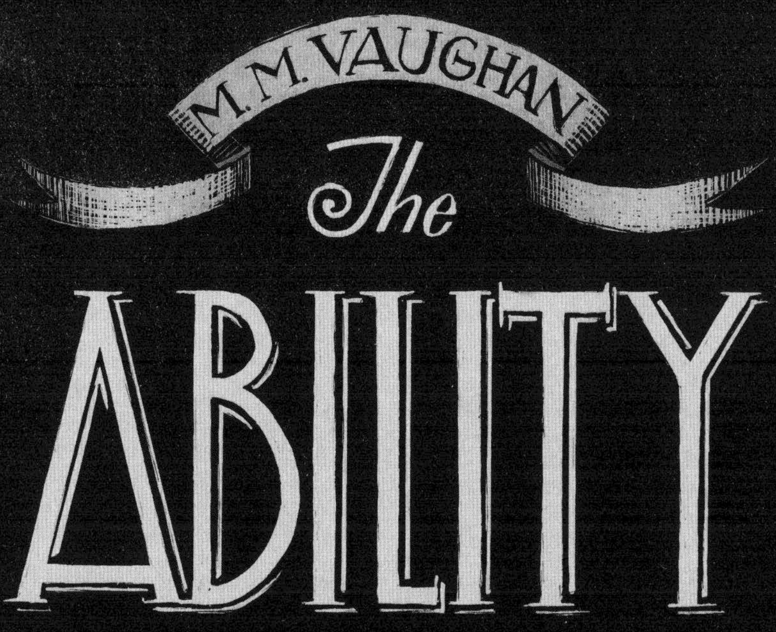

Margaret K. McElderry Books
NEW YORK LONDON TORONTO SYDNEY NEW DELHI

Many thanks to the following people: Stephanie Thwaites and Tina Wexler. Ruta Rimas, Courtney Bongiolatti, and the team at Simon & Schuster. My family and friends who read this first, especially Joanna McCracken, Alex O'Brien, and Laura McCuaig. And Mark.

MARGARET K. McELDERRY BOOKS
An imprint of Simon & Schuster Children's Publishing Division
1230 Avenue of the Americas, New York, New York 10020

Book design by Krista Vossen
The text for this book is set in Garamond MT.
Manufactured in the United States of America
0313 FFG
2 4 6 8 10 9 7 5 3 1
Library of Congress Cataloging-in-Publication Data
Vaughan, M. M.
The Ability / M. M. Vaughan ; [illustrations by Iacopo Bruno].—1st ed.
p. cm.
Summary: While Chris and five other twelve-year-olds learn to make the most of their mental abilities in a secret, government-run school last used in 1977, twins Ernest and Mort are studying under someone with much more sinister motives.
ISBN 978-1-4424-5200-8 (hardcover)
ISBN 978-1-4424-5202-2 (eBook)
[1. Psychic ability—Fiction. 2. Schools—Fiction. 3. Espionage—Fiction. 4. England—Fiction. 5. Science fiction.] I. Bruno, Iacopo, ill. II. Title.
PZ7.V4518Abi 2013
[Fic]—dc23
2012006613

For Emilia

. PROLOGUE .

Thirty Years Ago

"I have a bad feeling about this," said Edward, tapping his foot nervously. The sound of his shoe hitting the metal floor of the van echoed all about the enclosed space, masking the sound of the waves that crashed furiously at the foot of the cliffs that stood not far from where they were parked. *Tap. Tap. Tap.*

Anna gave Edward a warning look as their teacher, Mr. Cecil Humphries, turned round from the driver's seat, his face red with anger.

"Stop that right now or I'll throw your shoes out of the window."

Edward didn't say anything, but the tapping stopped. Mr. Humphries turned to Miss Arabella Magenta, sitting next to him in the passenger seat, and sighed.

"Honestly, what have I done to deserve this? As soon as this year is over, I'm moving to the country—as far away from any brats as possible."

"We can hear you, sir."

"Good," said Mr. Humphries, without looking back.

Anna said nothing as the four other children whispered around her. She felt the anxiety of the group deeply and hoped the mission would end quickly so that they could return to their school, far away from this desolate, dark landscape.

At that moment, exactly as their carefully planned schedule dictated, Mr. Bentley Jones was carrying the briefcase full of money toward the cottage by the cliff. Their view of the cottage was hidden by the wall of trees behind which they had parked the van, but Anna could see exactly what was happening—it was her and Clarissa's job that night to use their Ability to keep an eye on their teacher.

"Mr. Jones is nearly at the cottage. There's a light on in the window."

"Good," said Miss Magenta. "As soon as he's inside, we'll get out and move closer."

"Why do we have to get out? Can't we just do it from here?" asked Danny nervously.

"For goodness' sake, we've gone over this a thousand times," said Miss Magenta, looking exasperated. "If we're going to wipe the minds of these people, then we need to be within twenty feet of them."

"Can't we just give them the money?" asked Danny.

Anna, Edward, Clarissa, and Richard all nodded in agreement.

"Don't be ridiculous," said Mr. Humphries. "It will only be a short time before they ask for more, and then when will it stop? If we don't want people to find out about the Ability—and believe me, we don't—then we have to use Inferno on them. It's the only way."

"But we've never even practiced it—what if it doesn't work?" asked Clarissa.

"It will," said Miss Magenta, irritated. "It's been tried out in Italy, where the rules are more relaxed, and it worked just fine. Where is he now?"

Anna and Clarissa remembered what they were supposed to be doing and closed their eyes.

"He's not there yet—probably another minute."

Anna kept her eyes closed and watched Bentley Jones striding forward, head bowed low as he fought his way through the invisible wall that the vicious wind and rain had created.

"Don't do that!"

Anna opened her eyes and saw Richard, who was almost twice the size of the other two boys, flicking screwed-up pieces of paper resting on his knee in the direction of Danny.

"What? I'm bored," said Richard, seeing the look of disapproval on Miss Magenta's face.

Anna sighed and closed her eyes. They had been classmates for just over five months, and she was only slightly less irritated by Richard than she had been on day one, when he had spent the entire morning pulling her long braid of black hair and then laughing hysterically. Clarissa had told her it was a sure sign that Richard liked her—a thought that made Anna's stomach turn. The other two boys, however, Danny and Edward, had become her close friends. Edward was serious and calm, always trying to keep the peace between Richard and whoever he was irritating on any particular day; Danny, on the other hand, was sweet and clumsy, his head always stuck in a book.

"He's coming up to the door," said Clarissa. Everybody stopped and looked over at the two girls.

"Right, get ready to jump out. As soon as Mr. Jones gives the signal, you're all to leave the van and wait for our instructions. Understood?"

They nodded.

"Good. What's happening now?"

"He's knocking on the door. It's opening . . . It's . . . it's . . . an old lady in a dressing gown?"

"How strange. It's not exactly the image of a blackmailer that I had in mind," said Mr. Humphries to a similarly bemused-looking Miss Magenta.

"She's asking him if he's okay. Mr. Jones is holding up the briefcase," said Anna, trying to explain everything in as much detail as possible. "She's asked him if he'd like to come inside and warm himself up."

"And now?" asked Miss Magenta.

"He's gone inside, and there's a man there. An old man smoking a pipe. He's turning off the radio and walking over to Mr. Jones. They're shaking hands."

"What's the old lady doing?"

"She's putting the kettle on."

The group watched the girls intently as they took it in turns to describe the scene in detail. The old woman prepared the tea and carried the three steaming mugs over to the sofa on which Bentley Jones was now sitting.

"Mr. Jones says he's here to hand over the money. . . ."

"Yes?"

There was a pause.

"The lady said she doesn't know what he's talking about."

"Something's wrong. Something's very, very wrong," said Mr. Humphries, rubbing his hand across his greasy, thinning hair.

"I think we should get out and—"

Mr. Humphries was interrupted by the sound of the back doors swinging open. Two men in black hoods appeared before them. Anna, who up until that point had been watching the cottage in her mind, was taken completely by surprise. She screamed as the men reached inside and grabbed her, pulling her out onto the ground.

"It's a trap!"

Anna spun her head round in the direction of the voice and saw the figure of Bentley Jones rushing back toward the van.

The men grabbed her by the arms and legs and lifted her easily, then sped off in the direction of the cliffs, as she wrestled them in vain.

Danny looked about him at the others, all frozen in shock.

"Anna!"

He leaped out of the van before anybody could stop him and ran off in the direction of the men, the teachers and pupils following behind him.

Anna screamed as she watched Danny running to try to catch them, and then suddenly, without speaking, the men stopped. Anna watched as one of them moved his right arm around and lifted it up above her head. It took a moment for her to work out what she was looking at.

"He's got a gun! Danny, stop!"

Her voice was drowned out by the sound of a single shot fired. Anna watched as Danny fell to the ground. The men began to run again toward the cliffs, holding Anna tightly as she sobbed and tried to turn and twist her way free. Suddenly Anna remembered her Ability and closed her eyes, but it was too late. The men stopped and swung her backward, then forward, and released her. She flew up into the air, over the cliff's edge. The last thing that Anna saw, before she lost consciousness, was the black water of the sea looming closer.

"Quick, where's the knife?" said a deep voice that sent a chill down Anna's spine.

Anna opened her eyes and grimaced at the throbbing pain in her head. The ground she was on was moving and she realized that she was on a boat. It was pitch-black except for the light from a flashlight, resting next to her on the deck. She was lying down, her arms and legs tied, her clothes soaked and clinging to her skin. She shivered, then noticed that she was no longer wearing her jacket, which was now in the hands of a woman sitting at her feet. The woman passed the knife over Anna's head to a gloved hand.

Anna screamed as the man took her arm. She felt the blade cut slowly into her and then the sting as the pain began to register. Blood dripped down from her arm as Anna cried, tears running down from her emerald green eyes, and the woman leaned over to wipe her arm with the jacket.

"That's enough. Throw it into the sea. They'll find it in the morning."

"Why are you doing this?" asked Anna.

"Because, my dear, you and that Ability of yours are going to make us very rich indeed."

"They'll find me," said Anna, sobbing. "You won't get away with this."

"Oh, I don't think they'll look very hard. You'll be easily replaced."

"You don't know what you're talking about. They're my friends; they won't leave me."

"Look up."

Anna stopped crying and looked up. The cliffs loomed high ahead of them, and she could make out the light from the cottage window. Something near the building moved, and she squinted to try to make out what it was.

"That's right—that's the van you came in, with all your so-called friends inside, and it looks like they're leaving.

They've given up already," said the man, laughing.

Anna watched helplessly as the van drove off into the black night. It was at that moment that she realized the true hopelessness of her situation, and she began to scream, the sound of her anguish lost within the howling of the heavy storm winds.

. CHAPTER ONE .

Wednesday, October 17

Cecil Humphries, the government minister for education, despised most things, amongst them:

Cyclists.

The seaside.

Being called by his first name.

Weddings.

The color yellow.

Singing.

But at the top of this list was children. He *hated* them, which was rather unfortunate given that he was in charge of the well-being of every child in Britain. He knew, however, that the public was rather fond of them, for some reason he couldn't fathom, and so he had reluctantly accepted the position, sure that it would boost his flagging popularity and take him one step closer toward his ultimate goal: to take the job of his old school friend Prime Minister Edward Banks. Unfortunately for him, the public was far more perceptive than he gave them credit for, and kissing a couple of babies' heads (then wiping his mouth afterward) had resulted only in a series of frustrating headlines, including:

HUMPHRIES LOVES BABIES
(BUT HE COULDN'T EAT A WHOLE ONE)

The more he tried to improve his image, the more it backfired on him, which only intensified his hatred of anybody under the age of eighteen, if that were at all possible.

It was only fitting, therefore, that the person who would ruin his career and leave him a quivering wreck in a padded cell for the rest of his life would be a twelve-year-old boy.

The beginning of the end for Cecil Humphries began on an uncharacteristically warm, sunny day in Liverpool. It had been four days since he had been photographed by a well-placed paparazzo stealing chocolate from the hospital bedside of a sick child and only two days since he had been pelted with eggs and flour when the photograph appeared on the front page of every newspaper in the country. Even for someone well accustomed to bad press, this had been a particularly awful week.

Humphries looked out of the window of his chauffeured car, saw the smiling children, and sighed.

"Never work with animals or children. Anyone ever tell you that?" he grumbled. James, his assistant, looked up from his notes, nodded obediently, and said nothing, as he had learned to do.

"Different school, same brats," he continued as the car pulled up outside the school entrance. "It's like reliving the same nightmare every single time: a disgusting mass of grubby hands, crying, and runny noses."

He took out a comb from his jacket pocket and ran it through what remained of his hair.

"You know which ones wind me up the most, though?"

"No, sir," said James.

"The cute ones. Can't stand them, with their big eyes and irritating questions." He shuddered at the thought. "Do try to keep those ones away from me today, would you? I'm really not in the mood." Humphries adjusted his dark blue tie and leaned over to open the car door.

"What's the name of this cesspit?" he asked as he pulled back the door handle.

"Perrington School, sir. I briefed you about it earlier."

"Yes, well, I wasn't listening. Tell me now," said Humphries, irritated.

"You're presenting them with an award for excellence. Also, we've invited the press to follow you around while you tour the school and talk to the children. It'll be a good opportunity for the public to see you in a more, um, positive light. And we've been promised a very warm welcome," explained James.

Humphries rolled his eyes.

"Right. Well, let's get it over and done with," he said, opening the car door to a reception of obedient clapping and flashing cameras.

• • •

The teacher walked into the staff room and found Humphries and James sitting alone on the pair of brown plastic chairs that had been provided for them in the corner of the room.

"I am terribly sorry about that," said the teacher, handing Humphries a tissue from the box she had brought in with her.

Humphries gave a tight smile and stood up. He took the tissue and tried, in vain, to dry the large damp patch of snot on the front of his jacket.

"No need to apologize. I thought they were all utterly charming," he said with as much enthusiasm as he could muster.

"Well, that's very understanding of you. He must really like you—I've never seen him run up and hug a complete stranger before! I hope it didn't distract you too much from the performance."

"No, not at all," he said, handing James the wet tissue. James took it from him, paused to look around, and, not seeing a bin anywhere, reluctantly put it away in his pocket.

"They've been working on that for the last three weeks," said the teacher proudly. "I'm so glad you liked it. Anything in particular that stood out for you?" she asked.

Humphries hesitated and looked to James who gave a barely visible shrug.

"Yes. Well, the whole thing was marvelous," he said. The teacher waited for him to elaborate.

Humphries considered telling her that the best bit was when it finished, then quickly thought better of it.

"Hmm. Ah. Yes, I know. I rather enjoyed the part where the donkey hit the angel on the head. I thought the little girl's tears were most believable."

"Oh. Well, that really wasn't planned," she said, and quickly changed the subject. "Hopefully, the senior pupils will be a little less unpredictable. We've assembled everybody in the hall. There'll be about three hundred students there."

"And the press?"

"Yes, they're all there. We've set up an area for the cameras and journalists at the side of the hall."

"Good, good," said Humphries, looking genuinely pleased for once. "Shall we go through?"

"Yes, of course. Follow me," said the teacher. She led them out of the room, down the brightly decorated corridor, and through the double doors to face the waiting assembly of students.

Humphries walked in first. He stopped, smiled, and waved slowly, taking in the surroundings. The large hall was packed with children sitting on the wooden floor, all smartly dressed in their maroon uniforms, and the teachers sat in chairs that ran along both sides of the hall, positioned so that they could shoot disapproving glances at any pupil daring to misbehave. Humphries spotted the press area at the front and made his way toward them slowly, a wide, false smile on his face, stopping along the way to shake the hands of students, never taking his eyes off the cameras. He climbed a small set of steps and took a seat at the side of the stage. The headmistress took this as her cue and made her way to the podium.

"Ladies and gentlemen, boys and girls, it is my pleasure today to welcome Cecil Humphries, the education minister, to our school. Receiving this award is, without a doubt, the single greatest honor that has been bestowed on the school in its one-hundred-twenty-four-year history. Established as an orphanage by Lord Harold . . ."

Humphries stifled a yawn, cocked his head, and tried his best to look interested as the headmistress began a twenty-minute history of the school and its achievements. He felt his eyes grow heavy, but, just as he thought he might not be able to stay awake a second longer, the headmistress turned to face him. He quickly sat up and straightened his tie.

". . . and so I'd like you all to put your hands together for our esteemed guest, Mr. Cecil Humphries."

Another round of applause, and Humphries approached the podium. He looked over at the headmistress and gave her his warmest smile (which would be better described as a grimace), then turned back to the audience and cleared his throat.

"Thank you so much for that wonderful introduction. One of the most pleasurable aspects of my job as education minister is to visit schools and see the wonderful achievements of pupils and staff. Today has been no exception, and I thank you all for the warm reception you have given me. It is—"

Humphries was interrupted by a loud ringing sound in his ears. He shook his head and coughed, but the noise persisted. Looking up, Humphries saw the audience watching him expectantly. He tried to ignore the sound and leaned forward toward the microphone.

"Excuse me," he said, louder than necessary. "As I was saying, it is—" He stopped again. The high-pitched whining was getting louder, and he was finding it difficult to hear himself speak.

"I'm sorry, I seem to—"

He felt his ears start to throb in pain. He clutched his head and pressed at the side of his temples, but the noise kept rising in volume and seemed to expand and press against his skull until he thought it might explode. He reeled backward, struggling to stay standing. Out of the corner of his eye he saw James making his way toward the stage in a half run with a concerned look on his face. The pain was getting worse, and he felt the blood start to rush to his head. He struggled to look calm, aware that the cameras were rolling, but the pressure was building up against his eyes until his eyeballs started pushing out against their sockets. He put his arm out and felt for the side of the podium to try to steady himself, but the room started to spin, and he fell to the ground. He tried to push himself up, but sharp, stabbing pains began to spread across his whole body, each one as if a knife were being pushed into him and then turned slowly.

And then, as suddenly as it had begun, the ringing stopped. Humphries looked around, dazed, and slowly stood up, trying to gather his composure. He heard the sound of a child laughing, and the expression on his face turned from confusion to fury.

"Who is that?" he asked. *"Who is laughing?"*

Humphries looked out at the audience as the laughter increased in volume, but all he could see were shocked faces.

He turned and saw that James was beside him.

"Nobody is laughing, sir. I think we need to leave," whispered James, but Humphries didn't hear him, as the sound of the child's laughter was joined by the laughter of what sounded like a hundred others.

"They're all laughing. *Stop laughing!*" screamed Humphries at the stunned crowd, but instead the sound got increasingly louder until it became unbearable. He fell to the ground once more, his hands clutching his head, the veins on his forehead throbbing intensely from the pressure.

"Arghhh . . . HELP ME!" he shouted, his fear of dying overriding any embarrassment he might have felt at such a public lack of composure.

He looked up and saw a mass of flashing bulbs coming from the press photographers' pen to his right. Struggling, he turned his head slowly away, his face twisted in agony, and searched the crowd for somebody who could do something to help him. At the front, a teacher stood up and appeared to start shouting for help. All about her, children were crying in fear as they watched Humphries begin to roll around on the floor in agonizing pain, but the sound of them was drowned out by the unbearable noise of children laughing in his head. He felt his temperature begin to rise suddenly and watched helplessly as his hands started to turn purple. Desperately, he looked down from the stage for help and caught the eye of a pale young boy sitting in the front row below him, cross-legged and staring intently at him with an expressionless face.

Humphries froze. It was at that moment, with a sudden jolt of clarity, that he realized what was happening, and panic swept over him. Using all the strength he could muster, he pulled himself to his feet, and, eyes wide with terror and face a mottled purple, he jumped down from the stage and collapsed on the ground as the children in the front row scrambled to get away. The only child who remained was the pale boy in the crisp new uniform, who sat perfectly still and maintained a steady gaze as Humphries crawled forward in his direction, screaming unintelligibly, and then slowly raised his hands toward the boy's neck. Worry turned to panic as the crowd realized that Humphries was about to attack the child. The headmistress sprang into action, hitched her skirt up, and jumped down from the stage, grabbing the young boy by his shirt collar and dragging him out of harm's reach. Humphries raised his head slowly and turned to face the cameras. He opened his mouth and screamed,

"INFERNO!"

As soon as the word left his lips, Humphries collapsed to the ground, his eyes open but expressionless, his body quivering in fear, just as he would remain for the rest of his life.

CHAPTER TWO

Later that day

One hundred and eighty miles away, in central London, director general of MI5 Sir Bentley Jones turned away from the image on the television of Cecil Humphries being stretchered out of the school and sighed deeply. He walked over to the large window overlooking the river and looked up at the darkening sky above him, which mirrored the sense of unease that he was feeling. He stood motionless for a few minutes and watched the gray swirls of cloud gather above him, before a knock on the door shook him from his thoughts. He turned to watch as his secretary opened the door.

"Sir . . . ," she said, holding up a thick manila folder.

Sir Bentley nodded and mumbled a quiet thank-you as he took the folder from her. He watched silently as she left the room and closed the door. It was only then that he looked down at the folder in his hands, a folder that he had hoped never to see again, and read the thick black lettering on the faded label, which he himself had written thirty years earlier: INFERNO.

CHAPTER THREE

Wednesday, October 31

Christopher Lane sat in his usual chair in the school office and waited nervously, his class teacher staring at him intently from the seat opposite as if he might try to make a run for it at any time—which, to be fair, had crossed his mind. It was only Wednesday, and yet this was the third time this week that Chris had found himself sitting here, waiting for the headmaster to call his name. This time, however, he knew that the matter would have far more serious consequences.

Across the short corridor, and as yet unaware of the presence of his least favorite pupil, the porcine Mr. Tuckdown, headmaster at Black Marsh Secondary School for the last fourteen years, was looking forward to relaxing in his office with a cup of tea, that morning's crossword, and a ginger biscuit or two. Or three. Mr. Tuckdown sighed contentedly, slicked down the strands of greasy hair plastered across his bald head, and lowered himself into his exhausted black leather chair. Slowly, he unfolded the newspaper across the top of his empty mahogany desk and opened the top drawer to find a pen.

Margaret, the school secretary, knocked at the door.

"Your tea, sir?"

Mr. Tuckdown beckoned her in with his finger without bothering to look up.

"That'll be all for this afternoon," he said, as Margaret placed the cup of tea (milk and six sugars) next to the plate of biscuits in front of him. "I won't have any calls put through for the rest of the day; I'm rather busy."

"Yes, sir, of course. There's just the small matter of—"

"Yes?" he said, raising an eyebrow.

"Well, Mrs. Tanner would like to have a word. She's with Chri—"

"Christopher Lane?" interrupted Mr. Tuckdown, sitting up abruptly.

Margaret opened her mouth to speak, but she could see that Mr. Tuckdown was getting ready to explode, and she closed it quickly. She watched nervously as he got out of his seat and walked over to the window, mumbling angrily.

"That boy . . . that boy . . . honestly, Margaret, I curse the day he set foot in the school. *I am sick to death of him!*" he shouted, his face turning a mottled deep purple.

"Sir, the boy's standing outside," whispered Margaret.

"I couldn't care less. *I'm sick of you. Do you hear me, Christopher Lane? Sick of you!*"

Mr. Tuckdown took a deep breath and looked up at Margaret.

"The boy's been here less than two months, and he's already on his way to giving me a heart attack. My health is suffering, and *it's all his fault*." He grabbed a biscuit and swallowed it down in two gigantic bites.

Margaret, having edged her way back to the door, stood silently and watched as Mr. Tuckdown began to pace, beads of sweat forming on his forehead. He walked back and forth across the room, muttering under his breath.

Finally he seemed to calm slightly, and he stopped abruptly. A brief moment of silence followed as he looked down at the gold watch on his wrist and sighed.

"I suppose my tea break will just have to wait. Again. Give us five minutes and then come in and say there's an urgent call waiting," said Mr. Tuckdown. Margaret nodded and backed out slowly, leaving the door open. A moment later, after a hushed warning from Margaret about the headmaster's mood, Mrs. Tanner, form teacher for class 7C, entered the room followed by a boy almost as tall as her, his hands in his pockets and his head bowed in sullen anger.

"I'm sorry to interrupt you," said Mrs. Tanner, her lips pursed tight in a permanent sneer, her polished black heels *click-clack*ing smartly on the wooden floor as she made her way over to the headmaster's desk.

"Hurry up, Christopher," she said in a tight, shrill voice. Chris hesitated for a moment and then crossed the room to stand next to his teacher.

"Your visits are getting to be rather irritating, Mrs. Tanner," said the headmaster.

"I apologize, Mr. Tuckdown," said Mrs. Tanner, looking not the slightest bit sorry in Chris's opinion, "but unfortunately, this time it's rather more serious. You see, this morning I left my handbag under my seat in the classroom. At lunchtime I retrieved my bag, only to find that *someone*"—she looked over at Chris—"had been through my wallet and taken the money from it."

Mrs. Tanner and Mr. Tuckdown both turned to look at Chris. Chris made no attempt to speak. He looked down at his dirty, worn shoes and waited.

Finally Mr. Tuckdown got impatient.

"Well, boy? What do you have to say to that?"

"Nothing, sir."

"Nothing. How much did he steal?"

"Twenty pounds," said Mrs. Tanner.

Chris didn't move. His head stayed bowed.

"Twenty pounds, Chris. Where is it?" asked Mr. Tuckdown.

"I didn't steal it."

"Of course you did," said Mr. Tuckdown, "so where is that money now?"

"How would I know?" said Chris angrily. "I didn't steal it."

"Watch that tone of voice," warned Mr. Tuckdown. "Show me your pockets."

Chris silently put his hands in his trouser pockets and turned them out. They were completely empty.

"Well, that would be too obvious, I suppose, even for you. Clearly it must be somewhere else," said Mr. Tuckdown.

"I said I didn't take it," said Chris defiantly.

"So if it wasn't you, who was it?" asked Mrs. Tanner.

"I don't know," said Chris, looking up at Mrs. Tanner. It didn't surprise him to see the disbelief in her face.

"How convenient," said Mr. Tuckdown with a sneer. "Well, let's run through the possible suspects, shall we, Christopher? Could it be Emma Becksdale, our head girl? Or Ibrahim Lamos, who has never had a single detention in his six years here? Or could it be Jack Riggs, who has had more merits than any other pupil in the history of Black Marsh Secondary? What do you think?"

Chris stood silent.

"Or could it be, perhaps," continued Mr. Tuckdown, "the boy standing before me? This dirty little urchin of a boy, with holes in his trousers, who thinks uniform rules don't apply to him. The boy who has stolen food from the lunchroom more times than I care to remember and who likes to make smart-aleck comments to teachers and pupils just because he can't take a bit of a ribbing. The first-year who never brings in his lunch money and who arrives late into school every day. All the clues are there, Christopher, and I don't need to be Sherlock Holmes to work this one out."

He paused dramatically.

"The culprit is *you*, Christopher Lane. You are suspended for three days," he concluded. With that he took a biscuit from the plate and dipped it into his tea.

Mrs. Tanner smiled a rare smile, one that seemed to Chris to be reserved only for when he was punished.

"Thank you, Mr. Tuckdown; you've just made my day.

It seems that every cloud does indeed have a silver lining. Now, are you going to give me back the money?"

"I didn't steal it!" shouted Chris angrily.

"A thief and a liar. So be it. We'll send a letter home to your mother," said Mrs. Tanner brightly.

Chris felt tears of anger spring to his eyes, and he turned to leave before anybody could see.

"Three days of peace might be worth twenty pounds," he heard Mrs. Tanner say to the headmaster as he ran out of the office and down the corridor.

Chris didn't stop running as he passed the long line of classrooms, not caring who saw him or what they would think. He flew down the flight of stairs, two at a time, barging past students on their way to lessons, and out of the main doors. The rain was pouring down, but he hardly noticed as he crossed the playground and ran past the gates and down the empty street. He turned left into his usual shortcut, a small alleyway that led through to the busy road. Ahead in the distance he could see the traffic speeding past, blurred by the harsh rain. He leaned against the wet brick wall and caught his breath. Trying to calm himself, he began counting slowly, and after a while his breathing slowed. He pushed himself up from the wall, ran his fingers through his wet hair, and wiped his face with the bottom of his shirt. Leaning down, he slowly undid the frayed laces of his left shoe and rolled the wet sock off his foot. The crumpled twenty-pound note fell to the ground. He picked it up, wiped it off with his sleeve, and stuffed it into his pocket.

CHAPTER FOUR

Thursday, November 1

The next morning Chris woke up before his alarm clock went off. He lay in bed, and as the fog of sleep cleared, his mind began to recall everything that had happened the day before: the moment he had made the decision to steal from his teacher, his suspension, the guilt he had felt as he spent the money at the supermarket, and the lies he had told his mother when he'd got home. He thought about the plan he had come up with over the course of the previous evening, and though he was certain it was what he had to do, he felt no better for it. It was strange, he thought, how this day was special for all the wrong reasons.

Chris shivered and pulled the duvet up over his shoulders. He could hear the whistle of the cold wind coming in through the gaps in the rotting window frame, and he breathed out, watching the cloud of warm air rise up toward the ceiling, then disappear. He breathed in again and opened his mouth, but as he breathed out, something caught his eye, and he closed his mouth abruptly. Chris sat up. In the corner of his room, stretching from a shelf to the top of his bedroom door, a large web had appeared overnight, an intricate network of fine silver strings that glistened in the morning light. Chris pushed the covers back and walked over to it. A small brown spider, no bigger than a twenty-pence piece, was working at the web's edge, and Chris watched, fascinated, as it moved slowly along.

"That's some web you're building there," said Chris, reaching up to gently push against the web. It shook and the spider froze.

"I'm sorry," said Chris. "Don't stop."

As if the spider had understood him, it immediately set to work again.

Chris laughed. He looked at the spider.

"Stop."

The spider stopped. This time Chris didn't laugh. He looked at the spider, confused.

"Go on, spin your web," he said once more, quietly. Chris watched in wide-eyed amazement as the spider immediately started moving.

"How strange," said Chris, rubbing his forehead as he walked away. He dressed slowly, watching the spider as it continued to work, until he glanced over at his alarm clock and realized the time. He quickly did up the laces of his shoes, grabbed his bag, and took the small thin blue velvet box from his bedside table, pausing only briefly to look at the photograph beside it, a picture of his father in uniform taken two months before he was killed, when Chris had been only five years old.

"Sorry, Dad. I hope you understand," said Chris, putting the box into his bag and zipping it up.

Chris came down the stairs as quietly as possible. The hallway was dark even though it was eight in the morning and already light outside. He peered around the living room door and saw his mother asleep in the armchair, the blanket over her, just the way he had left her the night before. Most days he would go straight over to the window and open the curtains, but on this occasion he wanted his mother to stay asleep. He tiptoed past her to the coffee table and picked up his keys.

"See you later, Mum," he whispered, giving his mother a peck on the cheek as he walked back toward the door.

Chris's mother opened her eyes, and for a moment she looked just like she used to, a soft smile on her face.

"Where are you going?" she asked drowsily.

"To school," he said guiltily. "There's cereal and milk in the kitchen—please eat something when you get up. I went shopping yesterday, so there's plenty there."

Chris's mother took a deep breath and pulled the blanket down over her lap. She was dressed in the same clothes she wore most days: tracksuit bottoms and an old shirt of his dad's, which drowned her tiny frame. She looked up at him. The smile was gone.

"Haven't you gone yet?" she asked, rubbing her forehead to try to push away the headache that was beginning to form.

"I'm going."

She nodded blankly, leaned back in her chair, and closed her eyes, as if this brief conversation had drained her of all her energy.

"I'll be home straight after school. Do you need me to get anything at the shops?" he asked, but his mother didn't respond; she had fallen asleep again.

Leaning over, he pulled the blanket back up over his mother's shoulders. He put his keys in his bag, slung it over his shoulder, and walked out of the front door, closing it gently. He reached the end of his road and turned left. It was beginning to drizzle, and Chris quickened his pace, wishing he had taken an umbrella with him. He had no intention of turning back, however, in case his mother woke up again and asked him any questions. He hated lying to her, but, although she hadn't taken any interest in him or his schooling for many years, he still didn't want to do anything to disappoint her. He pulled up the collar of his jacket and headed off in the direction of the main road.

The rain had worsened by the time Chris reached King Street. Most of the shops hadn't opened yet, but the road was still full of people on their way to work and school. He walked slowly, ignoring the squelching from his shoes, and mulled over what had happened the day before. Although he didn't particularly like his teacher, he couldn't help but feel guilty about stealing from her, and he had spent all night trying to work out how he would rectify the situation. Sometime in the early hours he had come up with a plan, and only then was he able to fall asleep.

He was walking on autopilot, lost in thought, so much so that he almost walked past the pawnbroker's. Chris stopped and turned to face the shopfront. The windows and glass doors had been painted black so that passersby couldn't see who was in a situation desperate enough to trade their valuables for money. A sign on the door told him it was open, but a wave of doubt swept over him. After a few minutes of trying, and failing, to come up with an alternative, and with the rain seeping through his clothes, Chris took a deep breath, pushed open the door, and walked through the entrance into a dark and damp-smelling room. A bell rang to notify the staff there was a customer.

Chris stood awkwardly in the middle of the room, not sure what to do. He looked around at the glass cabinet that created a barrier between staff and customers around the shop. Behind it the walls were lined with shelves that looked as if they were going to buckle under the weight of the televisions, stereo systems, and larger electrical goods that had been crammed upon them. Inside the counter, past the dirty glass, jewelry, cameras, watches, and other small items filled the shelves. Every single item, he thought, represented somebody in a desperate situation like himself.

"Can I help you, son?" said a gruff voice to his right.

Chris turned and saw a surly-looking, thin, old man in a somber dark-gray suit standing behind the counter.

The man eyed him suspiciously as he approached.

"I have something I wanted to, uh . . ."

"Pawn?" said the man.

"Yes," said Chris.

"Well, get on with it. What is it?"

Chris fumbled in his jacket pocket. He took out the velvet box and placed it on the table gently, wishing that there were some other option.

The man picked it up and slowly opened it. For a moment there was complete silence as the man inspected it. Finally, he looked up at Chris.

"Son. Do you know what this is?"

"Yes. It's a medal."

"It's not just a medal. It's a very rare military medal, and a boy your age should not be walking around with one in his pocket. Who does it belong to?"

"Me."

"Well, you're either the British Army's youngest soldier or you're lying. Either way, I'm not interested." He closed the lid shut, put it on the counter, and pushed it toward Chris.

"Take it back before whoever owns it realizes it's missing." The old man turned to walk away.

"I own it," said Chris desperately. "It was given to my dad after he died, and it's mine now."

The man stopped and turned back to face Chris.

"He died when I was five."

"And your mum . . . hasn't she got something to say about you bringing this in?"

"No. My mum doesn't care. She hasn't been well since he died."

The man heard the falter in Chris's voice and saw how hard the boy was trying to keep his composure. He looked down at the box and then back at Chris. He softened.

"What do you want to be trying to get rid of it, then?" he asked.

"I don't want to get rid of it," said Chris, with more anger than he had intended. He took a deep breath to calm himself. "I'm going to buy it back. It's just . . ."

Chris hesitated. At that moment all he wanted to do was leave the shop and go back home, but he knew that he had no choice. Although it pained him to ask for help, he decided that he had to tell the man the truth.

"I'm in some trouble and I need the money."

The man considered this for a moment. Finally he spoke.

"Don't you have anything else you could trade in?"

"No, nothing," said Chris.

"Well, son, I'm sorry, but I can't take it. It's worth more money than I have here anyway. I wouldn't even know what to do with it. What's more, I'm not allowed to deal with under-eighteens," he said, pointing to the sign on the door.

Chris's face dropped. Deciding to come here had been the most difficult decision he'd ever had to make, and now he realized that it had all been for nothing. He picked up the box and put it back into his jacket.

"All right, thanks," he said flatly. He looked up at the man, hoping that he might change his mind, but the man remained silent, a strange blank expression on his face. Finally Chris turned and walked away from the counter.

"What's your name?" said the man, as Chris opened the door.

Chris looked back, surprised.

"Chris. Chris Lane."

"Right. Well, Chris, come back here."

He waited for Chris to come back in.

"I don't know what's wrong with me. I've come over all soft or something, but I'm going to give you some money."

"You'll take the medal?" asked Chris.

"No, son, I'm not taking the medal. That belongs with you. I'm going to pay you to do some work."

"Oh," said Chris, surprised. "It's just that . . ."

"That you need the money now, right?" asked the old man.

"Yeah."

"That's all right. I'm going to give you the benefit of my trust—and I don't often do that, but something's come over me today. I'll give you fifty pounds, and you can begin to help me sort this mess out. My back's not what it was, and I can't be doing any heavy lifting anymore," he said, nodding over at the piles of goods and boxes crammed on the shelves and floors all about him.

Chris was about to say yes, then hesitated.

"Pay me a hundred pounds and I'll do it all myself."

The man laughed.

"Hmm. You've got some nerve, son. I don't know—that's quite steep."

"One hundred. You'll never have seen this shop look better," said Chris, with a determination that surprised even himself.

The man looked at Chris, and after some consideration he smiled.

"Done. But you better live up to your word," he said.

"Thank you. I'll work hard," Chris said quietly.

The man looked Chris in the eye and smiled.

"I know if I can trust someone the moment I lay eyes on them. You won't let me down," he said, and took his wallet out from his pocket. From it he took five twenty-pound notes and placed them one by one on the counter.

"Now get out of here. Come back on Sunday, the sixteenth of December. We're closed that weekend. It'll be a good time to sort out the mess before the final Christmas rush."

"I'll be here. Thank you . . . sir."

"Frank."

"Thank you, Frank."

Chris took the money, folded it carefully, and put it in his jacket pocket. He smiled gratefully and hesitated, unsure of what to say.

"Go on, out. I'll see you in December," said the man sternly, waving Chris out.

Chris nodded, turned, and walked out into the street. There was a break in the rain, and the sun had managed to find its way through the clouds. He patted his pocket, smiled, and walked with purpose toward the bus stop shelter.

It was still early when Chris reached the entrance of his school. He had twenty minutes, plenty of time to do what he needed to do and get out again before class registration started. A few students were milling about but nobody took any notice of him. He had only been at the school for two months, and barring the run-ins with teachers and Kevin Blunt, the school bully, he had kept himself to himself. It wasn't that he didn't want to make friends; he just didn't want to explain why he always had to go straight home after school or why he never had any money to go to the cinema or do anything else that most children his age did. On this occasion, however, his ability to blend unnoticed into the crowd served him well. He made his way across the playground, through the main doors, and up the stairwell. He was just about to step out into the corridor when he heard the sound of a door opening ahead of him. Chris froze. Mrs. Tanner came out of the classroom, cup of tea in hand, and headed off in the opposite direction. Chris pressed himself up against the side of the wall and held his breath until she had gone through the doors at the other end.

With greater caution, he walked up to the door of his classroom and looked in. The room was empty. Not knowing how long he had before Mrs. Tanner came back, he darted in and made his way straight to her desk. Her handbag wasn't in its usual place. The thought briefly crossed Chris's mind that this was because of what he had done, but he pushed it away—he needed to concentrate on the task in hand. He checked once more behind him, reached into his pocket, slid open the top drawer, and carefully placed the twenty-pound note inside it. He went to close the drawer when—

Creak!

Chris jumped. He turned and saw a woman he didn't recognize standing in the doorway. The fitted gray suit, manicured nails, and blond hair perfectly in place all suggested that she wasn't a teacher.

"Hi, I'm just looking for the lunch hall. I seem to be going in circles and can't find it anywhere."

"Oh," said Chris, red-faced, "it's through the courtyard, upstairs, on the other side."

"Right. Of course. Are you busy? Could you show me where it is and give me a hand? I have to bring some chairs into the hall."

Chris hesitated, but, unable to come up with an excuse on the spot, he agreed.

"Yeah. Okay," he said, pushing the drawer closed behind him. He quickly followed the woman back out into the corridor.

"Thank you for doing this," said the woman from behind the stack of chairs that she was carrying.

"That's all right," said Chris. "What are they for?"

"I'm from the Ministry of Education. We're running some interviews today. How old are you?"

"Elev—I mean, twelve."

"Excellent. So that means I'll be seeing you again later—we'll explain it all then. What's your name?"

"Chris. Christopher Lane."

"Well, hi, Christopher, I'm Allegra Sonata—Miss Sonata," she said. She looked over and smiled as she put the chairs down. She opened the door into the hall and secured it on the latch so that it wouldn't close.

"I need them over there," she said, pointing to the other end of the hall.

They walked over and put the chairs down.

"I could really use a cup of coffee," said Miss Sonata.

"You could get one in the staff room. It's at the end of the corridor, upstairs."

"Pardon?" asked Miss Sonata, looking confused.

"You can get coffee in the staff room. It's upst—"

"No, I heard what you said, but how did you know I wanted coffee?"

It was Chris's turn to look confused.

"You just said so," he said.

Miss Sonata opened her mouth to speak, paused, then closed it again. She thought for a moment.

"What did you say your surname is?" she asked finally, picking up a folder from the table next to her.

"Lane."

"Lane. Hmm," she said, leafing through the folder. She stopped, then ran her finger down the page.

"Ah! Got you. You're class 7C, right?"

Chris nodded.

"Excellent. Your interview is at eleven forty-five. I'm looking forward to it."

Chris hesitated and then decided to tell her the truth.

"I'm not going to be here later. I'm, uh, suspended today," he said, embarrassed.

A look of surprise flashed briefly across Miss Sonata's face.

"Oh. I'm sorry to hear that," she said, considering her words carefully. She paused and looked at him, and a thought crossed her mind.

"I had something to do before school started. I'm going to go home before lessons begin," explained Chris.

"So how come you're in school today?" asked Miss

Sonata at the same time, then stopped and smiled as Chris finished what he was saying.

"You're an interesting boy, Chris," she said. "I'd like you to stay and do the test and interview anyway, before you leave."

Chris hesitated.

"It's okay. It won't take long. All you have to—"

"Christopher Lane!" shouted a voice from the other end of the hall.

Chris and Miss Sonata turned quickly to see Mr. Tuckdown standing in the doorway, blocking out the light coming through the door like a moon eclipse.

He stormed over, his face turning red with a combination of effort and anger.

"I knew you were stupid from the first moment I set eyes on you, but even I didn't think you were stupid enough to come into school when you'd been suspended!" shouted Mr. Tuckdown, who was now standing less than two feet away from Chris.

"Mr. Tuckdown, I was just asking Chris . . . ," interrupted Miss Sonata.

In his fury, Mr. Tuckdown hadn't noticed Miss Sonata standing there.

He wiped his brow with the back of his hand and took a deep breath.

"Miss Sonata, I'm sorry about this. I hope this boy hasn't been pestering you," he said, looking over at Chris angrily.

"No, not at all. In fact he's been helping me to bring some chairs in," she said.

"Helping himself to your belongings, more likely," said

Mr. Tuckdown with a sneer. "I'd check my pockets if I were you; this boy's got sticky fingers."

He turned to Chris again. "An explanation, boy. Now. Why are you in school today?"

"I forgot, sir," said Chris gruffly.

"Well, your forgetfulness has just got you another day of suspension. Perhaps that will give you some time to work on your memory. Unbelievable," he said, shaking his head. "Now I'm going to say this slowly, so you can understand: Don't . . . come . . . back . . . until . . . next . . . Wednesday. Now . . . *Get out!*"

Chris turned to walk out, but Miss Sonata stopped him with a hand on his shoulder.

"One moment, Christopher," she said, facing Mr. Tuckdown. "Mr. Tuckdown, I would very much like to interview him. If you would allow it, I'll have the test completed by the time school begins, and he can be on his way."

Mr. Tuckdown's face tightened, and he pursed his lips in anger, as if about to explode. Miss Sonata took a step back, startled. He opened his mouth, but instead of shouting, he started to laugh.

"Oh, Miss Sonata, I don't know what lies he's told you, but I can assure you that it would be an utter waste of your time. This child has as much chance of getting into an academy for gifted pupils as I have of putting on a tutu and dancing for the Royal Ballet. Now get out, Christopher, before I expel you permanently."

Chris looked at Miss Sonata but could think of nothing to say. He turned and walked out in silence, the eyes of Mr. Tuckdown and Miss Sonata on his back.

. CHAPTER FIVE .

Later that day

At a quarter to four, after a day of wandering around the local park aimlessly, Chris walked up to his front door. The curtains were still drawn and the mail was sticking out of the letter box, a sure sign that his mother had had a bad day. He walked in, dropped his bag, and entered the living room.

Chris's mother was sitting in the same armchair he had left her in that morning. She had changed clothes but was back under the blanket, staring blankly at the television screen, which cast a flickering dark-blue light across her face. Chris walked over to the faded curtains and pulled them open, letting the gray light of the winter sun into the room.

Chris's mother winced at the light.

"Hi, Mum," said Chris cheerfully.

His mother put her hand up to shield her eyes.

"Can you close them?" she asked. It wasn't so much a question as a demand.

Chris hesitated, knowing by the tone of his mother's voice that it was not a good day to antagonize her, but he decided to ignore her request.

"Mum, I thought we could go out."

"Out?" she asked.

"Yes, out. I thought we could go to the cinema or something."

Chris's mother turned and glared at him.

"Don't be ridiculous, Christopher. I haven't left the house since—"

"Since Dad died, I know. But that's seven years ago now. You can't sit in front of the television for the rest of your life. And people don't even visit us anymore—not since I could look after you. It's not good for you."

"Don't tell me what's good for me, Christopher," she said, her voice getting louder. "Nothing is good for me. Just bad luck followed by worse luck—that's the story of my life, and I'm not about to leave the house and let more misery pile up on top of the rubbish that I already have to deal with."

"I just thought today would be a good day—"

"A good day? I haven't seen a good day in years. What's so special about today that you think this one should be any different?"

Chris opened his mouth to speak, but his mother didn't wait for him to answer.

"Nothing. This day is as meaningless as yesterday, as the

day before that, and every single day before that one. Do you understand?" she asked, and then, without waiting for a response, she turned back to face the television.

"Close the curtains on your way out," she said, dismissing him.

Chris considered saying something in response but decided that he would be wasting his breath. He walked up to the curtains and closed them. He was about to turn to leave the room when the doorbell rang. He looked at his mother.

"Are you expecting anyone?" he asked, confused.

"Of course not," she said, looking at Chris accusingly. "Who did you invite?"

"I didn't invite anybody," he said.

"Tell them we don't want whatever they're selling. And that if they come around again, we'll call the police."

The doorbell rang again.

"I'll get it," said Chris redundantly.

Chris opened the door and saw Miss Sonata leaning on the railings in front of his house, searching through an open brown-leather briefcase. She looked up.

"Oh. Hello! I didn't think you were in. I was going to leave you a note."

She stood up and walked over to Chris, standing silently in the doorway.

"I'm sorry I got you into trouble today," she said.

"That's okay. It wasn't your fault," said Chris uncomfortably.

"Anyway, I hope you don't mind me turning up unannounced. I tried the home phone number on the school

records, but it wasn't working, so I thought I'd come round instead."

"Oh," said Chris.

"Can I come in? I just wanted to have a quick chat with you and your mum, if she's in."

Chris closed the front door behind him a bit.

"It's just that Mum's not been very well for a while, and I didn't want to upset her more, so she doesn't know I've been suspended. I spent the day at the park until school finished," he explained in a hushed voice.

Miss Sonata nodded.

"That's fine. I won't say a word. I just want to make an appointment for you to do the test. I'd really like you to give it a go."

"What's it for?" he asked suspiciously.

"It's for a new school—a very exclusive school—that the government is opening up soon."

"But . . . well . . . I'm not really a good student," he confessed, surprised that this wasn't already obvious enough to Miss Sonata.

"We don't care how you've done at school so far, Christopher. We want students who have something different to offer."

"Like what?"

"Creativity. Imagination. Other things like that," she said. "I know we only spoke for a moment this morning, but I have a strong feeling you'll do well."

Chris thought about it for a moment.

"I'll check with my mum."

"Great," said Miss Sonata. "I'll wait here."

"All right, I'll be back in a second," said Chris, leaving the door open behind him as he went back into the living room.

Miss Sonata leaned against the porch and waited. She heard the sound of muffled voices, and although she couldn't make out what was being said, she could tell the conversation was getting heated. She heard footsteps and a door slam.

"You do what you like . . . I'm going to my room!" shouted Chris's mother, and before Miss Sonata had a chance to look away, she appeared in the hallway.

"What are you looking at?" said Chris's mother, her hair matted and disheveled, her face lined and worn. Miss Sonata stood opposite her, suddenly conscious of her expensive haircut and her tailored suit, and shifted uncomfortably.

"Mum, please," said Chris, appearing beside her. He touched her arm to try to calm her, but she shrugged it off angrily.

"I'll come back another time; I don't want to cause any trouble," said Miss Sonata.

Chris's mother shrugged and turned to walk up the stairs. "You go ahead and do your test with him or whatever it is you want. I'm going to sleep. Don't bother making me any dinner," she said to Chris without looking back, and with that she disappeared around the corner of the landing, into the upstairs darkness.

Chris and Miss Sonata stood awkwardly for a moment.

"Are you all right?" asked Miss Sonata.

Chris nodded but said nothing. He was both embarrassed and upset in front of Miss Sonata for the second time that day.

"Do you want me to go?" she asked gently.

Chris shook his head. "You might as well come in now; Mum won't come down again tonight."

"Is there anyone I can call—maybe someone from your family could come round and help with dinner?" asked Miss Sonata.

"No, it's all right, honestly," said Chris. "This happens all the time. I'm used to it."

Miss Sonata hesitated and then closed the front door behind her. She had already been warned about Chris's home situation from a quiet word on the side with the school secretary, but she was still shocked when she walked in. The house was dark and in desperate need of renovation. The paint was peeling as a result of the damp patches behind it, and strips of it had come off over the years, exposing the bare brickwork. The carpet on the stairs was threadbare and coming up at the edges, though she could see that there had been clumsy attempts to fix it in place with tape. Above her hung a cable with a light fitting that was missing a bulb and farther down the hall she could see a couple of mousetraps on the floor. There was a smell of damp, and it seemed to be colder inside than it was outdoors.

"We're, er, having some work done to the house. Sorry," said Chris, not looking at her. She followed him silently into the living room.

Chris quickly walked over to the sofa and picked up the blanket so that Miss Sonata could take a seat.

Miss Sonata smiled and sat down. She opened up her briefcase on her lap and rummaged through it.

Chris took a seat at the other end of the sofa.

"There it is," said Miss Sonata, and pulled out a glossy printed card. She handed it to Chris.

"This is the school I was telling you about," she said.

He looked at the front. The words "Myers Holt Academy, Center for Excellence" were written across the top in an ornate gold script, and underneath there was a picture of a Regency townhouse with wide steps leading up to a black front door and a gold plaque. He turned the card over, but there were no more photographs, just a paragraph, which he read to himself:

The Myers Holt Academy is a newly established, government-approved school situated in the heart of Bloomsbury, directly opposite the British Museum. Places are limited and are offered to a select number of students for a period of one year only. In this time, the staff at Myers Holt will provide pupils with an intensive, specialized curriculum aimed at stretching and developing the mind in a small class setting. In addition, pupils will enjoy a range of extracurricular activities, ensuring that your child will leave Myers Holt with the skills to guarantee him or her success for the future.

For further information, please contact:

The Admissions Office
Myers Holt Academy
40 Montague Street
London WC1 6JO

"The interview only takes about ten minutes—plenty of time to see if you have what we're looking for. What do you think? It could be a very good opportunity," said Miss Sonata.

"It looks expensive," said Chris, studying the photograph on the front.

Miss Sonata smiled. "Actually, quite the opposite. We're very keen to admit students who will get the most benefit out of the education that Myers Holt will be providing, regardless of income or background. As such, we will cover all costs for schooling, including books and uniform and any other school-related expenses. Not only that, but we would also provide you with a full scholarship to fund all your further education."

"So I wouldn't have to pay for anything at all when I'm at the school?" he asked, checking.

Miss Sonata nodded.

"Not even lunch?"

"No, you'd be boarding, so all your meals would be provided."

"Boarding?" asked Chris.

"Yes," said Miss Sonata. "You would have phone contact and come home on holidays."

Chris thought for a moment.

"I'm sorry, but even if I did get in, and I don't think I would, I couldn't leave Mum on her own," he said.

Miss Sonata nodded sympathetically.

"I completely understand. All I can say is that it is a small school of only one class, as we want to be able to offer a very individualized curriculum. There is a maximum of six places available, and we are testing over two thousand pupils. If you were to be offered a place, then perhaps something could be arranged to help you both out. If not, well, you're in no different a situation than you're in now. In other words, you don't lose anything by taking the test."

Chris shrugged.

"Okay. I'll do it. When?" he asked.

"We could do it now," said Miss Sonata, "it'll only take ten minutes but, if you're busy, we could arrange for you to come to us instead. We're in Central London."

"I can do it now. I'm not doing anything." said Chris flatly.

"Okay, well, good." Miss Sonata looked around for a surface to work from, but the only one she could see, a small round coffee table by the armchair, was cluttered with a pile of old television guides.

"If you need a bigger table, we can go into the kitchen," said Chris, picking up the two mugs his mother had left on the floor.

Miss Sonata smiled and stood up. He led her down the hallway, through an archway, and into the kitchen at the end, which, although old and in poor repair, was immaculately clean. *At least his mother cleans the place*, she thought, then looked over and saw Chris turning on the taps to carefully wash up the mugs. At that moment she felt a great sadness for this young boy with too many adult responsibilities. She walked over to the small sunroom, which was dominated by an imposing oak dining room table surrounded by a collection of worn, mismatched chairs. She pulled one back and took a seat.

Opening up her briefcase, Miss Sonata took out a dark red folder and pen and waited as Chris prepared them each a cup of tea. She shivered and then noticed a bucket in the corner, full of water. Looking up, she saw that there was a panel missing from the glass roof. She decided not to say anything about it.

Chris sat down opposite her and placed the mugs on the table.

"Thank you," said Miss Sonata, placing her hands around the mug for a moment to warm them. "Right. Let's get going." She smiled. "As I said, we're not really interested in how you're doing in school. We value certain skills far more than academic results. As such, the set of questions I'm going to put to you is a little unusual."

"What kind of skills?" asked Chris.

"Imagination, observational skills, empathy, for example. That doesn't mean that you won't be learning mathematics and English and the other school subjects at Myers Holt, but we think that you'll make the most progress if we work on the way you think, rather than on the facts that you know. Does that make sense?"

"Yes," said Chris, although he didn't have a clue what Miss Sonata was talking about.

"Good," she said, opening up her folder. Miss Sonata took out a photograph and handed it to Chris.

"Have a good look at this, please, and in one minute I'm going to take it from you and ask you some questions about it," said Miss Sonata. She picked up a stopwatch he hadn't noticed before and pushed a button.

Chris quickly looked down at the photograph and saw that it was of a young boy, maybe four years old, with a large present in his lap. He was sitting on a carpeted floor beside a brightly lit Christmas tree, and on the left of the picture Chris could see the corner of a television set on a wooden cabinet. He tried desperately to take in as many details as possible, his eyes flitting across the picture until Miss Sonata asked him to stop and hand the picture back to her. She carefully opened the folder and placed it back inside. She pushed the closed folder into the center of the table.

"Now, please keep your eyes on the folder while I ask you some questions. Don't worry too much about getting the correct answer. Instead, try to let your mind go blank, and respond with the first answer that comes to your mind. If you don't know the answer, just say, 'pass.' Is that clear?"

Chris nodded, and Miss Sonata picked up her clipboard and pen.

"Number one. What color were the boy's pajamas?"

"Green-and-blue striped."

Miss Sonata wrote something on her paper. Chris looked at her for a reaction to indicate if he was correct, but saw nothing.

"Please keep your eyes on the red folder here," she said instead, tapping the table. "Question number two: What color slippers was the boy wearing?"

"He wasn't wearing any slippers," said Chris with confidence. "He had bare feet."

"Good. Question number three: How many presents were under the tree?"

"Six," said Chris, relieved that he had already anticipated that question.

Miss Sonata scribbled something quickly and continued: "Question four: What was the boy's name?"

Chris hesitated for a moment.

"I'll have to rush you. Just say the first thing that comes into your head."

"Matthew," said Chris, suddenly remembering the name in white lettering on the stocking that hung from the mantelpiece in the corner of the photograph.

"Finally," said Miss Sonata, "what was inside the present the boy was holding?"

Chris looked up, confused.

"There are no right answers to some of these questions, Christopher. You just say whatever comes to your mind," said Miss Sonata, reassuring him.

"Umm . . . a penguin?" As soon as he said it, he regretted it. It was a terrible answer.

Miss Sonata didn't show any reaction and calmly wrote it down.

"Is that all right?" he asked.

She looked up, saw his worried face, and laughed.

"You're doing just fine. Now, let's get back to your penguin. Tell me about it in a little more detail."

"Ummm," said Chris, looking back down. He put the picture of the penguin back in his mind and tried to give it some detail.

"It was wearing a yellow bow tie. With red dots on it. And a black top hat on its head."

Miss Sonata wrote his answer down and looked up again.

"Good, good," she said, putting her clipboard down. "That's part one finished. Are you ready for the next set of questions?"

Chris nodded.

Miss Sonata pulled out a folded map and opened it out across the table.

"Do you know what this map is of?"

Chris immediately recognized the river cutting across the page.

"Yes, it's London."

"Good, good. See this cross here?" She pointed at a small red *X* just north of the river in the middle of the map. Chris nodded.

"Now, I want you to look at it until your eyes go fuzzy and just let your mind wander," said Miss Sonata.

Chris focused on the center of the map and squinted until the details started to blur.

"Now imagine that you're dropping down from the sky, onto the red *X*. You break through the clouds and see the street below you. Tell me when you're standing on the ground and we'll begin."

As he watched the map blur in front of him, the thought briefly crossed Chris's mind that this was the strangest test he had ever had to take. Nevertheless, he followed Miss Sonata's instructions and imagined a blanket of gray cloud below him, rapidly looming larger as he fell toward it; then, for a brief moment, he saw nothing in his mind but a gray fog before suddenly emerging above the unmistakable London cityscape. He imagined himself slowly falling down toward the ground directly below him; he looked around and saw that the streets were alive with the traffic of people and cars, colorful dots moving in all directions. As he became accustomed to the bird's-eye view, he began to recognize familiar landmarks: the Thames, like a dark ribbon dropped on the landscape; Piccadilly Circus, with its lights in the distance; and the two fountains of Trafalgar Square below him. He imagined the statue of Nelson, high atop its column, not far in the distance. He concentrated on the scene below and watched as his feet gently landed on the gray sidewalk of the busy street. He looked about at people rushing past him, seemingly oblivious to his presence. He waited.

"Um, okay, now what?" he asked, after a long silence.

"What do you see?"

"People. A street. Cars."

"Can you be more specific? Can you tell me exactly what you see?"

Chris lifted his head, eyes closed, but the image seemed to be fading in his mind.

"I can't really see much. Everything is going gray, like a fog."

"Look down again, Christopher. I think you'll find the image will come back to you."

Sure enough, Chris looked back down at the table, and the image of the busy street started coming back to him.

"I see a family walking past me, and a row of cars waiting at the traffic lights."

"What buildings can you see?"

"There's a bookshop and a cafe next to it. And there's a theater on the other side of the road."

"Hmmm," interrupted Miss Sonata. "Okay. Can you walk to your right a bit and tell me what you see?"

There was a pause as Chris imagined walking quickly along the street.

"Yeah, Trafalgar Square's in front of me. There's a church on my left, and there are people sitting on the steps outside."

"Walk over to the church and look for a number on the pavement in front of the church."

"A number?"

"Yes, just have a look and see if you can see anything."

Chris approached the church steps, wondering if he needed to be avoiding walking into the crowds of people if this was all in his imagination. He walked along the pavement, looking down.

"Oh! I see it. There's a number spray-painted in red on the ground."

"Can you tell me what that number is?"

"It starts one-two-nine, but I can't see the rest—There's a group of tourists standing in the way."

"Okay, let's wait until they move away."

The room was silent as Chris watched the group of men and women arguing over which way up their map should be held. Eventually a woman stormed off in anger past him, and the group she was with quickly ran off to catch up with her. Chris walked up to the pavement slab and looked down.

"One-two-nine . . . one-two-nine . . . two-zero-two-five," he said slowly.

"Interesting, Christopher. Very interesting indeed," said Miss Sonata, writing something down. "Okay, we're done with that section. Well done. You can open your eyes."

Chris had forgotten his eyes were closed. He opened them, and the image he had seen vanished.

Miss Sonata folded up the map and put it away.

"One last question. What animal am I thinking of?"

He barely looked at her before the image of an animal popped into his mind.

"A fox."

Miss Sonata pursed her lips together in an effort to conceal a smile. "That's right! Lucky guess?"

"Yeah. Lucky guess," he said, smiling. He knew she would have said that no matter what animal he had picked.

"Well, we're all done. Good job," said Miss Sonata, packing away her folder.

"That's it?" asked Chris, confused.

"Well, we're all done with the interview. We'll let you know how you did as soon as possible. But there is one more thing. I hope you don't mind, but I had a chat with the school secretary earlier, and she explained that you might not be doing anything today. Anyway, I couldn't come by without anything, so I hope you don't mind if I invite myself to join you for a few minutes longer. . . ."

She opened her bag and carefully pulled out a white cardboard box. Chris watched curiously as she lifted the top flap, and he saw that inside was a perfect chocolate cake. She reached back into her bag and pulled out some paper plates and a blue-and-white-striped candle, which she pushed firmly down into the center of the thick brown icing.

"Happy birthday, Christopher," said Miss Sonata, looking up at him.

Chris smiled awkwardly, not knowing what to say.

"I—how—I don't know . . ."

Miss Sonata laughed.

"You can't celebrate your twelfth birthday without a cake!"

"Thank you . . . I—"

"No need for thank-yous," interrupted Miss Sonata cheerfully. "Help me carry this lot into the living room so we can celebrate."

Chris picked up the plates and followed Miss Sonata out of the kitchen, a wide smile on his face—finally, today was feeling special for all the right reasons.

. CHAPTER SIX .

Friday, November 2

Ernest Genever had been looking for his twin brother for over an hour and had checked almost every one of the fifty or so rooms in the house, to no avail. All he wanted was some company, somebody to play with, but Mortimer was nowhere to be found. Frustrated, he made his way along the polished wooden floor of the west wing as quietly as possible, avoiding the gaze of the dour-faced subjects of the oil paintings that lined the walls, and stopped at the final room on the corridor. There was a gold plaque mounted on the heavy wooden door with the words WHITEHALL GUEST SUITE engraved on it. He turned the handle slowly and opened the door, wincing at the loud creak of the unoiled hinges—an automatic reaction he had to any loud noise that might disturb his mother. He paused nervously for a moment until he was certain that he had not been heard; then, with a quiet sigh of relief, he entered.

The curtains were open, and outside the sun was still shining brightly, yet the room felt dark and oppressive, like a rarely entered exhibit hall in a museum. Dark antique furniture crowded the room, each piece chosen for its grandeur and value rather than for its look. Ernest barely registered this, however; it looked exactly the same as every other one of the unused guest rooms of Darkwhisper Manor, the only home he had ever known.

"Mortimer," he whispered, tiptoeing in slowly, "Mortimer, are you in here?"

As he walked around the room, checking in the wardrobes and under the four-poster bed, small clouds of dust scattered and shimmered in the stagnant air. There was no sign of his brother. Ernest stood up and wiped the dust from his trousers where he had been kneeling; then, resigned to the fact that he was just going to have to play on his own, he stepped back out into the corridor, quietly closed the guest room door behind him, and made his way to the playroom on the other side of the house.

"Ernest!"

Ernest jumped. He stopped dead on the landing and looked down to where his mother stood in the center of the marble foyer. Even looking down on her, he felt that she loomed tall, and her presence seemed to fill the enormous space below him. Dulcia Genever would have been beautiful if it weren't for the icy shield that seemed to surround her and made people want to turn away and run. Her black hair, not a strand out of place, contrasted starkly with her blue white skin, so pale it seemed to glow. She always wore, as she did on this day, a long black evening dress and a necklace of brilliant diamonds that caught the light as she moved, sending spears of dazzling white about her. But the only thing that people noticed about Dulcia when they met her were her eyes, completely black, transfixing anybody who dared to look into them.

"What are you doing?" she asked, accusingly.

"I'm looking for Mort, Mother," replied Ernest meekly. He averted his gaze from her piercing stare.

"I imagine Mortimer is practicing, as should you be. We have been waiting many years for this time, and you seem more concerned about playing."

Ernest hung his head, ashamed.

"Do you love your mother, Ernest?" asked Dulcia coldly.

"Yes, Mother, of course," replied Ernest. And he did. Ernest had only really known two people in his life—his mother and his brother—and it had never occurred to him to question his love for either of them. As much as his mother terrified him and as unkind as his brother could be, he was sure that this was because they wanted the best for him. Unfortunately, it seemed that no matter what he did or how hard he tried, he was a constant disappointment to them both.

"I see no proof of that when you choose to play instead of work to help me. Your brother performed admirably against Cecil Humphries, and he will need you to help him soon. You don't want to let your brother down, do you?"

"No, Mother."

"Well, then, go and study."

"Yes, Mother," said Ernest, and walked quickly away.

In spite of its name, the playroom was no more entertaining a place to be in than any of the other rooms of the manor. It was in fact a classroom, for the most part, and unnecessarily large, given that only two pupils had ever been taught in it. Ernest made his way toward the far end of the room, where two wooden desks faced an enormous blackboard, upon which his mother had written their homework for the day:

Read "The Theory of Telekinesis" by Boris Karparov
Test tomorrow at 9 am.
You will need to be able to move an object from one end of the room to the other.

Ernest sighed. He walked over to his desk and picked up the book waiting for him. The faded red cover was plain except for the gold-embossed title. He opened it up and flicked quickly through the yellowed pages to the back. In total there were four hundred fifty-seven pages, which he estimated would take him about twenty minutes to finish, about twice the time it took his brother. He slid onto the bench attached to his desk and began to read the introduction:

Telekinesis, from the Greek meaning "distant movement," refers to the manipulation and movement of objects using the mind, and . . .

Ernest scanned the rest of the page, then turned it and stared at the next one for a few seconds before turning the page once more. He continued to turn the pages every few seconds and had committed about two thirds of the book to memory when he heard the door open behind him. He turned his head quickly.

"Mort! I was looking for you," said Ernest, as his brother walked into the room carrying a small, plain cardboard box.

"I had better things to do than to play with you," said Mortimer matter-of-factly.

"Oh. Sure," said Ernest, trying to hide his hurt. "What's in the box?"

"Actually, Ernest, I've got you a present," said Mortimer, smiling.

Ernest stood up. He looked at his brother in disbelief.

"Well, don't look so surprised, stupid—you are my twin brother," said Mortimer, placing the box on Ernest's desk and opening up the top flaps.

"I know, but you don't normally—oh . . ."

Ernest looked up at his brother in amazement. Mortimer said nothing, watching as Ernest placed his hands inside the box and carefully lifted out the fluffy gray kitten. The kitten blinked a few times and looked up at him curiously; then, satisfied that he was safe, it curled up and closed its eyes.

"Ahh. He's lovely. I can't believe it. Thank you, Mort." Ernest hesitated. "Does Mother know?"

"Yes, I checked with her first. Right, are you ready to get on with our work?"

"Work?" said Ernest distractedly, rubbing his finger under the purring kitten's chin.

"Yes, Ernest. That's why I got the kitten."

Confused, Ernest looked up at Mortimer and saw an evil smile, a smile that he saw too often, spread across his brother's face.

"Oh, no, Mort. What are you going to do?"

Mortimer looked over at the blackboard, and Ernest followed his gaze.

"I would say that a kitten is an object, wouldn't you, Ernest?"

"I don't think that's what Mother meant, Mort," said Ernest, panicking.

"It's open to interpretation, Ernest," said Mortimer, grabbing the kitten from his brother's hands.

The kitten looked up, surprised. Its little legs hung limply from Mortimer's hands.

"You always get so. . . . *emotional*," said Mortimer mockingly, as he placed the kitten on the floor. The kitten looked around and then stretched lazily, ignorant of the danger it was in.

"Mort, please don't," pleaded Ernest, but Mortimer paid no attention. Ernest watched as his brother's eyes glazed over and stared at the kitten.

Whoosh. Ernest watched, horrified, as the kitten began to slide suddenly across the wooden floor.

"Nooooo!" cried Ernest as he watched the confused kitten build up speed, its legs desperately scrambling around for some way to stop. Ernest covered his eyes with his hands as the kitten smacked into the wall. *Thump.*

An agonizing silence followed. Ernest stood frozen on the spot in horror, unable to look up.

Meeeeeeow.

Ernest slowly dropped his hands and looked up to see the kitten shaken and disoriented but still alive and seemingly unhurt. It raised itself up on his four paws and tried to walk, but wobbled and dropped back down again.

Mortimer exploded into laughter. Ernest looked at him, horrified, as Mortimer struggled to get his breath back, but every time he tried to compose himself, he dissolved into fits of laughter again.

Ernest said nothing and walked over to the kitten. He sat down on the floor and placed the kitten on his lap and stroked it gently until he felt it begin to calm. After a few minutes, his brother's laughing died down. He heard his footsteps as he approached.

"Your turn, Ernest."

Ernest looked up at his brother but didn't reply. He wondered how somebody could look so like him and yet be so different. For a brief moment he felt a surge of hatred rise up through him, so unfamiliar that it took him by surprise.

"No."

"What?" asked Mortimer, shocked.

"No, Mort, I won't do it. It's cruel," said Ernest, with a resolve he had never shown in all of his twelve years.

"How dare you question me, Ernest. Do it now."

"No, Mort. I'm not going to hurt him. We can practice without using a kitten."

Mortimer said nothing as he considered this turn of events, while Ernest pretended to ignore him and stroked the kitten.

"Ernest?"

Ernest looked up. "Yes?"

"If you don't do it . . . I'll kill it. You know that my Ability is stronger than yours. If you don't do what I did, I'll make sure the kitten hits every one of these four walls before I throw it out of the window."

Ernest's eyes filled with tears. "Why, Mort? Why do you want me to do it?"

Mortimer shrugged.

"Because it's funny. And Mother thinks you need to learn to be tougher."

"Mother knows?"

"Of course. I told her that I think you aren't strong enough for the work we have to do, and she agreed. Now. Are you going to do it or not?"

Ernest hesitated.

"Ernest. You are my twin brother, and we both have the same purpose in life. I want only what's best for you. You know that."

Ernest thought for a moment; then, with a look of defeat, he lifted the kitten from his lap and placed it on the floor next to him. Mortimer smiled. Ernest stood up; then, looking down, he let his eyes glaze over. The kitten began to move slowly.

"Faster, Ernest."

Ernest furrowed his brow in concentration, and the kitten picked up pace.

Mortimer began to laugh.

"Yeah, Ernest! Go, kitten, go!"

The kitten sped past the desks and bookshelves and

was almost at the wall when it stopped suddenly, just next to the doorway.

Mortimer looked over at Ernest, who was already running toward the door. He watched as his brother scooped up the kitten in his arms and ran out, without turning back.

"Coward!" shouted Mortimer.

Ernest ran back along the corridor, down the steps two at a time, out the front door, and across the manicured lawns into the forest, while his brother watched him from the playroom window. Ernest didn't look back.

That evening, a few miles down the road from Darkwhisper Manor, a young family played delightedly with the new kitten that had appeared on their doorstep earlier in the day. Ernest watched them in his mind, a new trick he had only recently learned, and the relief of seeing the kitten happily chasing a piece of wool distracted him from the evil looks his brother was shooting him across the dinner table.

"Ernest!" His mother's sharp voice brought him back suddenly into the dining room.

"Sorry, Mother," said Ernest.

"I said I want you both to clear up the plates, then go upstairs and get ready for bed. I'll be up for your bedtime story in half an hour."

"Yes, Mother," said Ernest obediently, standing up.

Plates washed and teeth brushed, Ernest changed into his pajamas and got into bed. He turned to Mortimer, who was already under the covers of the bed beside him.

"I'm sorry, Mort. I just didn't want to hurt the kitten," said Ernest, the anger of earlier forgotten.

"Well, don't do it again, Ernest. We have to work together."

"I know," said Ernest.

"Maybe you're not as much of a wimp as I thought," said Mortimer.

Ernest smiled to himself, knowing that this was as close to an apology as his brother would ever offer him. He rolled onto his back, pulled the sheets up to his neck, and waited for the familiar sound of his mother's heels approaching.

The boys turned to see the silhouette of their mother standing in the doorway. She walked slowly to the antique cream-leather armchair between their beds and carefully arranged the skirt of her dress before sitting down.

"I heard there was some resistance to our work today," said Dulcia, her voice soft yet empty of any emotion.

Ernest looked across at his brother, horrified. Mortimer looked back and shrugged smugly.

"Ernest," said Dulcia, looking straight ahead, "I am concerned."

There was a pause, which Ernest chose not to break, certain that whatever he said would only serve to make the situation worse.

"Seven years ago, I chose the two of you to bring home from the orphanage, and since that time, have you ever wanted for anything?"

"No, Mother," answered the boys in unison.

"Have I not treated you both as my own flesh and blood?"

"Yes, Mother."

"And now I ask a simple favor: one year of your life dedicated to the repayment of my kindness. In return you will live a comfortable and wealthy life, and all of this"—she motioned around her—"will be yours. Tell me, Ernest, is that too much to ask of you?"

Ernest shook his head.

"Do you want to go back to the orphanage? Without your brother? I waited a very long time for twins to be given up so that I would have two children to teach the Ability to at the same time, but if you do not feel that you can cope, then I am certain your brother will manage without you."

Ernest felt tears form and wiped them away with the back of his hand.

"No, Mother. Please don't send me back. I'll be good."

Dulcia nodded, satisfied.

"The kitten may have seemed harmless, but what I am asking of the both of you requires resolve far greater than giving a kitten a few bruises. If you couldn't manage that simple task, how will I know to trust you to be able to look a person in the eyes and destroy them forever?"

Ernest sat up suddenly.

"But that's different, Mother. Those people hurt you. They are bad people."

Dulcia gave a rare smile.

"Well, that's true. Nevertheless, I need you to be strong in mind. I need you to do as your brother tells you, because we don't know what is going to happen, and it won't always be as easy as it was with Cecil Humphries. Your brother's Ability is stronger than yours, and I need you to trust him. Do you trust him?"

"Yes."

"Good. Now, lie back down in your bed, and I want the two of you to listen to me carefully. I have told you the story of what happened to me every night for the last seven years, and I've trusted that you will sense the fear and suffering I endured from when I was twelve years old and still known as Anna Willows. However, I know that to fully understand what happened to me, you must experience the night those traitors abandoned me, so that you can truly understand why I want them to suffer. Do you understand?"

The boys looked at each other and, reassured by the look of confusion on the other's face, shook their heads.

"Tonight I will allow you both to use your Ability to see for yourselves what happened that night."

The look on the faces of Ernest and Mortimer made it clear that they were none the wiser.

"I'm going to let you read my mind."

"Oh," gasped Ernest in surprise.

"However, there are some rules, and I expect you to abide by them or there will be serious consequences. Understood?"

Ernest and Mortimer nodded solemnly.

"I am going to think about the incidents that I want you to witness. If it is something I am thinking about, then where will you have to go to access the memory?" Dulcia looked over at Mortimer.

"In Reception, the first room you enter in the mind, where current thoughts are stored."

"Good. That means you must go no farther. Remember,

I know how far you have gone by how loud the ringing in my ears is. If you attempt to go any further than Reception, I will know, we will stop immediately, and you will be punished. Do you understand?"

Both boys nodded solemnly.

"Well, then, you may begin."

Ernest sat up as Mortimer did the same, and he turned to his mother. He focused on her eyes, black and still, and felt himself drawn into her mind until he was standing in a vast room filled with a single dark image that slowly surrounded him as he traveled back to the memory of a night thirty years earlier—a memory that started with his mother as a twelve-year-old child sitting with a group of other children in the back of a van.

The last thing Ernest and Mortimer saw, before their mother instructed them to stop, was Anna Willows looking in a mirror hanging in the cold, gray cellar that was to become her bedroom for the next six years, tears streaming down from her brilliant emerald-green eyes, calling for her parents.

Although the boys had heard the story of their mother's kidnapping every night for many years, the reality of the scene, the fear in the girl's face, had left them both shaken.

"But why did they leave you behind?" asked Mortimer after they finished.

"Because their lives were worth more than mine, in their eyes, and for that they should all suffer. Do you understand?"

"Yes, Mother," the boys replied in unison.

"You . . . you . . . looked so different," said Ernest, turning to face his mother. Dulcia looked back at her adopted son, and there was a sadness in her face that softened the piercing black stare of her eyes.

"The day they left me to work for those cruel and greedy people was the day I could no longer be Anna Willows. On the day of my twenty-first birthday, I killed them, and all this became mine. But I would give back all the money in the world for one more day as Anna Willows."

"But I don't understand. Why are your eyes black now—was that really you?" asked Ernest, confused.

"Nobody can know who I really am if I'm to succeed in my plan. Time makes many changes to a person's appearance, with the exception of their eyes—so I decided to mask mine behind these," said Dulcia, lifting her hands to her eyes. She opened them wide and removed the contact lenses.

The boys gasped as Dulcia turned to face them, the emerald-green eyes they had just seen appearing before them, and with them a sadness that Ernest had never seen.

"I have spent many years planning my revenge carefully and waiting until the two of you reached your twelfth birthday. Now, finally, my plan is coming together. You, my sons, are the key to my revenge, and so, finally, they will suffer as I did. That is why I don't want them to die—I want them to suffer for the rest of their lives, just as I've had to do. So now you know everything, and now, Ernest, I hope you understand why I need you both so much."

"Yes, Mother, I do."

"Good. Cecil Humphries will know what it is like to live

in terror, just as I had to do, and now it is time for the rest of them to suffer, and the more you can hurt them, the prouder I will be of you. Learn from what your brother did so well. Do you see how he used the Ability to hurt both Humphries's mind and his body? It was more than I asked of him, and it was . . . *perfect.* And you know I don't use that word very often."

Mortimer puffed up with pride.

"I want to do it again. When will we use Inferno on the others?" asked Mortimer.

"Soon, my child, very soon. Our preparations will begin tomorrow for Richard Baxter. In a few months' time, every one of those Myers Holt traitors will rue the day they left Anna Willows behind."

. CHAPTER SEVEN .

Tuesday, November 20

Chris sat down at an empty table with his lunch tray and picked up his knife and fork.

"This seat taken?"

Chris ignored the familiar voice of Kevin Blunt and started to eat.

"I *said* . . . is this seat taken?"

Chris continued to ignore him and stared down at his food. He took another mouthful, then felt a hand land hard on his back, causing him to jerk forward, and the food in his mouth spat out in surprise.

Behind him Kevin and his gang laughed. Slowly, Chris wiped his mouth with the back of his hand, picked up the fork he had dropped on the table, and went back to eating his food.

"Deaf *and* dumb," he heard Kevin say. Christopher felt him take a seat next to him, and, taking that as their cue, the other four boys standing with him also sat down.

"So, Twist," said Kevin, knowing how much Christopher hated that nickname, "if you're deaf and you're dumb, that means we can say anything and you wouldn't hear."

"Yeah, huh, like that he's stupid and poor, huh, huh," said Arch, with the deep voice of a grown man. Christopher glanced over briefly and saw Arch stuff a whole piece of pizza into his oversized mouth in one go. The tomato sauce spilled out around his mouth, but he didn't bother to wipe it.

"He's so poor, beggars give *him* money," said one of the boys. The gang all laughed except for Arch, who took a moment to work it out and then let out a loud guffaw, spitting out what remained of the food in his mouth back onto his plate. He picked up the chewed-up bit of pizza and stuffed it back into his mouth.

"Why ain't you laughin', Twist? Don't you think that's funny?" asked Kevin, the table falling into silence.

Chris took another mouthful and chewed silently.

"Too busy eating, I guess," shrugged Kevin, and for a moment Chris thought Kevin might leave it at that, but it seemed he was only just starting.

"Only meal he'll get all day," continued Kevin, to quiet giggles from the others.

"Yeah, his mum is probably too busy begging tonight to get him dinner."

Chris stiffened only slightly, but it was enough for Kevin to notice.

"Oh, don't like us talking about your mum? Why, does your mum live in a cardboard box or something?" he said, a wide smirk across his face.

Chris put his fork down and turned to face Kevin.

"Say another word about my mum and—"

"And what?" asked Kevin.

"And you'll be sorry."

"Oooooh," said all the other boys in unison.

"'Sorry'?" said Kevin, standing up. Chris stood up too and faced him square on.

"*You* are going to make *me* sorry? If I remember right, you were the one on the toilets' floor last week. You were the one who went down after only a few punches. *Sorry?* Don't make me laugh," said Kevin, leaning forward so that his face was less than an inch from Chris's.

Chris stood motionless, his eyes fixed on Kevin's.

"I just got one more thing to say," whispered Kevin. "Your mum is a thief and a beggar, and your dad wanted to die 'cause he hated you so much."

"Aaaargh!" exploded Chris. He pulled back his right arm with a clenched fist and drew forward to punch Kevin, but before he had a chance to make contact, Kevin suddenly staggered backward.

Chris watched Kevin's eyes widen in shock as his body was lifted up into the air. He didn't so much as fall back but fly back, as if he were a ball of paper that Chris had thrown across the room. The boys around him, and the rest of the students and staff, watched as Kevin flew up in an arc toward the line of students waiting for their lunch. He crashed faceup onto the food counter, sending trays, food, glass, and students flying about him. There was a silence as everybody tried to process what had just happened.

"Help me . . . ," came a voice from the counter. Everybody looked over at Kevin, firmly lodged in a deep tray of custard, a soggy piece of lettuce on his head, and started laughing. Chris looked around him and saw the rest of Kevin's group staring at him, their mouths hanging open in shock and their eyes full of fear. Chris turned to them to explain that he hadn't even touched Kevin, but before he had a chance to say anything, they all turned and ran from him, leaving Chris staring down at his hands and wondering what on earth had just happened.

Chris sat quietly in the seat next to Mrs. Tanner and watched Mr. Tuckdown pace the room back and forth. He had been in his office for an hour now and had listened to Mr. Tuckdown's outrage turn to delight as he realized that this might mean a lengthy suspension.

"One month at least, don't you think, Mrs. Tanner?"

"One month at the very least, Mr. Tuckdown," said Mrs. Tanner. "Maybe two months? After all, let's not forget the trauma and suffering he caused to poor Kevin."

"Yes, indeed, maybe two months. After all, this might cost us the rugby trophy, if Kevin's too upset to play in next week's tournament."

Chris rolled his eyes but said nothing.

In the last hour, between Mrs. Tanner and Mr. Tuckdown they had managed to justify increasing his suspension from one week upward, and Chris was starting to lose patience.

"Why don't you just expel me?" he asked, finally.

Mr. Tuckdown stopped in his tracks and turned to face Chris.

"Why don't we? Well, I can tell you now that it's not through any lack of wanting to. Unfortunately, it's not that easy to do these days," he said, almost sadly. Then he sighed and started pacing again, and with it Chris knew that another lecture was about to begin.

"You are a stupid, stupid boy, Christopher. A useless, scruffy, good-for-nothing boy who steals and lies and fights. A sneaky little thief who keeps interrupting my tea breaks. *A man can't work without his tea breaks, do you understand?*"

"He said stuff about my dad!" shouted Chris, his usual self-restraint finally broken after the events of the day.

Mr. Tuckdown took a deep breath and held it until he started to turn red, and finally he exploded.

"How *dare* you shout at me! It's not my problem if your dad died in a war we can hardly remember now, it's not my problem if your mother can't pull herself together, it's not my problem that you can't take a joke with your classmates, and yet, *and yet*, you *insist* on making it my problem. Well, to hell with the rules," he said to Mrs. Tanner. "We'll just say that he attacked a teacher." He turned to face Chris.

"Christopher Lane . . . you are expelled!" he shouted, and slammed his hand on the table. The sheer weight behind it caused the desk to shake, and his now-cold cup of tea toppled over onto his desk and over the plate of biscuits.

"Bravo!" said Mrs. Tanner rapturously, clapping her bony, wrinkly hands in delight.

Mr. Tuckdown smiled and took a soggy biscuit from his desk.

There was a knock on the door, and Mr. Tuckdown stopped mid-bite.

"Yes?"

"I beg your pardon, Mr. Tuckdown, but we have Sir Bentley and Miss Sonata from Myers Holt here to see you. They've been waiting a while, and"—Margaret lowered her voice theatrically—"I think they can hear everything you're saying."

"Oh, right, um, well . . . yes, well. Hmmmm. Best let them in." He turned to face Chris. "Get out, Christopher, and don't bother ever coming back."

Chris didn't need to be asked twice. He stood up, and—shoulders hunched, head down—he walked over toward the door.

"Christopher!"

Chris looked up and saw Miss Sonata standing before him, and an older, suited gentleman by her side.

"Hi, Miss Sonata," said Chris, turning red. He wondered exactly how much of the conversation she had already heard.

"Mr. Tuckdown, there's no need for the boy to leave—we won't take up much of your time," she said, placing her hand on his shoulder and turning him back into the room.

Chris was about to protest, but Miss Sonata and the man had already walked past him. Chris wondered whether he should just leave anyway and then decided he didn't want to make a scene in front of Miss Sonata. He looked over at Mr. Tuckdown, who shot him a glowering look before turning to his guests and replacing the frown with a large smile.

"Sir Bentley, Miss Sonata, how *wonderful* to see you!" sang Mr. Tuckdown, hand outstretched.

Sir Bentley shook his hand coldly, followed by Miss Sonata.

"Please, please, take a seat," said Mr. Tuckdown, pointing to the two empty chairs beside Mrs. Tanner. "Biscuit?" he asked, offering them a plate of biscuits swimming in cold tea.

Sir Bentley and Miss Sonata both shook their heads.

"Mr. Tuckdown, we'd like to just get straight to business," said Sir Bentley.

"Of course, of course," said Mr. Tuckdown, shuffling into his seat. "I assume this must be good news?"

"Well, yes, we rather think so," said Sir Bentley without expression. "You'll be pleased to know that someone here has been selected for entry into the Myers Holt Academy this year."

"*Wonderful!*" said Mr. Tuckdown, rubbing his hands greedily. "We dared not hope, but I must admit I did start to think about how the generous school prize would be used. I have been suffering terribly having to eat these awful school lunches and the money will be used to create a staff dining room with a private chef. It's not easy for us, having to deal with all this *stress*," he said, looking over at Chris. "The remainder of the prize will go a long way toward refurbishing my office. It is, after all, the most important room in the school."

"Yes, well, wouldn't you like to hear which student was accepted?"

"Of course, of course," said Mr. Tuckdown, distracted, wondering where his new leather chaise longue would look best. He nodded over by the far bookshelves and then turned back to Sir Bentley and Miss Sonata. "Yes, so who is it? Emma Becksdale? Anthea Sylvester? Lucas Longley? It's Lucas, isn't it?" he said eagerly.

"Actually, no," replied Miss Sonata. "The pupil accepted into Myers Holt Academy is Christopher Lane."

The room fell silent, and all eyes turned to Christopher, standing at the wall and clearly as much in shock as Mrs. Tanner and Mr. Tuckdown.

"Congratulations, Christopher," said Sir Bentley, smiling.

Chris's mouth dropped open, but no sound came out.

"But . . . ," said Mr. Tuckdown, beads of perspiration beginning to form, "but there must be a mistake. This boy is—"

"Stupid?" interrupted Sir Bentley. "Useless? Good-for-nothing? It may surprise you to know that Christopher's results were outstanding."

"Outstanding?" interrupted Mr. Tuckdown. "If the boy is outstanding at anything, it's cheating. You might want to check those—"

"Uh, hmmm," coughed Mrs. Tanner. "Mr. Tuckdown, perhaps we should remember the *benefits* of Chris being accepted?"

"Benefits? Oh . . . *benefits*," said Mr. Tuckdown, suddenly remembering the chaise longue and the chef. He thought for a moment and came to a decision.

"Well, then, so be it. Take the stupid boy. He's not

wanted here anyway," said Mr. Tuckdown, and picked up another soggy biscuit.

"Yes . . . about that," said Sir Bentley, standing up. Mr. Tuckdown looked up suspiciously and raised the biscuit to his mouth.

"We couldn't help but overhear your earlier conversation with Christopher, which ended with you quite clearly expelling him. Regretfully, as he is no longer of this school, Black Marsh will no longer be eligible to receive the prize."

Mr. Tuckdown froze, biscuit poised at his open mouth. His eyes widened in shock, and then he leaped out of his chair, knocking it to the ground behind him.

"B-b-b-b-but—but—," he spluttered, but Sir Bentley paid him no heed.

"Christopher, would you care to follow us out? Good day, Mr. Tuckdown," said Sir Bentley without looking at the headmaster, who was at this point leaning on the desk, taking frantic deep breaths.

Chris looked over at Miss Sonata, who grinned and waved him over. He looked over at Mr. Tuckdown and Mrs. Tanner and smiled.

"Yes, good day to you both!" he said, and walked out of the room for the last time.

CHAPTER EIGHT

"Well, that was a rather unexpected turn of events," said Sir Bentley to nobody in particular as they walked down the headmaster's corridor. Chris, who was still reeling from the news, said nothing. Never in his whole life, he thought, had he been chosen for anything. Well, not anything good. It was a strange feeling, a mixture of pride and worry: worry that at any moment now Sir Bentley and Miss Sonata were going to realize they'd made a terrible mistake. He looked over at Miss Sonata.

"Are you . . . sure?" he asked.

"Sure about what, Christopher?" she asked, putting a hand on his shoulder.

"Well . . . about me. Are you sure you meant to say my name?"

Miss Sonata laughed. "One hundred percent. Now, Christopher, will you please not worry about anything and enjoy the moment?"

Relieved, Chris smiled. "Okay."

"Good! Let's get moving—there's a lot we have to discuss," said Miss Sonata, giving him a gentle nudge out the main door.

Chris stepped onto the playground and followed Sir Bentley and Miss Sonata over to the gates, behind which were parked two identical dark-blue cars. Standing in front of the leading car were two men in black suits, their arms folded. Chris's eyes went immediately to the one on the left, easily the biggest man that Chris had ever set eyes on. His muscles bulged with the effort of folding his arms, and his suit jacket, which appeared to be two sizes too small, strained at the buttons. If he had been painted green, Chris thought, he would have looked uncannily like an action figure he had once owned. Chris turned his attention to the significantly smaller of the pair, a skinny man with a slicked-down side part, and then looked away uncomfortably when he realized that the man appeared to be staring directly at him, although it was impossible for Chris to be certain, due to the fact that the man was wearing sunglasses, which seemed a little unnecessary given that it was the middle of winter.

"Are those your bodyguards?" asked Chris.

"Yes, security is rather tight these days," explained Sir Bentley.

Chris nodded, impressed. He was about to ask if they were carrying guns, but Miss Sonata interrupted him.

"Sir Bentley and I are going to go to the school now. Would you like to come with us and we can talk a little bit more about the place we'd like to offer to you? We'll get a car to take you home when we're done."

"Yes," said Chris, still stunned by the events of the last few minutes.

"Great. I'm going in the other car. I'll meet you there," said Miss Sonata, who then walked quickly away toward the car at the back. Chris nodded, following Sir Bentley over to the two waiting guards.

"Christopher, this is John," said Sir Bentley. Chris looked up at the enormous man, who smiled down at him.

"Good afternoon," said John as he opened up the car door.

"And this is Ron," said Sir Bentley.

The smaller man gave a barely visible nod and then jerked his head round, as if expecting somebody to jump out at them at any moment.

"Right, let's get going. Next stop, Myers Holt," said Sir Bentley, getting into the car.

Chris squeezed into the seat behind John, who, despite having pulled the driver's seat all the way back, still looked uncomfortably squashed behind the steering wheel, which appeared toy-sized in his giant hands. Ron, who was waiting impatiently for Chris to get himself seated, took one last look around him before closing the door behind Chris and running round the back of the car to the passenger side.

"Gamma One en route," said Ron to nobody in particular.

John started the engine and drove off in the direction of Central London.

"Well, Chris," said Sir Bentley, turning to face him, "I imagine this day is turning out to be quite an unusual one for you."

Chris nodded. "That's an understatement," he said, and Sir Bentley chuckled.

"We'll discuss everything in more detail when we get to Myers Holt. Miss Sonata has already spoken to your mother to explain that you'll be with us this afternoon—she stopped by your house this morning to give your mother the good news."

Chris looked surprised.

"What did she say?"

Sir Bentley put his hand on Chris's shoulder kindly.

"She said that you were capable of making your own decisions, and I have no doubt that she's quite right. She says that she will agree to whatever you want to do."

"My mum is not very well . . . ," Chris began to explain.

"Since your father died," said Sir Bentley, "I know. Miss Sonata told me about your situation, and I must say, I'm impressed with how well you have coped. You should be proud of yourself."

Chris shifted uncomfortably, unaccustomed to compliments.

"Well, perhaps this will be the day that your life takes a new turn. Now, make yourself comfortable and enjoy the ride. I have a few bits and pieces to take care of, and I'll explain more when we reach Myers Holt."

Sir Bentley pulled out his phone from the front of the

briefcase by his feet and started tapping away. Chris sat back, looking out of the darkened window as they sped along the bus lane past the stationary traffic, and listened to Ron giving John a nonstop risk assessment of everything he could see.

"Ten o'clock, old woman by lamppost; three o'clock, teenager in a hoodie; blue car, black car, white van. Hold on, what's this?! Eleven o'clock, man carrying a suspicious package . . ."

Chris sat up, alarmed, and leaned forward to have a look.

"At ease . . . just the postman," said Ron, as the car drove straight past without slowing down. Ron turned back to face the front. "Silver car, black car. One hundred yards, red light. Fifty yards, red light. Twenty yards, red light, and stop, stop, stop . . . *stop! Red light!*"

John, who had not once broken the thirty-mile-an-hour speed limit, pulled slowly to a stop at the red light and, without a word, leaned over to turn the radio on.

"What are you doing? How are you going to hear what I'm saying with the radio on?" asked Ron.

"I'm not. That's the point," said John calmly. He pressed the on button and settled back into his seat as the sound of country music filled the car. Chris looked over at Sir Bentley, who was still working on his phone, completely oblivious to anything going on around him.

"Stand by your man . . . ," sang John in a low, tuneless voice, tapping the steering wheel to the music.

Chris watched Ron get more and more agitated as he looked back and forth from the road to John, who was now lost in the music.

"John? John. John. John," said Ron.

"John!"

John looked over at Ron. "Yes?"

"Green light."

John looked up.

"Why didn't you say so?" said John, pulling away.

In the rearview mirror Chris saw a small smile on John's face, and Chris stifled a laugh as Ron folded his arms and turned away, sulking.

Ten minutes later, having driven the rest of the way in silence, John pulled up outside a row of tall Regency buildings and stopped.

Ron jumped out and opened the door for Sir Bentley. Chris shuffled along the seat and got out behind him. He looked up at Ron and smiled.

"Thanks," he said, and Ron nodded without looking at him.

Chris followed Sir Bentley up the steep steps toward the front door, which he recognized from the brochure that Miss Sonata had shown him at his house. He stood patiently as Sir Bentley pressed the single gold buzzer by the door and waited, but there was no answer. Sir Bentley tried the brass knocker. This time Chris heard the sound of running footsteps and then a loud crash followed by thumping and scraping.

"Be right with you," called a muffled voice. Finally the door opened and a plump, ruddy-faced lady appeared, a dripping sponge in one hand. She looked out of breath and was wiping the sweat off her forehead with the edge of her old pink apron. Behind her Chris could see the cause of the commotion—a stack of filing boxes that had fallen and had been hastily pushed back against the wall, their contents still strewn across the filthy, stained carpet.

"Sir Bentley, how are you, sir?" she asked in a thick Irish accent, giving a slight bow.

"Very well, thank you, Maura. And yourself?" asked Sir Bentley, stepping carefully over the pile of papers.

"Ah, well, getting there," she said, leading them down the hallway, which was dimly lit by a single bare bulb. "Not much left to do now."

"Good, good," said Sir Bentley, and walked into a room to their right. Chris followed silently and looked about as Maura dragged some plastic chairs over from the corner to the large, stained table in the middle of the room. He wasn't sure what he'd expected but was nevertheless surprised by the state of the place. The yellow wallpaper—possibly once white, judging by the lighter squares that marked where pictures had once hung—was peeling and stained by the damp that was seeping through. Mismatched, faded curtains hung limply from the one window, which looked out over an empty concrete yard.

Maura wrung the sponge into an open black garbage bag and gave the table a quick wipe, which only made the stains on the table more visible.

"Well, that'll have to do," she said apologetically.

"Thank you," said Sir Bentley, and turned to face Chris for the first time since they had entered the building.

"Maura, this is Christopher Lane. Christopher, this is Maura, the best cleaner on these shores."

Chris looked at Sir Bentley to see if he was joking, but if he was, he was giving nothing away.

"Hi," Chris said, and Maura gave him a big smile.

"Lovely to meet you, Christopher. Now, a cup of tea?"

Chris shook his head.

"No, thanks."

"I'll bring you some water, then. Your usual, Sir Bentley?" she asked, and Sir Bentley nodded. Maura left the room and Sir Bentley took a seat.

Chris sat down opposite him and looked up to see Miss Sonata at the door. He felt hugely relieved to see a familiar face and smiled as she sat next to Sir Bentley.

"Right, let's get to work," said Sir Bentley, placing his briefcase on the table and pulling out some papers. "Miss Sonata, would you like to start?"

"Thank you, Bentley," she said, looking up at Chris. "Well, Christopher, welcome to Myers Holt, and congratulations."

"Thanks," said Chris.

"I must say, I'm not at all surprised that you're here today. I knew there was something special about you the day that we met, and your test results proved that."

Chris looked surprised and Miss Sonata laughed gently.

"Yes, really, your score was remarkable! I will give you a quick rundown of what we would like to offer you, and then you can have a think about what you want to do."

Maura walked back in with a tray of drinks, and as she served them, Miss Sonata began to explain how Myers Holt had been reopened after a long closure.

"The school is designed for only a small number of

children in order to ensure that you get a very personalized education, with a curriculum that is designed specifically for you. There will be five other children here, and you would all be expected to stay here during the week and return home on some weekends and all holidays. The place is offered to you until the end of this academic year, and then you would return to your old school—or, in your case, a new school, which we will help you find. While here, you would be expected to follow the rules and work hard at all your lessons. We will take care of the rest."

"The rest?"

"Yes, your food, clothes, books. We have the best teachers in the country here to make sure that you will go on to achieve great things. In return, all we ask is that you don't speak to anybody about the work that you are doing here."

"Why?" asked Chris. Sir Bentley sat forward.

"We ask for your discretion because the methods we use here are unique and could be misused. You will learn more about this if you enroll."

Chris nodded, intrigued.

"Do you have any questions for us?" asked Miss Sonata.

Chris thought for a moment.

"When would I start?"

"School begins on Monday. We'll be starting at midday to give you all a chance to have a look around and get yourselves settled slowly. Lessons will begin on Tuesday."

"And I have to sleep here?"

Miss Sonata knew what Chris was really trying to ask.

"We have taken your situation into account,

Christopher. If you accept the place, we will make sure that your household bills will be taken care of and that the necessary repairs are undertaken in your home so that your mother is more comfortable."

"But she doesn't cook or eat if I'm not there."

Miss Sonata gave a sympathetic smile. "I understand, Christopher; we will take care of that. You are only twelve years old, and your mother is an adult. It is time that you thought of what is best for you. Your mother will be fine. How does that sound?"

Chris took a moment to think, while Miss Sonata and Sir Bentley watched him patiently. He thought about the fact that he had been expelled that morning, about his mother at home, and about what going to this strange school might involve, and finally he came to a decision.

"I'm really sorry, but you don't know my mum. She can't manage, and I can't leave her. I'm the only person she has," said Chris.

Miss Sonata looked surprised, and Sir Bentley stood up.

"Christopher, this is your decision and it is not for us to put pressure on you, but please, will you reconsider? Perhaps if you were to look around the school?"

Chris shook his head sadly.

"There's no point. It wouldn't change anything. I can't do it. I'm really sorry to waste your time."

Miss Sonata pulled out a card from her briefcase and handed it to Chris.

"Here's my number. Call me if you change your mind."

"Okay, thanks," said Chris, stuffing it into the pocket of his jeans. "I'm going to go now."

There was silence as Chris stood up. Chris didn't know what else to say. He pushed the chair back.

"Christopher, wait," said Sir Bentley. "Don't make any decision now—give yourself the weekend to think it over. Your place will still be here for you."

Chris wished that they weren't being so kind; it made it so much harder to do what he knew was right.

"There's no point—give the place to someone else. I can't accept it."

Sir Bentley shook his head, and Chris could see his frustration. "I don't know if we made it clear enough how special you really are. We have tested thousands of children, and nobody came close to achieving what you did. If you choose not to come, then we won't be taking a replacement. The school is designed for six pupils, but that is only if we find six pupils who are capable enough to take on our training."

"Training?" asked Chris.

Miss Sonata looked up at Sir Bentley and shot him a strange glance.

Sir Bentley smiled dismissively. "Sorry, wrong choice of word. I mean schooling. Regardless, please give it some thought."

Chris shook his head. "It's not that I don't want to; it's just that I can't, and nothing is going to change that."

"Very well. I can't say I'm not disappointed, but I respect your decision. It's been a pleasure, Christopher," said Sir Bentley, shaking his hand across the table. "John and Ron will be waiting outside. They'll give you a lift home."

"It's all right," said Chris, just wanting to be on his own. "I can get a bus home."

"Are you sure?" asked Miss Sonata. "It's really no problem."

Chris shook his head. "I'd prefer to get the bus," he said, standing up. "I'm really sorry if I wasted your time, and . . . thanks. Bye."

"Good-bye, Christopher," said Sir Bentley.

"Good-bye," said Miss Sonata.

Chris walked out of the room and down the corridor back to the front door, shoulders hunched and head bowed low.

He opened the door to find Maura scrubbing the steps. She stood up to let him pass.

"See you next week, Christopher," she said, ruffling his hair as he walked past. Chris looked up, and she saw the look on his face.

"Are you all right, love?" she asked, looking concerned.

Chris was about to tell her that he wouldn't be coming back, then decided against it. He gave her a weak smile, then ran off before she had a chance to say anything more.

For the next few days, Chris felt as if his life had been put on pause. While his former classmates went about their lessons as normal, he cleaned the house, fixed the carpet down where it was coming up, and made all the meals, which he and his mother ate in silence in front of the television. His mother never mentioned the visit from Miss Sonata or the fact that Chris wasn't at school, and Chris didn't bring it up. All the while, Chris wondered what would happen now, expecting a knock on the door from social services at any moment to take him away. He knew that he had to find a place at a new school, but he didn't know where to begin, and he couldn't bring himself to ask Mr. Tuckdown for another chance.

On Sunday, five days after his meeting with Sir Bentley and Miss Sonata, Christopher came down from the attic, where he had spent the last three hours trying to fix a leak in the roof, to find his mother sitting in front of the television, as always. He watched her for a moment and, suddenly, for reasons he couldn't explain, all the resentment and anger that had been building up suddenly spilled over. He stormed over to the television and switched it off.

"I was watching that. Turn it back on!" said his mother.

"*No.* You can't just sit and watch television all day!"

If his mother was surprised by his shouting, she didn't show it.

"Yes, I can. I have and I will, and it's none of your business."

"Yes, it is! You're my mother—you're supposed to look after me!"

"You can take care of yourself."

"But I have to take care of you, too. *It's not fair!*" he shouted at her.

His mother looked up at him, her face full of anger.

"Nobody asked you to. I can take care of myself. I don't need you. All you do is moan, moan, moan."

"*Moan?* I don't moan. All I do is cook for you, clean your clothes, pay the bills, and take care of the house, and I never say anything. I turned down the place at that school, so I could stay here and look after you."

Chris's mother stood up and looked straight at him, and her face was twisted with hate and rage. At that moment Chris didn't recognize the person looking at him. "Well, you're not doing me any favors," she said, staring at her son. "I don't need you here trying to make me feel worse. As if I haven't got enough to worry about. Life would be easier if you weren't around."

Chris stopped, and all the anger left him.

"You don't mean that."

"Yes, I do," said his mother. "I want you out."

"What?"

"I said, I want you out. You're not welcome here anymore. If you're so big and clever, you can find your own way. Now . . . *get out!*"

She sat back down and picked up the remote.

Chris stared at her, tears running down his face, and then ran out of the house.

Chris kept running—past his neighbor's houses, past the locked gates of his old school, across the empty park, past lines of identical houses until, out of breath, he finally stopped. He looked around to get his bearings and realized that he had no idea where he was. It was getting dark, and the streetlights flickered on, casting an amber glow across the deserted street. He sat down on the pavement and shivered, realizing that he hadn't even stopped to pick up his coat. Wrapping his arms about himself, he tried to think of anybody that he could call and realized that he had nobody—that the only person he did have didn't want him anymore.

"Oi!"

Chris looked up. A group of teenagers was coming toward him on their bikes. Chris stood up.

The boy at the front, whose face was hidden by a scarf and cap, put his foot down to stop and climbed off his bike. He walked up to Chris and stared down at him.

"What you doin'?" he asked.

"Nothing," said Chris, starting to walk away.

The boy put his bike down against the pavement and ran to catch up with Chris. Chris didn't look back but started to walk faster. Behind him he heard the sound of footsteps quickening, and then he felt a hand on his shoulder.

"I said, what you doin'?" said the boy, still holding onto Chris's shoulder.

"I'm not doing anything," said Chris, trying not to show how scared he was.

"Looks like you're on our turf."

"I'll move," said Chris.

"Bit late for that. Give us what you've got and we'll call it quits."

Chris hesitated, then pushed the boy's hand off him and turned to run.

"Get him!" shouted the boy, and Chris turned to see the rest of the group get back on the bikes and begin to give chase.

Chris jumped over a low brick wall onto a grass verge and began to run along it, but it didn't take long for them to catch up with him. Before he knew it, he was on the ground and his pockets were being turned inside out. Coins fell out, and one of the boys picked up a rumpled note.

"A fiver . . . nice. I'll have that," he said, and stuffed it into his jacket pocket. "Where's your phone?"

"I don't have a phone," said Chris, just wanting them to leave him alone.

"Everybody has a phone," said the boy, checking Chris's pockets.

"I don't have a phone," repeated Chris angrily.

The boys checked the rest of his pockets and realized he was telling the truth.

"Waste of time," said one of them, and kicked Chris's leg. "Let's go."

Chris lay on the ground and watched them leave, cycling off into the darkness. He sat up slowly and rubbed his leg, then stood up and shook the grass and dirt off himself. Bending down, he ran his hand over the grass to see if they had missed any coins, but there was nothing except a crumpled-up white card that he didn't recognize. He picked it up and walked over to the light of the streetlamp and saw Miss Sonata's name. It was all he had.

After a while he found a phone box and dialed the operator.

"I'd like to reverse the charges, please," said Chris.

"What number are you calling?"

Chris read out the mobile phone number on the card.

"And your name?"

"Christopher Lane," he said, and waited as the phone began to ring.

"Hello?"

"Hello, I have a call from Christopher Lane. Will you accept the charges?"

"Yes," said Miss Sonata, and there was a pause.

"Thank you," said the operator. "Your call is being put through."

Chris waited, and there was a click.

"Christopher? Are you okay?"

Chris opened his mouth to speak, but instead he started to cry.

"What's wrong?"

Chris wiped the tears from his face.

"I don't know. Mum threw me out and I've just been mugged."

There was a pause.

"I'm coming to get you. Look around you, can you see anything—a road sign?"

Chris scanned his surroundings and saw a sign up ahead on a low wall.

"Cambridge Place," he said.

"I'll be there in ten minutes. Don't move."

Chris put the phone down and went out onto the street.

"There you go, love," said Maura, and placed a large mug of steaming hot chocolate in front of Chris.

"Thank you," said Chris.

"Miss Sonata's just organizing for someone to go round to your house and tell your mum that you're here. She'll be back in a moment. Now, drink that down you, pet; it'll warm you up. I'm going to make your bed up and get you some dinner—you must be famished."

Chris nodded.

"Well, I won't be too long. Miss Sonata will bring you downstairs in a moment."

Maura left the room and closed the door behind her before Chris had a chance to ask her what was downstairs. Not wanting to think too much, Chris looked about for something to distract him, but the office was still as bare as it had been the last time he'd sat here—there were still no books on the shelves, and the desk and chairs were still the only items of furniture in the room. To kill time, he started to count the coffee cup stains on the table, until he was interrupted by the sound of the door opening once more. He turned around, expecting to see Miss Sonata, but instead Sir Bentley entered the room. He walked over to Christopher and shook his hand.

"How are you?"

Chris shrugged his shoulders. "Okay, I guess."

"I came as soon as I heard."

"Sorry," said Chris, feeling embarrassed at being the cause of so much disruption.

"Not at all. We were all still working—everything's been rather rushed to make sure we're ready for tomorrow. But first we need to work out what to do with you. What do you want to do?"

Chris thought for a moment. "Can I still come to school here?"

Sir Bentley nodded.

"Yes, the place is still yours if you want it—it won't be too difficult to arrange that. But I should say, Chris, that as much as we would like you to be a pupil here, that is by no means your only option. We could make some phone calls and find you somewhere to stay while this"—he paused, choosing his words carefully—"situation with your mother is sorted out."

"I want to come to school here," said Chris without hesitation.

"Are you sure? You seemed quite hesitant earlier this week, and if you came here, we'd need you to be prepared to throw yourself fully into your studies. Do you understand what I mean?"

Chris looked up at Sir Bentley.

"I will work harder than everybody else here. I will work twenty-four hours a day, if you want me to."

Sir Bentley smiled.

"I don't think that will be necessary—but I like your enthusiasm. So it's agreed, you will be joining us as a pupil here?"

Chris nodded. "Yes, sir."

"Very well, then," said Sir Bentley and offered Chris his hand. "Welcome to Myers Holt."

Chris shook his hand and then watched as Sir Bentley took out some papers from his briefcase and leafed through them until he came to the one he was looking for. He pulled it out and placed it in front of Chris.

"This is the Official Secrets Act. I explained the other day that you may come into contact with some confidential information. Therefore, we require all our pupils to sign this. It means that you agree not to discuss anything sensitive that you learn here. Read through it and sign here, if you agree."

Chris quickly scanned the page and picked up a pen lying on the desk and signed it.

Sir Bentley took the page and returned it to his briefcase, then pulled out a small machine.

"Finally, we don't use keys here—so I'll need your thumbprint. Place your thumb here."

Chris placed his thumb on the pad of the machine and watched as a red light scrolled up the pad.

"Wonderful! Now, I'm sure that Maura's rustled up some delicious food for you. Let's go get you some dinner."

Sir Bentley stood up, and Chris followed him out of the room and across the hallway. He waited while Sir Bentley opened a door and switched a light on. There was a flicker as the fluorescent strip lighting warmed up to reveal a small kitchen. Chris looked confused but followed Sir Bentley, who motioned for Chris to pass him and stand by the sink.

Sir Bentley closed the door and walked over to the kettle on the middle of the work surface.

"Tea?"

"Um, no, thanks," said Chris.

"Very well, then, I'll do the honors."

Chris watched as Sir Bentley pressed the button on the side of the kettle. There was a click followed by a blue flash, and then the room began to shake.

"What . . . ?"

"No need to be alarmed," said Sir Bentley, chuckling. "The room is a elevator. Activated by my thumbprint when I press the kettle's switch. Ingenious, I think you'll agree. Boils water, too," he added, looking rather pleased with himself.

Chris was too shocked to comment. Instead he held on to the side of the sink as he felt the room fall suddenly and then begin a thirty-second descent before coming to a smooth stop. The switch in the kettle clicked back into the off position, and steam poured out of the top.

Chris watched curiously as Sir Bentley opened the door to the sound of faint classical music. He couldn't quite believe that they had really moved, but sure enough Sir Bentley stepped out to reveal a spacious, bright entrance hall with closed doors leading from it on all sides. Chris walked out onto a dark green carpet decorated with gold fleurs-de-lis.

"Good for the brain," explained Sir Bentley, referring to the music, "and it masks the sound of the underground trains above us."

"Wow," said Chris. He was about to ask how far belowground they were, when he was interrupted by the sound of a door opening. Chris looked over to see Ron, the security guard from the other day, enter the room, still wearing sunglasses, followed by John, who had to stoop low to pass under the doorway.

"Ah, John, Ron. You remember Christopher from the other day," said Sir Bentley, putting his hand on Chris's shoulder.

They nodded in unison.

"He'll be joining us at Myers Holt," said Sir Bentley.

"We weren't expecting any pupils tonight," said Ron, looking Chris up and down.

"He's starting a bit early," said Sir Bentley. "The rest will be here tomorrow at midday as planned."

John nodded, but Ron didn't look quite as appeased.

"If you don't mind me saying, sir, this is a bit of an inconvenience. I haven't got all the security-clearance paperwork ready."

"You're very capable, Ron; I'm sure Chris won't mind if you just ask him a few questions and he can do the paperwork tomorrow with everyone else."

"Very well, sir. We'll only be a few minutes," said John.

"Excellent," said Sir Bentley. "Call me when you're done; I'll be in my office."

Chris watched as Sir Bentley walked off toward the same corridor through which Ron and John had entered.

"Right," said John, "we just need to have a look through anything that you're bringing in."

"Where's your bag?" asked Ron, walking round the back of Chris.

"I, um, didn't bring anything," said Chris.

"Hmm . . . very suspicious," said Ron, lifting up his sunglasses and staring directly into Chris's eyes. "We're going to ask you some questions now, and before we begin, it might interest you to know that I can smell a lie from fifty feet away."

"Honestly, I'm not carrying anything," said Chris.

"We'll be the judges of that," said Ron, stepping back. "John, do you want to start?"

"Really, Ron?" asked John. "The boy's not even wearing a jacket."

"That's precisely the kind of thinking that gets people killed, John," said Ron.

"Oh, for goodness' sake," said John, turning to Chris.

"Fine. Are you carrying any weapons—knives, guns, bombs, or anything else like that?" asked John.

Chris shook his head. "No."

"Excellent. That's all we needed to know," said John, looking satisfied. "Ron—you want to ask anything else, or can I get back to my dinner?"

Ron looked over at John and glared at him. He turned to Chris.

"Are you a terrorist?"

"No," said Chris, surprised.

"Have you ever been a terrorist?"

"Um, no," said Chris.

Ron stared at Chris for a few moments. Chris stood awkwardly, not knowing where to look.

"He's telling the truth," confirmed Ron. John rolled his eyes, and Ron turned back to Chris to continue his interrogation.

"Are you carrying on you any of the following items: gunpowder, dynamite, fireworks, flares, cooking fuel, gasoline, bleach, nitric acid, any radioactive materials, knives of any kind, scissors, firearms, ammunition, screwdrivers, tear gas, or anything else that could be used to inflict injury on another person?"

Chris shook his head. "I've got nothing on me at all."

"Turn your pockets out," ordered Ron.

Chris pulled the pockets of his trousers out, and Miss Sonata's business card dropped to the ground.

"Well, well, well, what's this? I thought you said you weren't carrying anything at all," said Ron, bending down to pick up the card. "I told you I could smell a lie."

Chris hesitated. He wondered if Ron was joking with him, but if he was, he was doing a good job of keeping a completely straight face.

"It's just a business card. What are you worried about—paper cuts?" said John, rolling his eyes.

"I *know* it's a business card, John, but that's not the issue," said Ron. "What if it *had* been a grenade?"

"It's not a grenade, though, is it, Ron?" said John.

"You're missing the point, John. It *could've* been a grenade, and if we'd left the security clearance up to you, the first we'd have known about it would've been when we got blown up to pieces halfway through our spaghetti Bolognese. I don't want my brains splattered across the walls. Do you, John?"

John shook his head slowly, as if he couldn't quite believe what he was hearing. He turned to Chris. "Don't take any notice of him; he has trust issues."

"Call it what you like, John, but I haven't been killed yet, have I?" said Ron.

"Good for you, Ron. Are we done now?"

Ron nodded, handing Christopher back his card. "I'm satisfied the boy doesn't pose a threat. I'll get Sir Bentley," he said, walking away.

Moments later Sir Bentley returned and dismissed Ron and John.

"Hope they didn't give you a hard time," said Sir Bentley.

"It wasn't too bad," said Chris.

"Excellent. They're good men. The best. They may seem a bit . . . odd, but that's probably exactly what makes them as good at their jobs as they are. It may take them a

at home," he said, and patted Chris on the shoulder as he made his way past him. Chris smiled back, then walked around the sofas and up to the bookshelf built into a section of the back wall and filled with brand-new books. He scanned the titles and recognized a few of them as latest bestsellers that had only recently arrived in his local library.

He walked back over to the sofa and sat down; then, realizing that he had the room to himself, he took his shoes off and flopped backward. He peered over the arm of the sofa and saw a remote control, which he picked up; then he realized that there was no television. He sat up and looked around, but he couldn't see a screen anywhere. Chris put it back down on the table and noticed a brass button next to the lamp. Out of curiosity he pressed it, then jumped at the sound of something buzzing in front of him. Looking up, he saw the large oil painting of the English countryside that hung above the fireplace begin to turn into the wall until it revealed an enormous television behind it.

Chris grinned, picked up the remote, and curled up on the sofa as the screen came to life.

"I see you worked out the television," said Maura, walking in with a large tray.

Chris jumped. He quickly sat up as Maura placed the tray in front of him. On it was a plate of roast beef, Yorkshire puddings, and vegetables, a small boat of gravy, and a tall crystal glass filled with apple juice.

While Chris tucked into his dinner, Sir Bentley was on the telephone in his office, down the hall.

"Yes, Prime Minister, we have everything in place and ready to go. We just have to hope for a bit more time so that we can train them up. . . . I know, I know, but what option do we have? As soon as they're ready, we'll send them out and see what we can find out. . . . No, sir, at the moment we have no further information. . . .Yes, it could be a coincidence, but I don't believe Cecil would have mentioned Inferno unless it was absolutely necessary. . . . No, he hasn't muttered a word since that day, and it doesn't look good. Unfortunately, whoever did this to Cecil clearly knew what they were doing—his shutdown appears to be quite irreversible. . . . Of course, Prime Minister, I'll keep you updated and let you know as soon as work is underway. . . . Thank you, Prime Minister, I appreciate that. All the best."

Sir Bentley put the phone down slowly and rubbed his hands over his silver-gray hair. He opened up the file in front of him and pulled out a black-and-white photograph of the strange-looking pale boy in a crisp uniform, cross-legged, staring up at Cecil Humphries.

"Who *are* you?" he said to himself.

"And here . . . is your room," said Maura, opening up the door. "You'll be sharing it with another lad, Philip. Ever so . . . eccentric. Lovely, too, of course. I'm sure you'll get along like a house on fire."

"Thanks," said Chris, and walked out into the open air—or at least that's how it felt, as the walls of the small room had been painted from top to bottom in a realistic landscape of rolling hills, with distant trees silhouetted against the moonlit night. There were two small wooden cabins, like miniature log houses, on either side of the room, with beds above them that could be reached by ladder.

"Wow," said Chris.

"It's lovely, isn't it?" said Maura, smiling. "This way you won't feel like you're stuck underground the whole time. Now, that's for you to do your homework in," she continued, pointing to the door of the cabin on the left. "There's everything you'll need in there for your studies tomorrow." She walked over to another small door to the right, which was camouflaged by the landscape. She turned a handle and pressed a switch. A light came on, and she moved to the side to let Chris see in.

"This is your wardrobe space, and past the other door is your bathroom."

Chris peered in and saw empty clothes rails on both sides with drawers below them. At the end of the dressing area, he could see a small bathroom with a toilet, a sink, and a shower stall against the far wall, which from what he could make out, seemed to be moving.

Chris walked into the room, curious, and his mouth dropped open in amazement.

"Are those real jellyfish?" he asked, staring in wonder at the wall, which was, it turned out, a giant aquarium filled with gently pulsating jellyfish floating around.

Maura shuddered.

"Not my cup of tea, I can tell you. They told me it's supposed to be calming—though for the life of me I can't see how anyone could relax when they're showering next to hundreds of deadly creatures! What's wrong with a blooming goldfish in a bowl, I say."

Chris couldn't have agreed less—he thought the jellyfish were beautiful. He stared at the wall, hypnotized, until Maura called him back into the bedroom and broke his trance.

"We'll sort you out some clothes tomorrow," she said. "In the meantime, there's a toothbrush and a towel on your bed. Now try to get yourself a good night's rest. You'll need it. Big day tomorrow!"

"Thanks," said Chris. "This is amazing."

"Ah, well, I'm glad you like it. I'm off now. Night, night, love," said Maura, and walked out, closing the door behind her.

Chris climbed up the ladder and sat on the edge of his bed. He looked around at his new room and was filled with a strange feeling—a mix of excitement, trepidation, and loneliness.

He kicked his shoes off and lay back on the bed. It was only then that he noticed that the ceiling was black, except for a bright moon in the far corner and a thousand twinkling stars. He stared up at them, then saw a comet shoot across the top of the room.

"How strange," said Chris, but he was too tired to think. He closed his eyes and fell into a deep sleep.

· CHAPTER NINE ·

The next morning

Chris woke to the sound of birds singing and a warm light on his closed eyes. He opened them and saw clear blue skies above him.

"What . . . ?" Chris sat up, disoriented, then remembered where he was. Amazed, he looked around him and saw that the landscape was now bathed in morning light. The grass of the field about him glistened with dew, and the trees in the distance swayed gently in the breeze that he could hear whispering faintly about him. Chris leaned over and touched the wall. It felt cool and smooth, like glass, and Chris realized that he was looking at a screen.

There was a knock on the door.

"Can I come in?" said a voice Christopher recognized as Maura's.

"Yes," called Chris, and Maura opened the door, carrying a mug. She walked over to Chris's bed and passed it to him.

"Now, I know it's early, but you'd better drink that up and have a quick shower. I'll see you in the Map Room. There's a car waiting for you upstairs."

"A car?"

"Miss Sonata arranged for you to go buy some new clothes. You can have some breakfast when you get there."

Chris hesitated.

"What's wrong, love?"

"It's just that . . . well, I don't have any money to buy clothes."

Maura smiled. "Don't worry your head about that. Miss Sonata explained that you had to leave home in a bit of rush."

Chris reddened, wondering exactly how much Maura knew.

"There's nothing to be embarrassed about, love," said Maura gently. "We all need a bit of help sometimes. Now, Miss Sonata's taken care of everything. You just enjoy yourself."

"Really? I could pay it back when—"

"Don't be so silly," interrupted Maura. "You don't have to pay anything back. Every growing boy needs new clothes once in a while, so will you stop your worrying and finish up that cup of tea?"

Chris nodded gratefully and took a sip from the hot mug.

"I'll see you in the Map Room in ten minutes," said Maura as she walked out.

Chris took another sip, then left the mug on the shelf by his bed and climbed down the ladder. He showered quickly, watching the jellyfish circle gently around the aquarium, then dressed in the clothes he had arrived in.

He met Maura in the Map Room, and they took the kitchen elevator back up to the ground floor. This time he activated the kettle himself with Maura's permission, much to his delight.

Out in the street, which was still dark, Chris found Ron standing at the bottom of the stairs by the waiting car. John, he saw, was already squeezed into the driver's seat, ready to go.

"Have a good time, love, and we'll see you back here in a couple of hours," said Maura, as Ron opened the door and shooed Chris inside.

"Thanks," said Chris, as the door closed behind him.

"Mornin'," said John, starting the engine.

Chris smiled. "Hi," he said, fastening his seat belt.

"Right," said Ron, "let's go. Cleaver and Hawkes."

"The department store?" asked John, checking.

"Cleaver and Hawkes?" asked Chris. He had expected to be taken to a supermarket to pick up some jeans and a couple of T-shirts, not to London's most exclusive department store.

"Affirmative," said Ron.

Chris didn't respond—he was thinking about the last time he had been inside Cleaver and Hawkes on a cold day in late December, when he was four. His father was on leave from the army and had taken him there with his mother to look around and do some Christmas shopping. He still remembered it now—the carol singers greeting the throngs of shoppers, the enormous Christmas tree in the marble foyer and the smile on his parents' faces as they watched him run about the toy department in amazement. It was one of the few clear memories he had of his parents together.

"So, doing a bit of shopping?" asked Ron, interrupting Chris's thoughts.

"Um, yes," said Chris.

"Just shopping, nothing else?"

"Um, no. Just shopping," said Chris.

"You can trust us, Christopher," said Ron, sounding, Chris thought, a bit annoyed. "We need to be kept in the loop to protect you. So I'll start again. Going to do a bit of shopping, Christopher?"

Chris didn't know what answer Ron was expecting. "Yes. I'm getting some new clothes."

"That's nice," said Ron, staring at the road ahead, sunglasses on. "Just popping out to get a couple of designer belts and some cologne?"

"I don't think so," said Chris, confused. "Just some trousers and a couple of tops, probably."

In an instant Ron unbuckled his seat belt and jumped round in his seat, facing Chris.

"What are you really doing?" he shouted.

John looked round in surprise and grabbed Ron by the arm.

"For goodness' sake, Ron, calm down," snapped John, still driving.

Ron did up his seat belt, breathing heavily. "I know, I know," he said, taking deep breaths, "but he's not telling us everything, and you know I don't like secrets, John."

John didn't respond. Instead he looked in the side mirror and swerved to the side of the road, where he stopped the car and pulled up the hand brake. He turned to Ron, while Chris sat sheepishly in the back.

"Look, Ron, you need to calm down. The boy doesn't have to tell you anything. If he says he needs to get some socks, then we're going to drive him to get them, 'cause that's what we're paid to do."

Ron shrugged his shoulders and turned his head to look out of the window, while Chris sank back into his seat, wishing he could disappear.

Finally Ron spoke. "It's just . . . well . . . something's not right, John. Twelve years in Special Forces—personal bodyguards to the Queen, for Pete's sake—and now they've got us living in a cellar, minding a bunch of kids—doesn't that seem a bit strange to you, John?"

John thought about this for a moment before responding.

"You've got a point, Ron, I'm not denying it, but we're just here to do what we're told," he said, and with that he pulled back out onto the road and they continued their journey in silence.

"We'll wait here for you," said John when they finally pulled up outside Cleaver and Hawkes.

"Thanks," said Chris quietly, glad to get out of the car.

Chris stepped out onto Regent Street and looked around. Although the sky was beginning to lighten, the streetlamps were still on and the sidewalks were mostly empty. Chris looked up at the clock above the entrance. It was only seven thirty in the morning. He walked up to the doors and saw that, although the lights were on inside, the sign on the door said they were still closed. He was about to turn back and tell John they were too early when he saw a lady in the distinctive Cleaver and Hawkes navy-and-gold uniform approach. She smiled and unlocked the door.

"Christopher Lane?" she asked, and Chris nodded, surprised.

"My name is Victoria. Welcome to Cleaver and Hawkes. Please, come in."

Chris walked in and looked around at the sprawling shop floor. All about him, members of staff were rushing around, preparing to open up for the day.

"Follow me. Personal Shopping is up on floor six."

Chris followed Victoria to the lobby elevator, and she pressed the call button.

"Have you been to Cleaver and Hawkes before?" asked Victoria, as they waited for the elevator to arrive.

"Um, only once," said Chris, but he didn't elaborate and Victoria didn't ask.

They entered the elevator and Chris saw himself in the mirror. He looked tired and disheveled, even after his shower, and he suddenly felt very out of place.

Victoria saw him looking at himself and smiled warmly.

"You'll enjoy this, I promise you," she said reassuringly. Chris smiled awkwardly.

The elevator opened out onto a dark lobby surrounded

by illuminated glass cases filled with expensive watches, ties, and belts. A large vase of flowers stood on a pedestal in the center and to the side were two armchairs behind a glass coffee table.

"Take a seat, Christopher, and I'll just make sure your fitting room is ready."

Chris sat down and watched Victoria walk quickly down the hall. He looked at the neat stack of magazines fanned out in front of him and picked up the one with a car on the front cover.

He had barely opened the front page when he heard footsteps approach from ahead of him and looked up to see a man with slicked hair and a scowl walking in his direction. As he neared, the man spotted Chris and stopped suddenly. Chris sat uncomfortably while the man looked Christopher up and down, then flinched in horror at the sight of Chris's worn-out shoes.

"Young man, do you know where you are?" he asked in a snooty voice.

Chris opened his mouth to reply, but the man didn't give him a chance to speak.

"You are not allowed up here. This is for our VIP customers only. Now, get out of here before somebody sees you. We have a reputation to uphold," he said, and plucked the magazine from Chris's hands, then wiped the cover with the corner of his Cleaver and Hawkes jacket.

"I was—" said Chris.

"Just leaving. Yes. Now get out before I have to disinfect the place."

"Ahh, Julian, there you are!"

Julian and Chris looked up to see Victoria.

"I see you've met Christopher. Christopher is a guest on the Millbank account."

Julian's eyes widened in shock.

"The Millbank account?" repeated Julian.

"Yes," said Victoria, "he is a personal guest of Sir Bentley." She raised her eyebrows on Sir Bentley's name, as if to stress the importance of it.

Chris watched as Julian processed the information and squirmed.

"Yes, of course," said Julian uncomfortably. "Christopher and I were just sharing a little joke." He turned back to face Chris and gave a small bow.

"Would you like to follow me, sir. Your fitting room is ready for you."

The fitting room was larger than his bedroom at home, and Chris looked around in awe at the opulent surroundings. Large vases of fresh flowers surrounded him, and an ornate crystal chandelier hung from the ceiling. The room was almost empty, except for a long cream sofa in the center; a changing cubicle to the side, cordoned off by a heavy blue velvet curtain; and a tall, ornate mirror at the other end. Chris noticed the light carpet, which looked as if it had never been stepped on, and then behind him with sudden panic, hoping that his dirty shoes hadn't left a mark. Thankfully, they hadn't.

Julian took a measuring tape and notebook out of his jacket pocket and began to take notes as he measured Chris. Chris stood awkwardly as Julian rushed round him with the tape, moving his arms and legs around as if he were a puppet. Both stayed completely silent throughout, until finally Julian stepped back with a sheepish smile.

"Thank you for your patience, sir. I'm all done. If you would care to take a seat while I make some notes. Breakfast will be served in just a moment."

"Okay, thanks," said Chris, still feeling very much out of place. He walked over to the cream sofa and sat on the edge of it awkwardly, his back straight and hands on his lap, while Julian began to scribble numbers furiously in his little black notebook.

After a few minutes Victoria walked in, followed by another woman pushing a cart covered with a white tablecloth. On it was a lavish selection of pastries, toast, cereals, juices, tea, and coffee and a collection of magazines. Victoria directed the trolley over to Chris, then handed Julian a clipboard, and Julian scurried off.

"Miss Sonata forwarded a list of items you'll need. We'll just put together a selection for you to choose from and bring them up to you. In the meantime, enjoy your breakfast."

"Great, thanks," said Chris, standing up as Victoria walked out of the room. He looked over at the feast on the table and picked up a croissant. Taking an enormous bite, he took the car magazine on the top of the pile and sat back on the sofa. *Maybe this isn't so bad after all*, thought Chris as he began to relax.

Two hours later Chris walked out wearing crisp new jeans, a white shirt, a green sweater, a black jacket, and a pair of brand-new sneakers. Behind him Julian and another member of staff carried bags laden with new clothes and shoes and loaded them up in the trunk of the waiting car.

"Thank you very much, sir. I hope you've enjoyed your time with us, and, well, I'm terribly sorry for the misunderstanding earlier," said Julian, shaking Chris's hand.

"It's fine," said Chris cheerfully, getting into the car. "I had a great time. Thank you."

Julian bowed his head gratefully. "No, thank *you.* I very much hope you'll visit us again soon," he said, closing the door behind Chris.

"Thanks for waiting for me," said Chris to Ron and John, as the car pulled away.

"Not a problem," said John cheerfully, clearly trying to make up for Ron sulking in the seat next to him.

"Can't believe it," muttered Ron, looking out the window. "He really *was* doing some shopping."

John leaned over and turned the radio on, much to the relief of Chris, who was for once quite happy to sit back and listen to country music.

Maura greeted Chris on his return to Myers Holt and helped him carry the bags down to his room, cooing the whole way about how handsome he looked in his new clothes. Chris had to admit he felt good, although a bit embarrassed at all the attention.

"The other children will be here in a couple of hours," said Maura as they hung up the clothes in his room. "Are you looking forward to it?"

Chris shrugged. "Yeah, I guess."

"You'll get along grand," said Maura, reassuring him,

but Chris wasn't convinced. He always felt like an outsider around other children, partly because he didn't know anything about the latest films or toys and partly because he knew that none of them were worrying about paying bills or taking care of their parents. Maybe this time would be different, he hoped.

Chris spent the next couple of hours watching television and playing pool against himself. Finally, at half past eleven, the door opened, and Sir Bentley walked in with a girl in a pink dress and pink cardigan following behind him, sniveling.

"Good morning, Christopher," said Sir Bentley. Chris laid the cue down on the table and walked over.

"This is Daisy Fields. Daisy, this is Christopher Lane."

"Hi," said Chris. "Cool name." The girl took one look at him and burst into tears.

Sir Bentley patted the girl on the back awkwardly.

"Daisy is a bit upset about saying good-bye to her parents. Perhaps you could reassure her. I'll, uh, leave you to it," said Sir Bentley, making a quick exit.

Chris and Daisy stood awkwardly facing each other, not speaking. Daisy looked down at the floor, her straight blond hair covering her face, and brushed the tears away with the back of her hand.

"It's all right here," said Chris, trying to reassure her.

Daisy nodded but didn't look up.

"Look at this," said Chris, and walked over to the button by the armchair. He pressed it, and the television appeared from behind the painting.

He turned back to Daisy, who was looking at the screen. She smiled weakly and sniveled.

"That's nice," she said quietly.

"You can watch whatever you want," said Chris, handing her the remote control. Daisy took it and walked over to the sofa. He watched her take off her shoes, pink also, and curl up on the sofa. Chris stood for a moment, wondering what to do next, then finally walked back over to the pool table and resumed his game.

Ten minutes later the door opened again, and Sir Bentley walked in behind a boy and a girl. The girl was wearing a blue tracksuit and had light brown skin and piercing green eyes, which were framed by a mass of wild dark hair. The boy next to her was chubby, and his face was covered in freckles. His hair had been shaved close to his head, and he had an air of confidence about him that was immediately obvious.

"All right," he said to Chris. Chris nodded.

"Christopher Lane, this is Rex King and Lexi Taylor," said Sir Bentley. Lexi nodded at him but didn't say anything. Chris returned the nod.

"Where's Daisy?" asked Sir Bentley, and Chris pointed over to the back of the sofa. Slowly, they saw the back of Daisy's head appear and look round. Her eyes were bloodshot, and she looked terrified.

"What's up with her?" asked Rex.

"She's missing her parents," said Chris.

"Blimey, it's only been five minutes," said Rex, and Daisy burst into tears once more.

"Yes, well, perhaps you could try to cheer her up," said Sir Bentley. "I imagine the others won't be too long; I'd best get upstairs to greet them." Sir Bentley walked out and left the children standing in the room.

"Fancy a game?" Rex asked Chris. Chris nodded and walked over to the pool table to set up the balls.

"What is this? Some kind of boys' club? I can play too," said Lexi, following behind them.

"Actually, I think you'll find you can't," said Rex, chalking up his cue.

"What makes you think that?" asked Lexi, angrily.

"Well, let me see. Oh yeah, that's right—you're *a girl*."

"Who you calling a girl?"

"You," said Rex with a smirk, "or aren't you a girl?"

A flustered look crossed Lexi's face, replaced quickly by a frown.

"Whatever. Just let me play."

Rex shrugged his shoulders. "Fine. Just don't cry like Princess Snotty over there when you lose."

A loud sob came from behind the sofa.

"Hey, come on," said Chris.

"Sorry. Didn't realize she was your girlfriend," said Rex.

Chris rolled his eyes and passed the cue to Lexi.

"Make sure you win and shut him up," said Chris, standing back to watch.

"Stay out of it, rich boy," said Rex, looking Chris up and down. Chris looked confused for a moment and then realized that Rex was looking at his new clothes. For a moment he considered correcting him, then decided to keep quiet. "You can break," said Rex, turning to Lexi. "Probably the only shot you're going to get."

Lexi walked up to the table with a determined look on

her face. The boys watched as she placed the cue awkwardly over her hand. She pulled back and slammed the cue forward, completely missing the white.

Chris grimaced.

"Ouch. That's embarrassing," said Rex. "Two shots to me."

Lexi looked at the cue as if it were to blame, as Rex fired off the balls in all directions, potting three. He took a couple more shots and then finally missed.

"Feeling sorry for you," he said as Lexi leaned down to try to line up the shot. She pushed the cue forward, but instead of hitting the red, the white ball went straight into the corner pocket.

Chris put his hand to his forehead, shaking his head in disbelief and embarrassment for Lexi.

"Argh!" cried Lexi in frustration. She kicked the table.

"Oh, dear," said Rex, laughing. "Looks like it's going to be a short game after all."

"I'm sick of this," said Lexi, putting the cue back in the rack.

"Don't say I didn't warn you," said Rex.

"Want to show the girls how it's done?" asked Rex, offering Chris the cue.

Chris shook his head. "No, thanks," he said, turning away.

"Suit yourself," said Rex, shrugging his shoulders.

Lexi and Chris left Rex playing on his own. They walked over to the sofa next to the one that Daisy was sitting on and sat at opposite ends.

"What are you watching?" Lexi asked Daisy. Daisy shrugged, still huddled in a ball.

This is not going well at all, thought Chris. He couldn't have been more grateful when Sir Bentley opened the door once more and walked in with two boys.

"And these are the last two students. This is Sebastian White," said Sir Bentley, placing his hand on the shoulder of a good-looking boy with olive skin and black hair. "And this is Philip Lowry," he said, gesturing toward a skinny, pale boy in a three-piece brown suit and glasses.

"Ready for a day at the office?" Rex asked Philip from the other side of the room. Philip smiled.

"Dress to impress," he said.

"Impress who? My grandmother?" laughed Rex.

"Rex, perhaps we could try to tone down the humor," said Sir Bentley, sternly. He turned to the two boys next to him.

"Philip, Sebastian, this is Christopher, Lexi, Daisy, and Rex." Philip gave a small salute, and Sebastian bowed.

"Encantado."

"Eh?" said Lexi.

"It means 'enchanted.' I am Spanish," explained Sebastian in a strong accent.

"Knock it off! Your dad's from Manchester," said Rex, walking over. "You were standing outside when I came in—I heard him. You're about as Spanish as a Sunday roast."

Sebastian curled his lip and glared at Rex.

"Half-Spanish. My mother is Spanish, and I lived there until last year. You are . . . *un idiota*," said Sebastian, waving his arm at Rex dismissively.

"Boys, boys. Enough!" said Sir Bentley. "You are all

going to have to learn to get on. And Rex, if you can't say anything nice—"

"Don't say anything at all. Yeah, I hear that a lot," said Rex, sulking.

"Perhaps this will be the last time, then. If you don't think you can manage to conduct yourself properly at Myers Holt, then we have no need for you here. Do you understand?"

Rex nodded.

"Right then, let's start again. Why don't you all take a seat and we'll begin."

Rex plopped himself down between Chris and Lexi, and the other two boys sat next to Daisy, who by this point had managed to stop crying and was sitting up.

Sir Bentley pressed the button by the lamp, and the screen flipped back round to the painting, which he stood in front of. All the children, apart from Chris and Daisy, who had already seen it, looked impressed. Sir Bentley walked over to stand in front of it and addressed the children.

"Welcome to Myers Holt. I hope you'll enjoy your year here with us. You have all been picked for your unique talents, of which you will all become aware very soon. In the meantime I'd like to remind you that you all signed the Official Secrets Act, and what you learn here is not to be discussed outside of this facility. This is very important. Do you understand?"

The children all nodded in unison.

"Good. You will learn more later, but I will say this. Your stay here will teach you many things, and you will leave Myers Holt with an academic foundation that will stay with you for life. Of that I can assure you. However, there are other reasons that you are here. To put it simply, as pupils of Myers Holt you will be expected to do some work for the government in addition to your studies. Some of you may not feel comfortable about this, and at the end of today, when you have been given more information, you will be asked to make a decision as to whether you choose to remain here or prefer to leave. That is a personal decision for each one of you, and I can't stress enough that you are under no pressure to stay."

The children said nothing, but they were all leaning forward, intrigued, when the sound of the door opening disturbed them. Chris turned and saw Miss Sonata walk in, smiling. She walked over to Sir Bentley and, even though she was wearing a gray somber pinstripe jacket and skirt, she looked very young standing next to him.

"I think you have all met Miss Sonata," said Sir Bentley.

"Good morning, everybody," said Miss Sonata brightly.

"Miss Sonata is my right-hand man, if you will. She will also be teaching your curriculum lessons. You'll meet Ms. Lamb tomorrow—she was unable to join us today. She is deputy headmistress at Myers Holt and will be teaching you most of your other lessons."

"What other lessons?" asked Lexi.

"Everything will be explained in due course," answered Sir Bentley cryptically.

"Miss Sonata, I'll leave you to it. Once again, welcome to Myers Holt," he said, and walked out.

Miss Sonata waited for the door to close and then turned back to face the children.

"So, let's show you around," she said.

The children all stood and followed her out of the room and into the hallway.

"This is the dining room," said Miss Sonata, walking over to a door opposite. She opened it, and the children jostled to look inside. The room was rectangular and bathed in light. Large French windows ran along three sides of the room and looked out over fields. Chris recognized the view as one similar to the landscape in his bedroom. Between the windows, on bare brick walls, hung baskets filled with overflowing ivy and plants. Philip walked over to one of the windows and pressed his face up to the glass.

"The windows are screens," explained Miss Sonata, "designed to disguise the fact that you are living underground. The light comes from specially designed sun-replicating bulbs, which will give you plenty of vitamin D and make sure that the plants thrive. And, unlike upstairs, the weather is always fine," she said, smiling.

"Breakfast is served at eight in the morning, lunch at twelve, and dinner at seven. There is always fresh fruit and snacks available here," she said, pointing to a table in the corner with a white-and-red-checked tablecloth, on top of which sat an enormous bowl of fruit, cheeses, yogurts, and other foods that Chris couldn't make out from where he stood, "so you can help yourselves at any time."

Rex walked over to the table and grabbed three oranges, stuffing them all into his pockets.

"I could get used to this," he said, picking up an apple and taking an enormous bite out of it.

"I'm glad you approve," said Miss Sonata, smiling,

and changed the subject. "Why don't I show you your bedrooms."

The first room they came to was Chris's.

Miss Sonata turned to Philip. "You'll be sharing with Christopher," she said.

"Looks like it's me and you, then, Pedro," said Rex to Sebastian. Sebastian grimaced, while Chris and Philip smiled at each other in relief.

Miss Sonata moved on to the next room without comment.

"So this one is Rex and Sebastian's room, and the one next to it is Lexi and Daisy's. You can have a look around later. We'll move on to the school area. I think you'll like it," said Miss Sonata, leading them back down the hallway and into the entrance foyer.

Miss Sonata stood by the door directly opposite the elevator and waited for the children to join her, then opened the door. Chris walked in, and his mouth dropped open in amazement. He looked around him and saw that the other children had exactly the same expression on their faces.

An enormous glass dome towered above and around them and extended all the way down to the ground. It was made up of the screens he had seen in the other rooms and projected a vast landscape of fields under a perfect summer sky, with gentle wisps of clouds passing by above their heads. In front of him was a large, gentle hill with an enormous blossom tree in full bloom at its top. Chris knelt down on the stone pathway that ran around the vast room and touched the vibrant green grass in front of him. He was shocked to find that it was real.

"Oh, it's beautiful," said Daisy, and she smiled for the first time that day.

"This is the Dome. Over on the other side of the hill is the swimming pool and changing rooms. The classroom wing is over here," said Miss Sonata, leading them to the right. They stopped at one of the glass screens, and Miss Sonata turned a handle, revealing another hallway with the same yellow-and-cream-striped walls and green carpets as the rest of the facility. She led them to a wooden door marked with a gold plaque: CLASSROOM.

Miss Sonata led them into a large white room, with sash windows looking out over a river. At the front was a white-board and a long table that faced two rows of glass desks. The chairs behind them were large and comfortable with tall backs, and each one was covered in bright colors.

"Oooh, I want the pink one," said Daisy.

"It's all yours," said Lexi.

"What is this?" asked Sebastian, pointing to the wall behind them. Chris turned to look and saw a diagram that took up the whole wall. It looked like another map, but instead of buildings there were rainbow-colored boxes, each one labeled in ornate black script with titles such as LIES, FEARS & PHOBIAS, PEOPLE, BRIEF ENCOUNTERS, and even one called EMBARRASSMENT.

"Ahh, this is your mind map. You will learn more about it later," said Miss Sonata, looking up at the clock on the wall. "It's nearly lunchtime. I'll quickly show you your think tanks."

Miss Sonata led them back out into the corridor and into a dark room. The room, as far as Chris could see, contained only six large cubicles standing in a line, each one glowing a different color.

"Again, all will be explained," she said, closing the door. "Now, Maura will be waiting."

Miss Sonata led them back down into the Dome and up to the top of the hill, where Maura was laying out food on picnic blankets.

"Lunch is served," she said, handing them each a plate.

"Enjoy," said Miss Sonata. "Sir Bentley will be back in an hour; he'll be taking you for your first lesson."

The children all nodded, their mouths already full.

"So, what do you think those think-tank things are?" asked Lexi after they had stuffed themselves full of food. It was the first time any of them had spoken since they had sat down.

"Torture chambers," said Rex, "definitely torture chambers."

Daisy's eyes widened in horror. "Why would they want to torture us?" she asked.

"That's how they get you to learn. Nothing makes you remember your times tables faster than the threat of having your fingernails ripped out slowly," he said, holding his hand up to Daisy's face and pretending to rip out his thumbnail.

"That is highly unlikely," said Philip matter-of-factly. "Fear reduces performance. Fact."

"He's winding you up," said Lexi, pushing Rex's hand away from Daisy.

"Well, don't say I didn't warn you when you hear the sound of the drill start up," said Rex.

"Far more likely to be a computer-based teaching program," continued Philip, ignoring Rex. "I read about it in this month's *Science Review*."

"*Science Review*? I'm sorry, *how* old are you?" asked Rex.

"Old enough to know my times tables," replied Philip, and the others sniggered.

"Get a life, Einstein," said Rex.

"I guess we'll find out in a moment," said Chris, spotting Sir Bentley looking over at them from the entrance to the classroom wing. Daisy stood up and smoothed out her dress, and they all walked down and followed Sir Bentley into the classroom.

Chris walked in last and took the blue seat at the front by the door, and Sir Bentley made his way over to the whiteboard. He cleared his throat and began.

"As you all know, my name is Bentley Jones, and I am headmaster of Myers Holt. This is in addition to my role as director general of MI5, which some of you may have heard of."

"MI5? So you're a spy?" asked Philip incredulously.

"No, not a spy, though I do have spies that work for me. Ultimately, my job is to protect the United Kingdom from threats on our shores. As you can imagine, this is an extremely difficult job, but for the most part we're very successful at keeping Britain safe. However, from time to time, situations arise that are beyond even our usual resources, and we have to be creative in ways to tackle them. Myers Holt, the home of MI18, is one of those ways."

"There's no such thing as MI18," said Philip matter-of-factly.

"There's no such thing as MI18 *on paper*, Philip, but that doesn't mean it doesn't exist. MI18 was formed during World War Two as a top-secret agency that employed children to help them with their intelligence efforts."

The children all looked at each other in confusion.

"The reason we have picked the six of you is that you all have particular talents that can help us. And by 'us' I mean the United Kingdom. Myers Holt was established to help nurture those talents and use them in ways that will be of great good, and in return you will learn more than you could from a lifetime of schooling. I think, perhaps, the best way to explain is to give you a demonstration. First, do any of you speak Swahili?"

The children all shook their heads.

"Good," he said, and picked up a stack of books on his table. He handed one to each child.

Chris looked at the cover of the book. *A Beginner's Guide to Swahili.* He opened up the book to a page in the middle, on a section about emergencies. Phrases in Swahili were followed by their translation in English. He stopped at one of the English sentences and read.

Please could you call an ambulance. My friend requires immediate medical attention.

"I'd like you all to close your books and listen to me carefully," said Sir Bentley. Chris put the book down and looked up.

"When I ask you to begin, I want you to open the book up to the first page. I don't want you to read it, or even to try to understand or remember what you are looking at. All I want you to do is to *look* at the page—a quick glance will do—and then move on to the next page. There are"—he picked up the book on his desk and turned to the back page—"one hundred eighty-five pages in this book. That should take you about five minutes to glance through. Right, off you go."

Chris opened up the book and did exactly as instructed, glancing briefly at each page, then turning to the next. He tried to concentrate, but his mind kept wandering, trying to work out what the point of the exercise was. He reached the end and closed the book, just as the others did the same.

"Good," said Sir Bentley. "Lexi. Please translate the following into Swahili." He picked up the book and let it fall open. "'There is a fire in the garden.'"

"Uh, I don't speak Swahili," said Lexi, flustered.

"Actually, you do. Don't think about it; just say it."

"Um. *Kuna moto bustani pale.*" The children looked at Lexi in amazement. Lexi looked around to see who had said that, as if she couldn't believe that those words had come out of her own mouth.

"Excellent and absolutely correct, as you can see if you turn to page thirty-two."

"What? That's impossible. Or a fix," said Rex, looking annoyed.

"Entirely possible, Rex. Perhaps you could do the next one: 'Where is the nearest police station?'"

Rex opened his mouth, but instead of delivering the sentence in nonsense words, as he had intended to do, he answered in perfect Swahili.

"Kituo cha polisi kipo wapi?" His eyes widened in surprise.

"Now Chris," said Sir Bentley, and Chris sat up straight. "'I want to go to the cinema tonight.'"

Chris hesitated.

"Again, don't think; just speak. Your brain will do the work without you realizing."

Chris tried again.

"Nataka kwenda sinema leo usiku."

Chris couldn't believe it and felt complete confusion. He had spent three years learning French and could barely remember the numbers to ten.

Sir Bentley repeated the task with Daisy, Sebastian, and finally Philip, who were all left with the same shocked expression on their faces.

Sir Bentley gathered up the books and put them back on his desk.

"Does anyone know what percentage of our brain, on average, human beings use?"

Philip put up his hand immediately.

"Ten percent," he answered.

"Exactly right. However, during World War Two, a man named Walter Vander stumbled onto something through sheer chance. He discovered that children, beginning on the day that they turn twelve—the transitional year from child to young adult—are able to use their brains to their full capacity. This lasts until the last day of your twelfth year and then stops as suddenly as it started. During this time, if you know how, it is possible to learn the most incredible skills, which are as powerful as they are, unfortunately, short-lived. We call this power the Ability, and it is the reason that you are all here today."

Sir Bentley paused to let the information sink in. Finally, Chris put up his hand, looking as confused at the other children in the room.

"Yes, Christopher?"

"So, you're telling us that we have this Ability, that's why we're here?"

"Actually, all children have it at the age of twelve, to varying degrees. The reason that we asked the six of you in particular to come here is because you have all recently turned twelve and, although every child we tested can be trained to use the Ability, some have more of a natural talent. That is what the test you took was designed to show us." Sir Bentley walked round to the back of his desk, opened a drawer, and took out a remote control. He pressed a button, and a screen came down from the ceiling in front of the whiteboard. He pressed another button, and the screens on the windows turned off, leaving the room pitch-black. They heard a click, and the screen in front of them lit up with the image of a boy underneath a Christmas tree, the same photograph that Miss Sonata had shown Chris back at his house.

"You'll all remember this, I'm sure," said Sir Bentley, "but here is a picture that you won't have seen before."

He pressed a button on the remote, and the photograph was replaced with another similar one, but in this one the present had been opened and the boy was holding a stuffed penguin with a yellow bow tie and a top hat.

"This photograph was stuck behind the one that you were looking at. Without realizing it, you were all able to see past it using your Ability and reveal what the little boy was holding."

Lexi gasped loudly as Chris's jaw dropped open in amazement.

Sir Bentley turned back to face the screen. He pressed the button, and this time a photograph of a street scene appeared. Chris immediately recognized the steps leading up to the church, and, looking at the bottom of the screen, he saw the same red numbers spray-painted onto the pavement that he had read out to Miss Sonata.

"This question tested your Ability to use remote viewing. Has anybody ever heard of remote viewing?"

Philip put up his hand.

"Surprise, surprise, Einstein knows the answer," said Rex.

Sir Bentley shot Rex a disapproving glance. "Yes, Philip?"

"It's when you use the power of your mind to view distant places using a picture or coordinates."

"Exactly right, couldn't have explained it better myself. In this case you all looked at the map and were able to see the location as it was at exactly that moment and imagined yourself walking around it. The stronger your Ability in this area, the closer you would have landed to the numbers on the pavement. As I'm sure you understand, this is a fantastically useful tool in gathering information by, for example, viewing confidential files in a locked cabinet.

"Finally, Miss Sonata asked you all what animal she was thinking of—a fox. A deceptively difficult question that requires you to access somebody's mind. A couple of you were able to do this without hesitation—an impressive feat indeed. And so," said Sir Bentley, turning the screens on the window back on and filling the room with light once more, "you are now familiar with the Ability. As pupils here, you are officially agents minor for MI18. Any questions?"

Philip raised his hand.

"So we'll be working for you?"

"You will be studying, but as you have learned from your short introduction to Swahili—that won't take up too much of your time. As for your role as agents minor, you will be asked to help us with gathering some information."

"What kind of information is this you want?" asked Sebastian.

"Forget Swahili; Pedro needs *The Beginner's Guide to English*," laughed Rex.

"Rex!" boomed Sir Bentley. "My patience wears thin quickly. Pull yourself together and keep your mouth closed unless you have something positive to say." Rex looked surprised at the rebuke and looked down at his desk.

"In response to your question, Sebastian, we are looking for some answers. The Ability is incredibly powerful, and if the wrong people were to find out about it, it could cause a great deal of harm. Unfortunately, that seems to be exactly what has happened. You may remember that a few weeks ago a man called Cecil Humphries suffered a breakdown on national television while visiting a school."

"Who is Cecil Humphries?" asked Daisy.

"The politician who stole chocolate from that sick girl's bedside," said Philip.

"Oh, that's not nice."

"Well, no," said Sir Bentley. "He was, nevertheless, a government minister and was once a teacher here at Myers Holt."

"I thought it was a new school," interrupted Rex.

"No, not exactly," said Sir Bentley. "Myers Holt opened during World War Two as a school for just one class of very special children each year. Here the pupils were taught, as you will be, to use their Ability so that they could help the government with gathering information. It ran for many years within this very building as the headquarters of MI18 until, thirty years ago, it was closed down. At that time, believe it or not, I was actually a teacher here, as was Cecil Humphries.

"It was never the intention to reopen the school, until Cecil, before he was . . . incapacitated, managed to let us know that the cause of his breakdown was someone using the Ability on him. We believe we know the boy who did it, but we have no more information about him other than what he looks like and that he has mastered some incredibly complex techniques using the Ability, techniques that he must have been taught to use. It turns out that he was not a pupil at the school where the incident occurred, and despite our best efforts we have come to a dead end. However, we know that there is somebody out there using the Ability for harm, and that is of great concern to us. And so, after nearly thirty years, we have made the decision to reopen Myers Holt. We hope you will be able to help us find out who the boy is and how he learned to use the Ability. Any questions?"

Philip raised his hand. "So how come I have never

heard of this? If every child who is twelve has the Ability, then we would all know about it."

"Interesting question, Philip," said Sir Bentley, and Philip puffed up with pride.

"The answer to that is that most people do not want to believe what they do not understand. Children who are not trained to use the Ability, for the most part, will never know exactly what they were capable of during their twelfth year. Any strange activity will normally be dismissed as coincidence and ignored. Any other questions?"

"Why did you close Myers Holt?" asked Chris.

Sir Bentley shifted uncomfortably. "It's a difficult answer, but I'm going to be completely honest with you all. Our last mission was not a successful one. We had become complacent and decided to experiment using a new technique called Inferno that requires close proximity to the target. In doing so, we placed our agents minor in a dangerous situation that had tragic consequences."

"Tragic? Did somebody die?" asked Daisy, horrified.

"Well, yes. On that terrible night, two children lost their lives. Myers Holt was closed the following day."

The children all gasped.

"But," said Sir Bentley, putting his hand up to get their attention, "we have learned our lesson. We would never ask you to do anything that would place you in any danger. If we had any doubts about that, you would not be here today. I will live with the events of that night for the rest of my life, and it is not without careful consideration that we decided to reopen the facility. Your safety will be of my utmost concern. That is my solemn promise to you all."

"Forget it! I have better things to do than to get myself killed," said Rex. For once, the others nodded in agreement with him.

"And that is your decision. As I said earlier, at the end of today you will be asked whether you choose to stay here. If you decide not to, then you will be free to leave and return to your old schools. However, if you decide to stay, you will not only have the opportunity to save lives and serve your country, but you will also be given skills that will help you to achieve great things in your own lives. It may interest you to know that one of my former pupils at Myers Holt was Edward Banks."

"The prime minister?" asked Chris.

"Yes, the prime minister. He came from a broken home and struggled at school. By the age of ten he could barely read. When he was twelve years old, he was accepted into Myers Holt, and only a few years later he was the youngest-ever law graduate of Oxford University and went on to become a very successful lawyer before deciding to turn his hand to politics. As I said, Myers Holt will give you the tools to become extremely successful in any field of your choosing."

"But," interrupted Philip, "I don't understand. If you lose the Ability at thirteen, then what use will that be?"

"You will lose the Ability, but you will retain all the information you learn in that time. Imagine, by July of next year you could all be speaking ten languages fluently and be working on university-level mathematics with ease. It will change your lives for the better, that I can guarantee you.

"Well, I think you've heard enough from me for one day. And now I would like to introduce you to somebody who will explain our Mind Access Program—MAP, for short. Follow me," he said.

They walked down the hallway and into the think-tank room, where six cubicles glowed and hummed in the darkness. Sir Bentley switched on the light to reveal a stout old man kneeling on top of the lime-green cubicle with a screwdriver. He looked up in surprise, wobbled, and then fell from sight, landing on the floor below with a crash.

Sir Bentley hurried round and helped up the old man, who was red-faced and flustered.

"You rather took me by surprise," explained the man.

"Of course, of course, are you hurt?" asked Sir Bentley, looking concerned.

"No, not at all. I'm well padded," he said, patting his stomach. He adjusted his glasses and turned to face the children.

"Well, well, our new recruits."

"Children, this is Professor Ingleby. He is the chief engineer for the government research-and-development division, and he has kindly agreed to help us design the most effective training program possible to teach you how to use your Ability."

"Delighted, delighted!" he exclaimed, walking round to shake each of the children's hands vigorously. "And what fun we have in store for you!"

His enthusiasm was contagious, and the children all smiled, even Rex.

"These cubicles have been built with each one of you

in mind. Using information gathered from your school records and your interviews, you have been assigned a teacher that will best suit your personality to guide you through the program. Inside, you will have an opportunity to learn how to use your Ability. The program is as realistic as possible and reacts to your brain waves—you can control it by thinking. Isn't that marvelous?"

Philip nodded enthusiastically.

"Unfortunately," said the professor, "we have not yet managed to develop a computer program that can truly replicate the human mind, and so for that you will also have lessons outside of this classroom. I'll say no more, but let you enter the wonder of MAP." He picked up a clipboard and peered over his glasses.

"Sebastian, you are in the green cubicle. Philip in purple. Lexi in orange, Christopher in red, Rex in blue, and Daisy, I believe you rather like the color pink."

Daisy nodded enthusiastically.

"Fabulous! Now, off you go. Enjoy! And don't forget your seat belts," said the professor.

"Seat belts?" asked Daisy as they walked over.

"So you can't move when the drilling starts," whispered Rex in her ear, as he stepped into his cubicle.

Chris quickly walked over to his one and turned the handle. Inside was a built-in armchair that took up the entire space and a red harness that appeared to buckle in the middle. Chris strapped himself in and pulled the belts tight, just in case. He leaned back into the chair, and the door closed in front of him automatically, leaving him in complete darkness. He waited a moment and was just beginning to wonder whether he needed to do something to start the thing up when all the walls began to brighten slowly, until all he could see was blue sky around and above him. He looked down, just past his feet, and saw green fields far below him. Chris turned his head, and the chair moved round until Chris faced forward again, at which point the chair stopped. Chris smiled. He turned his head the other way, and the chair followed his gaze round once more; then he quickly spun his head in the opposite direction, and his whole body quickly followed.

He was about to try it again when he felt the chair lean forward slightly, and the vast emerald expanse below him filled the screen. The chair tilted forward again suddenly, taking Chris completely by surprise, and stopped when he was almost horizontal with the floor. His hands moved instinctively to the harness, and he held on tightly as the full weight of his body pushed down onto it. Suddenly he felt himself dive forward and fall through the sky toward the sea of green below him. He wasn't sure if he was moving or the image was, but the effect was convincing enough to make Chris feel as if he were really flying, not sitting in a box.

As he neared the ground, he straightened up and saw a meadow of white flowers in the distance, and standing in the middle of it was the distant but unmistakable image of a woman dressed in red. As he glided toward her, the image became clearer, and he was able to see that she had long, straight brown hair that was held back on one side by a single yellow flower. She wore a deep red dress with a long skirt that reached the ground and swayed gently about her in the breeze. She looked up, saw Chris approaching, and waved. She was, without a doubt, the most beautiful woman that Chris had ever seen, and when she smiled at him, he felt a deep calm wash over him. He came to a stop and realized that he was now sitting up straight again.

"Good morning, Christopher," she said in a gentle voice.

Chris said nothing, but stared into her eyes, hypnotized.

"My name is Cassandra," she said, "and I will be your teacher. Are you comfortable? Can I get you anything?"

Chris still didn't speak, wondering what would happen next.

"Christopher, don't be nervous. I am a computer program, but you can talk to me. I can respond to you as any human would. Are you comfortable?"

"Erm, yes," said Chris in a robotic voice, leaning forward into an imaginary microphone, so that the computer could understand him.

"That's wonderful. Sit back and relax; I can hear you clearly."

Chris sat back stiffly.

"Perhaps some water will help," said Cassandra, and Chris felt a low rumble beneath his right arm. "Lift up your armrest," she instructed him gently.

Chris moved his arm and pulled up the armrest to reveal a lit hatch with a bottle of water in it. He picked it up, twisted the cap off the bottle, took a deep gulp, and then placed it back in the armrest and closed it. He looked back up and Cassandra smiled.

"Better?"

Chris nodded.

"Good. As I said, my name is Cassandra, and my task here is to teach you to use your Ability. But I have limitations. I will guide you through the basics, but then you need to use your skills with real people and their complex minds. Does that make sense?"

"Yes," said Chris, a little more relaxed.

"Good. Then we'll begin."

The picture zoomed out again, leaving Cassandra on the ground below him. He felt himself soar backward, until she was just a red dot in a green landscape, and then turn sharply. He flew forward, passing over more fields and into a stretch of fog, which dissipated to reveal a small cottage with a thatched roof, surrounded by a dark forest. The door of the cottage loomed large in front of Chris and, once it took up the full screen, opened to reveal a dark room with two stools and a wooden table. Cassandra was sitting on one of the stools, smiling at him, and on the table stood a plain white candle with a small flame—the only light in the room. Chris turned his head and the chair followed, revealing the back of the room, which was in almost complete darkness. Chris squinted and leaned forward, making out the faint silhouette of what seemed to be a large dresser.

"Come, sit with me," came Cassandra's voice from behind him. Chris turned to face her, and the picture took him deeper into the room, until he was facing her across the table.

"The easiest skill to begin with is telekinesis. Have you heard of that?"

"No," said Chris.

"That's the power to move or manipulate objects with your mind. We're going to start with a very simple task. All I want you to do is focus on the candle's flame. I want you to focus on it getting bigger and then smaller again. You must think of nothing else, just the candle, and see the flame in your mind doing exactly what you want it to do. Do you understand?"

"Yes," said Chris.

"Okay, off you go."

The picture turned to the candle, and Chris looked at it intently. He imagined it getting bigger, and the flame flickered slightly.

"Good. That's excellent; keep going," said Cassandra. "Imagine it getting bigger and smaller."

Chris imagined the flame bigger, and the flame flickered slightly more before he heard a small pop and it disappeared, leaving him in total darkness.

He heard the sound of a match being struck, and the flame appeared again.

"Now, the problem there was that you weren't giving the candle your full attention. You have to forget that I'm here or that the candle is not real. The only thought in your mind should be about controlling that flame. If it helps, make the thought exaggerated. Imagine a huge flame coming out from it and then a tiny one."

Chris was determined to impress Cassandra. He turned his attention to the candle and focused on its flame getting bigger. There was another flicker, like the first time, but Chris ignored it, and slowly the flame began to get larger.

"Good, Chris, wonderful! Don't stop."

The flame continued to grow until it was about a foot high, and then he imagined it getting smaller, and the flame began to diminish until it was the size it had been at the beginning.

"Keep going, Chris; make it bigger again."

Chris put all his energy into the thought and willed it to get larger, and the flame began to rise again, faster and faster, until there was a flash and the whole of the screen around him turned white.

Chris jumped, and he put his hands up to shield his eyes from the blinding light.

The light faded, and Cassandra appeared in front of him again, the candle glowing brightly.

"Well, Chris, I think we could call that a successful first attempt. I'm very proud of you."

Chris blushed. "What happened?" he asked.

"You managed to make the whole cottage explode. Not quite what I had in mind, but it does tell me that you have incredible potential, Chris. The only problem is that the more power you have naturally, the more harm you can do with it. You'll have to learn how to control it. But that's what I'm here to teach you. And now, for the second half of the lesson," she said, "follow me."

As Cassandra stood up, Chris's point of view rose as if he were on his feet. He watched her turn and followed her out of the cottage door and along a stone path, which led into a dense forest. He stopped and watched Cassandra as she walked ahead, following the path into the forest until all he could see was the faint flash of red from her dress and then nothing. He leaned forward in his seat and watched the forest close in on him, as if he were running to catch up with her. When he did reach her, he found her standing in a dark clearing, the trees leaning over so that the sun filtered through the leaves, casting a green glow about them.

"Look down, Christopher," said Cassandra, and his eyes followed hers down to the screen under his feet and found that he was standing in the center of a circle of pebbles.

"This is your safe area. When you see anything approach, use your Ability to push it away back into the forest before it crosses the circle. Let's practice," she said, and he saw that she was holding a small red ball. "Are you ready?"

Chris nodded, and Cassandra disappeared, only to reappear a moment later at the edge of the clearing. She was kneeling down. He watched her carefully as she swung her arm back gently and released the ball toward him.

"Look at it and imagine it flying backward into the forest."

Chris stared at the ball for just a moment and watched as it slowed, came to a stop, and then flew gently backward into the air, straight into Cassandra's hand.

"Well done. Let's try it again," she said, but she was gone, and the voice was now coming from behind him. He turned his head and the chair moved his body round to face her. He looked at her and realized her hand was empty and that the ball had already traveled halfway toward him. He stared at the ball quickly and willed it backward, but this time the ball didn't slow down and instead flew backward violently, hitting Cassandra in the face and knocking her to the ground. Chris looked at her in shock.

"I'm so sorry—I didn't mean to . . ."

Cassandra gave a small laugh and picked herself up. "No harm done. I don't think you need any more practice, though; let's begin. In a moment you're going to have a series of animals enter the clearing. Your task is to use your Ability to make sure they don't eat any of the food," she said, then disappeared.

"Food?" asked Chris, looking around him; then, saw that the pebbles beneath his feet had been replaced by pieces of cheese.

Chris looked around nervously in anticipation, but nothing happened. Sure that there was something behind him, he turned quickly, saw nothing, and then turned back, but the clearing was still empty. He jerked back the other way and suddenly found himself spinning around faster and faster until the trees surrounding him blurred to become a black stripe. He held on to the sides of his chair and tried to keep his head straight. He was starting to feel sick.

"Just think of yourself standing still," came Cassandra's voice in a soft whisper—as if she were standing right next to him.

Chris imagined standing still and the chair immediately stopped. He sighed in relief, but before he had a chance to relax, he heard a rustle coming from the tree ahead. Chris sat up straight and stared at the leaves, his heart beginning to pound, and waited for the animal to appear.

Squeak!

Chris looked around.

Squeak!

He looked carefully at the leaves and saw a small brown nose and whiskers appear.

Ahh, cheese, he thought, watching the little brown mouse scuttle forward nervously. Chris looked at it, wondering if he should begin, when he saw the mouse's nose begin to twitch, and then suddenly sprinted forward, its little legs pushing up the earth about it, creating a small dust cloud that raced toward him.

Chris looked at the cloud and willed it to turn away.

No sooner had the thought crossed his mind than the mouse froze and the dust settled.

Chris couldn't believe how easy this was.

"Sorry, little mouse, no cheese for you today," he said, and pushed the mouse away in his mind. The mouse squeaked, then turned and fled, back into the darkness of the trees.

Before Chris had a chance to congratulate himself, he looked down to see that the cheese had been replaced by carrots. A twig snapped to his left, and he turned to see a rabbit, which only managed two small hops toward him before Chris stopped it dead in its tracks. The rabbit's eyes widened, and then it turned and hopped frantically away back the way that it had come.

Chris was finding his stride now, and he spun around to find a cat, crouched down, ready to pounce for the fish lying by Chris's feet, but before it had a chance to jump, Chris stared at it and it cowered backward, meowing sadly as it retreated. Seconds later Chris turned to see the striking blue eyes of a white wolf from behind some leaves. He looked down and saw large pieces of fresh meat laid out neatly about him. The wolf stepped out from behind the cover of the undergrowth and snarled. It rushed forward, but Chris was ready for it. He looked it in the eyes, and the wolf stopped and lay down a few feet in front of him. It turned on its back, its paws in the air, and looked at Chris pathetically. Chris didn't blink. Finally the wolf stood back up and ran away.

Chris looked about him, waiting for the next animal to come into view, when he heard the crashing sound of branches being ripped out. He heard a loud, low growling sound, a sound that shook Chris from his complacency. As the sound neared slowly, Chris started to feel nervous. He looked down at his feet, but this time there was nothing, just the dry earth about him.

"Where's the food?" asked Chris, looking around frantically as the growling got louder. "I can't see the food!" he said, beginning to panic. He took deep breaths and tried to tell himself that it was just a harmless computer game, but he wasn't entirely convinced—it all looked and sounded so real. The growling continued, louder still, and Chris tensed up. *Maybe*, he thought, *this machine really can hurt me*, and the more he thought it, the more convinced he was that it was true.

His train of thought was broken by a sound close by, and he snapped his head round to see a set of large claws reach out from behind a tree and pull at a branch on the edge of the clearing. It snapped easily and fell to the ground. Chris held his breath as an enormous brown bear stepped out into the clearing. Chris looked at the bear and realized that it was staring directly at him. It was only then that he realized that *he* was the food.

The bear stood up on its hind legs and let out a deep, loud roar that shook the trees about it. Chris jumped and leaned as far back in his chair as he could, and at that moment he forgot that he was supposed to be using the Ability or that the animal wasn't real. At that moment all Chris could think about was that he was about to be ripped to pieces, and he watched in horror as the bear attacked, lunging forward.

Chris raised his arms instinctively to protect himself.

"Your Ability, Christopher, use your Ability," said Cassandra's voice.

Chris closed his eyes in panic and tried desperately to remember how to use his Ability, but his heart was pounding and he found it impossible to focus. He looked up and saw the jaws of the bear open wide in front of him, and then suddenly the screen around him turned black.

Chris realized he was sweating. He wiped his brow with the back of his hand and breathed in deeply.

The screen began to lighten, and he was once again surrounded by woodland. Cassandra was standing in front of him, smiling.

"You did very well."

"I didn't, really; I couldn't control the bear. I thought . . . I thought it was going to kill me." As the words came out of his mouth, he realized how ridiculous they sounded.

Cassandra laughed. "You're quite safe in here, Christopher, I promise. You did very well—the very fact that you reached that level tells me that you are an extremely talented boy, so don't be so hard on yourself. It was, after all, your first lesson. You will have plenty more practice—soon you'll have bears flying all over the place!"

Chris felt his heart rate slowing. He smiled.

"That's better," said Cassandra. "How are you feeling?"

"Good. Tired."

"That's to be expected; you worked hard. Have a moment to get yourself together. Drink your water and have some chocolate to get your energy back up."

Chris lifted up the hatch and took out the water and a bar of chocolate that hadn't been there before.

"Thanks," said Chris, taking a bite out of the bar.

"You're welcome. I'll see you tomorrow for your next lesson. And Christopher . . ."

"Yes?"

"I'm proud of you," she said with a smile. The image of Cassandra faded and then the screens brightened, until all about him was the image of water swirling gently about him. Classical music started playing, and Chris leaned back in his chair and breathed out deeply. After a few minutes he took his last bite, washed it down with some water, and unbuckled himself. The door in front of him opened, and Chris stood up and reentered the classroom, which was again dark, lit only by the glow of the cubicles. As he stepped out, the doors around him also opened, and he was joined by all the other children.

Professor Ingleby was waiting for them by the door, eyebrows raised and hands clasped in anticipation.

"Welcome back, welcome back! Did you enjoy your adventure?"

"Fantastic!" exclaimed Sebastian.

"Amazing!" said Lexi.

Chris nodded enthusiastically. "Yeah, it was awesome."

Philip walked over to the professor and shook his hand. "Outstanding," he said, and the professor grinned enthusiastically.

"I was scared at first, but I kept telling myself it wasn't real, and after a while I really enjoyed it!" said Daisy, smiling.

"Scared?" said Rex, stepping out from the back. "You were scared of *bubbles*?"

"Bubbles?" they all asked in unison.

Rex looked about him, confused.

"Yeah, bubbles. A candle and some stupid bubbles floating about."

"A candle, yes, but I see no bubbles," said Sebastian.

"Me neither," said Philip.

Rex shifted uncomfortably. "So you didn't all stand in a meadow with some stupid military guy screaming at you to move the bubble to the left?"

Lexi giggled. "No, did you?"

The professor walked over to Rex and put his hand on his shoulder.

"Now, now, let's be kind, children. Perhaps telekinesis isn't for you, Rex. I'm sure there are other areas that you excel at," said the professor.

"I wouldn't be so sure," said Lexi. She gave Rex a smug smile.

Rex glared at her, then turned suddenly and stormed out of the room.

"Oh, dear, he seems rather upset, poor chap. Perhaps

you'd best go console him. Your lessons are finished for the day."

The children all thanked the professor and left quickly, back into the garden, where they ran up the hill and collapsed around the foot of the tree.

"Do you think it's true?" asked Chris.

"What?" asked Lexi.

"This Ability thing. I mean, it was a good computer program, but I can't believe that we can really do what Sir Bentley said. Do you think we really do have the Ability?"

"Of course it's true!" exclaimed Daisy. "They wouldn't lie to us."

Philip shrugged. "Chris has a point; we don't know anything about this place."

"Well, there's only one way to find out," said Lexi, standing up.

"What are you going to do?" asked Daisy, looking concerned.

Lexi reached up and pulled a leaf from the branch above her head. She placed it on the ground and stood back up over it, arms crossed, and stared down at the ground.

For a few seconds nothing happened, and then the leaf began to shake and rise slowly, until it was standing on its stem.

The children all watched intently as the leaf rose slowly up in the air and hovered in front of Lexi's face. Lexi didn't blink, her focus completely on the leaf, which began to rise up farther and then started spinning in circles in the air.

"It works!" cried Lexi, as the leaf flew down and began

to circle Daisy's head, then suddenly fell to the ground before rising up again.

"I've got it now," said Philip, excited. "Look, I'm going to put it in the swimming pool." No sooner had he said the words than the leaf began to spin and then dive down to the back of the Dome, where it hovered for a moment over the still waters of the swimming pool before landing gently in the center.

The children all watched the leaf floating in the blue waters before Sebastian broke the silence.

"Incredible!" he said.

"What's happening?" cried Daisy.

The children all turned to see that Daisy was cross-legged and hovering a foot above the ground.

"It works on people, too!" said Lexi, laughing, watching as she lifted Daisy up higher, so that she was hovering above them, her legs kicking from under the skirt of her dress.

"Help!" screamed Daisy.

Lexi laughed as Daisy continued to rise up.

"Put me down!"

And then, as if from nowhere, Ron and John appeared, running toward them up the hill. Ron grabbed Lexi and lifted her, pinning her arms to the side, and Daisy dropped down, hitting the grass with a thud.

Ron, who was still holding Lexi by her arms, looked up at John, who was helping Daisy to her feet. Chris and the others sat completely still in shock.

"What now, John?" asked Ron, breathing heavily and looking confused.

"I haven't got a clue, Ron," said John.

"Let the girl go, Ron," said a voice. Chris turned and saw Sir Bentley striding purposefully up the hill.

Ron looked up at John, as if he wasn't sure what to do, and John gave him a nod. Ron stood up slowly, leaving Lexi to sit up, unhurt but in shock.

"This girl was . . . well . . . I don't know what she was doing, to be honest, but it didn't look good," explained Ron, brushing the grass off his trousers while never taking his eyes off Lexi.

Sir Bentley nodded. "I understand. I should have briefed you sooner. Meet me in my office in ten minutes and I'll explain. I need to talk to the children first."

"Yes, sir," said Ron and John in unison.

Sir Bentley watched Ron and John walk out of the Dome. Only when the door closed behind them did Sir Bentley turn to face the group. Chris saw the anger in Sir Bentley's face and suddenly felt very nervous.

"You must never, never, use the Ability on one another. Or on any person, for that matter, unless you have a teacher with you. Do you have any idea how powerful the Ability is?"

The children all looked sheepish and stayed silent.

"What you are learning to do could kill someone if you're not careful—that's no exaggeration. We have to be able to trust you to follow the rules. If you can't do that, then Myers Holt is not the place for you. Do you understand?"

Sir Bentley looked about at the children and, seeing the looks of remorse on their faces, he softened.

"I suppose you weren't to know. Just . . . don't do it again. I don't want to see any of you come to harm. Understood?"

They all nodded.

"Good. Now," he continued, looking around him, "where's Rex?"

"We don't know," said Chris. "He left the class before we did."

"Yes, Professor Ingleby explained what happened. He can't have gone far," said Sir Bentley.

Sure enough, they all followed Sir Bentley back into the student quarters and into the Map Room, where they found Rex standing at the pool table, arms folded, staring at the balls on the table, eyes scrunched up in determination.

Lexi laughed and walked over to the opposite end of the table as the other children and Sir Bentley walked over to the sofas. She looked down at the felt, and after only a few seconds the balls all exploded in movement, bouncing off the sides of the table and into one another. Lexi turned her head toward one ball and then the next, sinking each one with only a quick glance. Within seconds all the balls were potted, and she looked up at Rex, a sneer on her face.

"Maybe you should stick to bubbles," she said.

Rex, bright red in the face, looked up at Lexi, tried to think of something clever to say, then stormed off toward the door. Sir Bentley stepped back and put a hand on his shoulder to stop him.

"Rex, you have skills too; otherwise you wouldn't be here, I promise you. Give it time—you will find out what they are."

Rex shrugged his shoulders. "I don't even care."

"Yes, you do," said Sir Bentley, "and that's good. Determination is the key to success. You mustn't give up at the first hurdle."

Rex looked up at Sir Bentley, and the children could all see that his eyes were red.

"Come now, join us," said Sir Bentley gently. "I know this has been a hard day, but it will get easier. Maybe we could all start again as friends." Sir Bentley looked over at Lexi with a nod of his head toward Rex.

Lexi sighed. "Fine. Just stop being such a baby, Rex, and sit down."

Rex considered the idea and then, after a pause, straightened himself up and walked over to the armchair by the fireplace.

"Wonderful, that's everything back to normal, then," said Sir Bentley. "And now I must ask you all if you would like to stay."

Chris, Sebastian, Lexi, and Philip all nodded enthusiastically.

"Daisy?"

Daisy pursed her lips together in thought, then smiled. "I'd like to stay."

"And Rex?"

Rex shrugged his shoulders. "Yeah, fine, I'll stay. Even stupid bubbles are better than an hour of history at my school."

"I'm glad to hear it," said Sir Bentley. "I have great faith in each and every one of you to make this the most successful team at Myers Holt yet. Now, I must go and have a chat with Ron and John, who probably have quite a lot of questions for me. Your dinner will be served in an hour, and then I suggest you all have an early night—you have a full day of lessons tomorrow." He turned to walk out, then stopped and turned back.

"One more thing. I want to stress to you again how powerful the Ability is. I know that you'll all be keen to try out the new skills you'll be learning here at Myers Holt, and we encourage you to do so . . . within reason. It might also interest you to know that the metal lead blocks the Ability. The entire facility is lined in it—it's there to protect you and to make sure that you only practice the Ability within the confines of the school. As for your teachers, well, it's simply not practical for us to wear lead—the whole head would have to be covered, including the eyes. Instead, all the teachers have been trained to block you from entering their minds. It might be worth remembering that, if you are considering testing out your Ability on any of our members of staff, though I'm sure I can trust you all not to attempt such a thing. Is that understood?"

"Yes, sir," they replied.

"Good. Well . . . that'll be all. Good night—I'll see you all tomorrow."

Dinner was served by Maura in the dining room, the classical music barely audible behind the sound of the children discussing the day's events enthusiastically.

"He was old, a bit like my old headmaster, and he talked in a really slow, low voice," said Lexi, describing her teacher from the training program.

"What was his name?" asked Daisy.

"Prometheus!" said Lexi, laughing. "I had to ask him, like, ten times, and he kept saying it really slowly—Prooo . . . meee . . . theee . . . us," she said, in a low, booming voice, imitating him.

"Mine was called Baltasar," said Sebastian. "He just wear a white shirt and jeans, and he speak in Spanish, too."

Chris told them all about Cassandra.

"Ahh, she sounds lovely," Daisy said. "Mine was a bit like that too—her name was Astra."

"Bet she wore pink," said Rex.

Daisy nodded excitedly, not noticing the sarcasm in Rex's voice. "Yes, she did! A beautiful, long pale-pink dress, and it glittered in the sun."

"That sounds just lovely," said Rex, eyes rolling.

"It really was," said Daisy dreamily.

"What about yours, Philip?" asked Chris.

"He had a long white beard and was wearing white robes. His name was Zeno."

"And yours was in the military?" Chris asked Rex.

"Yeah. He was nasty, too. Kept shouting all the time—don't know why I got one like that. I'd prefer a teacher in a dress, like Einstein's."

"Not a dress, a *robe*," replied Philip, annoyed.

"Dress, robe, whatever—still better than being shouted at for an hour," said Rex, putting down his knife and fork. "I'm going to have a shower."

Rex left the room, and the rest of the children followed him out soon after and said good night.

Back in their room, Chris gave an amazed Philip a tour of their moonlit bedroom.

"What's in the cabins under the beds?" asked Philip.

"I don't know; I didn't really look before," answered Chris, opening the door of his cabin. He stepped inside and saw a small desk with a lamp on it, which Chris switched on. Chris sat in the comfortable swivel chair and looked up at the books that lined the shelf to his side, most of which were A-level textbooks. He opened up the drawer of the desk and found it full of new stationery and exercise books.

"We have PE first thing tomorrow . . . swimming," called Philip from the inside of his own cabin.

"Where did you see that?" asked Chris.

"Look inside the Myers Holt folder, on the shelf."

Chris looked up and saw the plain spine of a black folder on the far end of the shelf. He pulled it out and opened it up on the desk. It was empty except for a set of new dividers and a laminated timetable at the front. Sure enough, Chris saw that they had PE first lesson on a Tuesday, followed by Mind Access with Ms. Lamb at ten thirty and think-tank training after lunch, and they ended with Academia with Miss Sonata.

Chris closed the folder and stepped back into the bedroom. He peered into Philip's cabin and saw Philip scanning the pages of one of the books from the shelf.

"I'm going to have a shower; do you want to go first?" asked Chris.

"No, you go ahead. I want to finish some extra advanced physics that I'm working on," said Philip without looking up.

"Okay," said Chris. He turned to walk away, when a knock at the door interrupted them.

"Come in," said Chris, and the door opened.

"It's your mother on the phone, love," said Maura. "Do you want to talk to her?"

"My mum?"

"Yes, she asked if she could speak to you, but you don't have to, pet, if you . . . don't feel ready."

Chris reddened, very aware that Philip was listening.

"No, it's fine. Where's the phone?"

Chris followed Maura down the hall, past the other bedrooms and into a small room equipped with only an armchair and a phone on a small table. He waited until Maura closed the door behind her, then picked up the handset.

"Christopher?"

"Hi, Mum. Is everything all right?" Chris asked, still worried about her despite everything that had happened.

"I'm doing okay. Chris . . . I'm so sorry. I shouldn't have told you to leave."

It was the first time that his mother had ever apologized after an argument, and any anger that Chris might have been feeling disappeared completely in that instant.

"It's all right, Mum."

"No, it's not. Your teacher came round and made me realize that I wasn't fair on you. She offered to get me some help, and I said yes."

"What kind of help?"

"They made me an appointment to see a doctor."

"You're leaving the house?" asked Chris, amazed.

"Yes. Tomorrow," she said, and Chris could hear the nerves in her voice.

"You don't have to, Mum, if you don't feel well enough."

"I do have to. I can't go on like this."

"Do you want me to come home?" asked Chris.

"No, darling, I need to do this myself. Are you having a nice time?" she said, suddenly changing the subject.

"Yeah," said Chris, "it's good. Did you eat?"

"Yes, the supermarket delivered some food today. I don't want you to worry about me; just enjoy your new school."

"Okay, Mum."

"Good. I'm going to bed now; it's been a long day. And Christopher . . ."

"Yes?"

There was a pause.

"I love you."

Chris didn't speak for a minute. He hadn't heard those words for years.

"Chris? Are you there?"

"I love you too, Mum," said Chris, finally, and put the phone down. He walked back out into the corridor, lost in thought, and bumped straight into Ron and John.

"Hi," said Chris sheepishly, not looking up. They both stopped in front of him and then stood back to let him pass without a word. Chris, not knowing what else to say, walked between them toward the door. He was about to reach over to turn the handle when Ron spoke.

"Is it true?"

Chris stopped and turned round.

"Is what true?" he asked.

"That you have . . . you know . . . special powers," said Ron, as if it pained him to ask such a ridiculous question.

"Yes, I think so," said Chris.

Ron didn't respond, and there was an awkward silence as the two guards stared at Chris, arms folded, obviously trying to work out if he was telling the truth. Finally John spoke.

"Prove it."

Chris hesitated. "What?"

Ron looked up at John and nodded in agreement.

"Do something to prove it's true—make a rabbit appear or something."

"I can't make a rabbit appear from nowhere" said Chris, taken aback.

"What can you do?" asked John.

Chris shrugged his shoulders. "I don't really know; it's only the first day. We can learn stuff quickly and move things—"

"Anything?" interrupted Ron.

Chris shrugged his shoulders. "I don't know; I think so," he said.

"Lift John up in the air," said Ron.

"What?" asked Chris.

"Told you it couldn't be true," said Ron, and John, his arms folded, nodded his head.

"No, no, I *can* do it . . . I think . . . but, um, I'm not allowed to. If Sir Bentley—"

"We can keep a secret if you can. Sir Bentley's gone home anyway."

Chris looked around, trying to decide what to do.

"All right," he said finally, "I'll do it."

Ron smiled, but John didn't look quite as pleased.

"Wait. Just . . . you know . . . don't get carried away—just an inch or two."

Chris nodded and turned to face John, relaxing his eyes until they started to lose focus. He concentrated on lifting John up, and within seconds John's body began to shake slightly, and his gigantic feet lifted slowly off the ground.

Both Ron and John looked down in amazement.

"Uh, I don't like this," said John as he rose up higher. "I really don't like this," he repeated, sounding increasingly nervous. He waved his arms in an effort to stay vertical as Chris left him hovering a foot off the ground, and then suddenly he shot upward, smashing into the ceiling with his head.

Chris, his focus broken, looked up, horrified, and watched as John fell back to the floor, landing on his feet. John rubbed his head.

"I'm so sorry," said Chris, not knowing what to do. "I'm only learning—I haven't practiced much."

Chris was shaking with nerves as Ron and John both looked up to the ceiling. Chris followed their gaze and saw a large circular dent in the plaster. For a moment there was silence, and then, at the same time, Ron and John started laughing.

"That's unbelievable!" said Ron.

"Are you okay, John?" asked Chris, still concerned.

"Better than the ceiling," said John, his body shaking

with laughter, and then, without another word to Chris, they both turned away, still chuckling.

"I don't like this," squealed Ron as they walked off, imitating John by flapping his arms frantically.

"Shut it, Ron," said John, as they turned the corner and disappeared.

Chris smiled, not really knowing what to make of what had just happened, and headed off back to his bedroom.

That night, while Philip slept, Chris lay in bed thinking about how much his life had changed in such a short space of time. It was a strange feeling, as if a weight had literally been lifted off his shoulders, and yet in some ways he felt unnerved by it, as if he might suddenly wake up and find that this had all been a dream. Barely twenty-four hours had passed since his arrival at Myers Holt, and yet the overdue bills, the desperation he had felt as Frank had refused his offer of his father's medal, and the arguments with his mother all seemed like faded memories from another life, and when Chris finally fell asleep, he did so with a contented smile on his face.

working too. So go change and have a quick drink. See you all tomorrow and . . . don't be late!"

Ms. Lamb walked into the classroom and found the children already sitting at their desks, their hair still damp, chatting amongst themselves. She slammed the door shut to get their attention, and their heads all snapped round to see a short woman wearing high-heeled turquoise leather boots that didn't look as if they could support the rather large-framed body they were carrying. Never had a name been less suited to the person who owned it. The green leather suit she wore seemed to be made to fit somebody much smaller, and younger, and she had on so much black eye makeup that it made her look like a panda in costume. And if that wasn't bad enough, Chris could swear that Ms. Lamb had a mustache.

Chris heard Rex stifle a laugh behind him.

"Good morning," she said, not smiling. "Sit up and stop being silly," she barked at Rex. "I am Ms. Lamb, and I will be teaching you how to use your Ability for Mind Access." She walked over to her desk and placed on it the pile of books she was carrying. "So . . . ," she said, looking over at each one of them, "*this* is what I have to work with." She didn't look impressed.

"You," said Ms. Lamb, pointing to Sebastian, "what do you know about Mind Access?"

"I . . . not know nothing," said Sebastian.

"No, clearly not. Anybody else?" she said, looking at the rest of them. Nobody moved.

"Why doesn't that surprise me," she said, rolling her eyes.

"You—girl in pink—what is telepathy?"

"I—I—don't know," said Daisy, looking very nervous.

"Telepathy—the ability to send and receive thoughts. Repeat."

"Telepathy. The ability to send and receive thoughts," repeated the children.

"This is the most important skill that you gain with the Ability."

"We can read minds?" exclaimed Rex.

"Be quiet, boy!" barked Ms. Lamb. "You—hand these out," she said to Philip, pointing at the pile of books.

Philip stood up and passed the books round. Chris looked down at his spiral-bound copy. It had a faded red cover and the same diagram as the one painted on the wall, below the words, in thick black lettering, THE ABILITY TRAINING MANUAL.

"We have not had enough time to update this from the last edition, printed in 1962. Much of the information is irrelevant, as you will be learning it in the think tanks. For our purposes we are interested in chapter four onward only. Turn to that page now."

Chris turned to the start of chapter four and saw the diagram on the cover spread out over two pages.

"This is a map of the human mind. It is not an accurate representation, of course, but it is the simplest way to organize the information you will have to access. Glance at it and commit it to memory," She paused a few seconds. "You, girl with the frizzy hair."

"Lexi."

"Not interested. Now, look up and tell me what the

first long yellow box is at the bottom of the map."

"Reception," said Lexi, gruffly.

"Finally, a correct answer. This is where you hold current thought. Whatever you are thinking about at the present time is held here. Beyond Reception," continued Ms. Lamb, as the class listened attentively, trying to keep up, "is a complex web of rooms that are all linked. Those links are represented by roads in this diagram. You can imagine yourself walking around a town when accessing somebody's mind, and that will make it easier to navigate. You should imagine the colored blocks as buildings, each one filled with filing cabinets containing all the information that the mind has stored. The files that are most vivid in a person's memory will be on the lower floor. As you climb up, you will be accessing vaguer memories and information. On the second floor are the files that contain information that a person can access with some work: When you have something on the tip of your tongue, that would be on that floor. The top floor houses information that the person is not aware they hold and that will only move down to the ground floor if something external literally jogs the memory. Are you all keeping up?"

The children all nodded.

"Right. Finally, before we begin our lesson, you must all learn how to stop somebody else from accessing your mind. If somebody uses their Ability on you, you will hear ringing in your ears the moment that they enter the Reception area. That ringing will increase in volume until the person passes through the door that leads out into the mind's city, or leaves the mind entirely. The stronger somebody's Ability, the quieter the ringing in your ears. If, at any time, you hear ringing in your ears, you may stop it by immediately filling your Reception area with a block. A block is a thought strong enough to prevent somebody from moving farther in. Examples of good blocks are nursery rhymes or songs that you are very familiar with. Concentrate on repeating this over and over again in your mind until the person is forced to leave and the ringing in your ears stops. Anybody can use a block, you do not have to be twelve years old, so if you are even contemplating trying this on myself, or any other member of staff, you will be stopped immediately and suffer the consequences. Understood?"

"Yes," replied the children.

"Very well. Now, you, you, and you, close your books," she said, pointing to Chris, Lexi, and Rex. "The rest of you, turn to the next page in your manuals. On it you will see a list of objects. You are to concentrate on the list so that an image of each thing appears in your Reception area. I will give you a few minutes; then I will ask the person sitting next to you to list the objects you were thinking of. To enter the mind, simply look at your partner and focus on looking past their temple. Simple as that. And no blocking for now. You may begin."

Chris turned to Philip, and Philip looked down at the manual. Chris looked at the side parting of Philip's hair, and before he had a chance to imagine any map or room, he saw the list of objects as clearly as if he were looking at the manual himself.

"Go on Chris, start," whispered Philip.

"I already did," replied Chris.

Philip looked confused. "But I didn't hear any ringing."

"Stop talking!" said Ms. Lamb.

"We've already finished," explained Chris, looking round at Lexi and Rex, who were staring intently at Sebastian and Daisy, respectively.

"I hardly think so," said Ms. Lamb. "You were supposed to read the whole list."

"I did," said Chris.

"Very well, list them now."

"Scissors, a candlestick, an apple, a paper clip, a truck, and the sun."

Ms. Lamb looked surprised, then annoyed. "It's not reading somebody's mind if the person simply reads the list out to you," she said, furious.

"I—I didn't," said Philip, surprised and a little confused. "It's just, I didn't hear any ringing."

Ms. Lamb considered this for a moment. "Well, you obviously weren't paying attention. Right," she said, looking up, "the rest of you can stop now. You—yes, you—tell me what was on the list."

Lexi closed her eyes. "Ummm, scissors, a candlestick, an apple, and a paper clip."

"And . . . ," said Ms. Lamb.

Lexi hesitated. "That's all."

"No, that's not all. You, freckles, what else?"

Rex looked nervous. "A truck and the sun?"

"Correct. Good. At least I have one person in this class useful for something."

Rex looked thrilled. He turned to Lexi and grinned.

"Oh yes, ha-ha! I am Rex, reader of minds; you can bow to me now."

Lexi curled her lip and turned away from him, disgusted. To Chris's surprise, Ms. Lamb made no comment.

"Now we'll try this again with the same people looking at the list on the opposite page, but this time you are going to try to block the person the moment you hear the ringing in your ears."

Philip straightened his jacket and looked down at the page opposite. Once again Chris was able to see the list immediately.

"I can't hear anything," said Philip, staring intently at the page.

"That's because I've already done it," whispered Chris, looking apologetic.

"Again? I haven't even picked what I'm going to use for my block yet."

Chris shrugged, then looked up to see Ms. Lamb looking over at him with a disapproving stare.

"Talking again? I suppose you've finished, have you?"

"Umm, yes. I didn't mean to, but I had already done it before Philip started blocking me."

"You're supposed to use the block," said Ms. Lamb to Philip.

"But . . . but . . . I didn't hear anything again. I hadn't even started reading the list."

"Have you seen this book before?" asked Ms. Lamb, staring at Chris.

Chris reddened. "No, honestly, I haven't. I don't know what's going on."

"Well, if you think you're so clever, maybe you can come up here and do a demonstration."

Chris sunk back in his seat. "I'm sorry, I'll—"

"I *said*, get up here."

Chris stood up from behind his desk and walked over to where Ms. Lamb was standing.

"All of you can stop now," said Ms. Lamb, and the rest of the class looked up. Chris stood awkwardly, shoulders hunched.

"I don't like cheats. It's pointless and a waste of everybody's time," said Ms. Lamb, addressing the class.

"But I didn't cheat," said Chris, shocked.

"Well, we'll soon see about that. If you're so brilliant, then I'll expect you'll have no problems reading my mind before I block you. You have one minute to find my least favorite color. That will be in the Dislikes building which is next to—"

"Fears and Phobias," said Chris.

"Fine, begin," said Ms. Lamb, irritated.

Chris looked at Ms. Lamb and tried to ignore the hair that lined her upper lip. He looked at her temple, and immediately he imagined himself in a room with a door up ahead. He walked straight across to the door, opened it up, and saw he was standing on an empty street lined with buildings of various sizes and colors. Streets led off in all directions, but Chris, having memorized the map, knew exactly where he was going. He raced ahead, out of habit looking both ways as he crossed the street, and down another main road toward an enormous green building that stood in the center of a group of buildings ahead of him. He reached it and looked up to see a sign above the door that read DISLIKES. Chris hurried inside and entered a room full of filing cabinets lined up in rows. Chris rushed along them, checking the white label on each one.

Food . . . places . . . transport . . . people, said Chris to himself, noticing how large the PEOPLE cabinet was. *Ahhh . . .* He stopped at a small, one-drawer filing cabinet labeled COLORS and opened it up. Inside was a single folder, which he opened up. A cloud of orange exploded about him.

Excited with his success, Chris rushed out to return to Reception, when he spotted the sign above the building next to him: FEARS & PHOBIAS.

A quick look might be useful, thought Chris, then ran in through the front door and opened the bottom drawer of the first enormous filing cabinet he came to. He took a bulging folder out of it. As he opened it carefully, a scene appeared before him. He saw Ms. Lamb at a table, on her own, crying in the middle of a desolate gray landscape. The words "Being Lonely" appeared above, hovering.

Chris grimaced uncomfortably, closed the folder quickly, and rushed back out onto the main street, back to Reception, where the sound of Ms. Lamb singing "London's Burning" filled the room. Chris walked straight through and out the door into a bright light. He squinted, then opened his eyes to find he was staring Ms. Lamb directly in the eyes. He looked away quickly.

"Pathetic . . . *pathetic,*" said Ms. Lamb. "You didn't even try. Not so easy when you don't have a book to cheat with is it, young man?"

Chris opened his mouth to speak, but Ms. Lamb raised her hand to stop him.

"I don't want to hear your excuses. You have to look into my mind and try to access it to gain the information we've asked you for. If you can't even enter the Reception area, then you really are wasting your time in my lessons."

"But I already did," said Chris.

"No, you didn't. What do you take me for? I can hear when you're using your Ability by the ringing in my ears."

"I did!" said Chris, getting annoyed.

"Fine, then, what is my least favorite color?"

"Orange," said Chris defiantly.

A flash of confusion crossed Ms. Lamb's face. "A lucky guess, of course. Sit down."

"And you're most scared of being lonely," added Chris in anger, immediately regretting the words as they left his mouth.

Ms. Lamb stared at Chris, her face turning red with a combination of embarrassment and fury. "You—you—how *dare* you?"

Chris heard the gasps from the other children, but he didn't dare to look round.

"Get out, all of you. Take your manuals and practice for tomorrow's lesson."

Chris couldn't get out quickly enough. He grabbed his manual and rushed out the door. He waited at the foot of the hill in the Dome, and the other children appeared moments later. As soon as they saw him, they burst into laughter and Chris, in spite of the trouble he knew he was going to be in, started laughing too.

CHAPTER ELEVEN

A few hours later

While the pupils of Myers Holt enjoyed afternoon tea discussing their think-tank lesson where they had learned to drive a car using only the power of their minds, property developer Richard Baxter was sitting in his brand-new four-wheel drive, parked in the middle of a vast construction site, which—if today's meeting went well—was to become his largest development project yet. Baxter looked around at the cranes and bulldozers and imagined them being replaced by the enormous concrete tower blocks that were going to make him a *very* rich man, as long as he could convince the planning office to sign on the dotted line.

"You're a winner," said Baxter, looking at himself in his rearview mirror. "You're a winner, you're a winner, you're a winner," he repeated under his breath, fastening the yellow hard hat under his chin and grabbing his briefcase. He stepped out onto the dirt floor beneath him and strode out purposefully toward the group of people talking amongst themselves in the distance, not noticing the two identical boys ducking down behind the steering wheel of the bulldozer next to him.

"Good morning," said Baxter, as he approached the group of people. "Baxter, Richard Baxter," he said, shaking each person's hand with a vicelike grip. "Thank you for coming down today. I'm sure the changes we've made will impress you."

A stern woman with a clipboard under her arm nodded. "Perhaps you could start by showing us around," she suggested.

"Of course, of course . . . Sheila," he said, reading her name badge. "Why don't we begin here. At the moment we are standing in what will be the lobby of the Baxter Building, the largest of the five towers. As you suggested, we have now reduced the number of apartments from seven hundred to six hundred—a considerable reduction, I'm sure you'll agree."

A young man stepped forward, scribbling something in the notebook he was holding. "Mr. Baxter, as far as I can work out, that still means that the apartments won't allow enough space for a kitchen."

Baxter dismissed this comment with a wave of his hand. "I think you'll find kitchens are out of fashion these days—young people want fast food and takeout; they don't want to be slaving over a hot oven for hours. But," he added quickly, noticing the look of concern on Sheila's face, "we have allowed for a counter in each bathroom that is big enough for a small microwave and a toaster. So . . . problem solved," he said, grinning.

Sheila nodded and looked down at her clipboard. "And what about the green space we asked for?"

"Ahhh, yes! Well, I think you'll be very pleased to hear that we have incorporated a multiuse park area for the residents. Baxter Park will bring nature back to urban living," he said grandly, reciting the line he had been practicing all morning. "Children will have the use of a swing, and there is even a park bench for people to sit on."

"One swing and a park bench for more than five thousand people?" asked the young man. Baxter curled his lip at the interference.

"Yes, well, perhaps we could double that," said Baxter, placing his hand on Sheila's arm. "So I'm sure you'll agree that we have taken your concerns seriously. Now all you have to do is to sign here, and we can all be on our way. I'm sure you must be very busy."

Sheila hesitated. "Well, yes, I suppose . . . ," she said. "Do you have the papers?"

"Of course," he said, tapping on his briefcase. He walked back over to his car and placed his briefcase on the hood. He smiled to himself as he pulled out a pen and a piece of paper and laid them out in front of him. "Now if you just sign . . . ohhh," he said, turning to see that Sheila had somehow managed to transform herself into a clown with full makeup. He shrank back, terrified.

"Why . . . why are you dressed like a . . . clown?" he whispered, his eyes wide.

"Mr. Baxter! I find that rather insulting," said the clown, looking down at the enormous yellow buttons on the front of her oversized red jacket.

"You—you know," said Baxter.

"Know what?" said the clown, tilting her head so that the tip of her conical hat pointed toward him, the frown that was painted on her face curling farther downward.

"That . . . that I'm scared of clowns," cried Mr. Baxter, and he began to whimper.

"Mr. Baxter, are you okay?" asked a voice. Baxter looked over and saw that the young man was also dressed as a clown and, looking round, that so were the other people in the group. The clown who had spoken walked over to him, his curly orange wig looming nearer.

"Stay away," he said, putting his hands up to his face and pressing his back into the front of his car. *"Stay away!"* he shouted.

"Mr. Baxter, I don't think you're well," said the female clown, leaning over toward him.

"Aaargh!" cried Baxter, pushing the clown backward. He started to run, but the rest of the group closed in around him.

"Mr. Baxter, I think you need to sit down," said an old clown with a large single tear painted on his white face. He took Baxter by the arm.

"Get off me!" screamed Baxter as he pushed the old clown backward to the ground.

"What do you think you're doing?" demanded the clown in the green wig as he helped the old clown up to his feet.

Baxter looked around at the growing group of clowns surrounding him and realized with horror that he was trapped. He put his hands up to his mouth and screamed as loud as he could.

"SOMEBODY HELP ME! I'M SURROUNDED BY CLOWNS!"

A large clown that Baxter hadn't noticed stepped out suddenly from the crowd, his enormous purple shoes causing him to waddle as he strode toward him. Baxter looked up and saw the clown's red nose and black-rimmed eyes staring down at him.

"Mr. Baxter, I think you need some help," said the clown sinisterly.

"Oh, oh . . . oh . . . please don't kill me," whispered Baxter, beginning to hyperventilate.

The clown's eyes narrowed. "I'm not going to kill you; I just want to help you, Mr. Baxter. Don't be scared," said the clown, raising his arms. Baxter saw the giant yellow gloves coming toward him and, with pure panic sweeping over him, he realized that the clown was about to strangle him. Baxter's very worst fear of coming face-to-face with a killer clown now appeared to be a reality. He staggered backward as the clown approached him, and he bumped into the crowd that encircled him. Baxter turned round and saw what appeared to be hundreds of colorful conical hats and white faces with painted frowns looking at him. The clowns all watched as Baxter screamed and began to run around in a circle trying to escape, until finally he collapsed on the ground, sobbing.

The group of clowns looked down with curious expressions as Baxter finally turned silent, and then his eyes rolled to the back of his head and he fainted.

• • •

Ernest giggled.

"See, that wasn't so hard," said Mortimer, watching as Richard Baxter was strapped onto a stretcher and wheeled toward the waiting ambulance. Sheila and her colleagues gathered around the vehicle, dressed exactly as they had been on Baxter's arrival. They watched in shock as the doors closed and the ambulance sped off in the distance.

"I can't believe he was scared of clowns," said Ernest, amazed, jumping down from the cabin of the bulldozer they had been hiding in. They walked behind Baxter's car and turned out into the street.

"It's easy if you know how. You just have to find exactly what they're most frightened of and replace everything in their mind with that one thought so they think that it's real."

Ernest nodded, deeply impressed, although a part of him felt a bit sorry for the man, even though he would never have admitted it.

"Quick, let's get back to Mother," said Mortimer, breaking into a run.

"She's going to be so happy," said Ernest, following behind.

CHAPTER TWELVE

That evening, while Ernest and Mortimer were treated to a sumptuous banquet by their mother, and the pupils of Myers Holt were relaxing in the Map Room, an unmarked car pulled up outside 10 Downing Street. A waiting police officer with an umbrella opened the car door and escorted Sir Bentley in through the front door.

"The prime minister's expecting you," said the butler. Sir Bentley followed him down the hallway and into a dark study, where he found the prime minister standing by an open fire.

"Prime Minister," said Sir Bentley, shaking the prime minister's hand.

"Please, Bentley, call me Edward; we've known each other for more than thirty years now. I got your message—what's the urgent news?"

Sir Bentley looked at the prime minister. "Richard Baxter has been the victim of Inferno."

"What?" exclaimed the prime minister, louder than intended. He coughed. "When?"

"Today, this afternoon. He's in the hospital now, but it looks irreversible—the doctors say that there's not much they can do for him."

"Poor man," said the prime minister sadly, looking down at the roaring fire. After a few moments, he looked up. "What is going on?"

"I don't know," said Sir Bentley, "but we're going to find out. You obviously remember Richard Baxter; he was a pupil at Myers Holt when you were there."

"My roommate," said the prime minister, walking over to the bar in the corner of the room and pouring them each a drink. He walked back over and handed one of the crystal glasses to Sir Bentley.

Sir Bentley took a sip and continued. "As you also know, Cecil Humphries was a teacher at the same time. The coincidence is just too great. The only pupils not to have their knowledge of the Ability wiped at the end of their time at Myers Holt were the last set of pupils we trained—we just closed down after . . . that night . . . and as far as I knew, nobody ever spoke of the Ability again . . . until now. I have spent the last few hours trying to work out what this could all be leading to and I'm afraid that I can only come to one conclusion: Your life is in danger."

The prime minister considered this carefully. "I understand. But not my life only, is that right? You were also there."

"Yes, I imagine that I'm a target too, if the pattern continues. The only other people who are still alive and were there that year are Lady Magenta and Clarissa Teller. Everybody else is either dead or locked up in a hospital room."

"Do you think one of them could be responsible for this?"

"I really can't, but I keep asking myself who could have knowledge of Inferno and be able to train children to use it. Danny Lyons and Anna Willows both died that night. Jenkins and Basil both died of old age some years ago. We know where Cecil and Richard are, so that leaves you, me, Clarissa, and Arabella Magenta. If you were training up twelve-year-old children to use the Ability, we would know about it."

The prime minister smiled at the thought.

"And if I were responsible, then I wouldn't be bringing it to anybody's attention. That leaves only the two of them."

"And where are they now?"

"As you know, Clarissa only leaves her home in the Outer Hebrides once a year, for the Antarctic Ball. She spends the rest of her time writing her books. Lady Magenta is still in London, hosting dinner parties every night. I've had my men watching them both, and they've seen nothing suspicious at all."

"So what now?"

"It's still early in their training, but I have some very talented pupils. I'll take them tomorrow to meet Lady Magenta and Clarissa and see if they can find out anything."

"Very well," said the prime minister, nodding. "You know that you have my full support and any resources that you need."

"Edward, you must take care. I'm afraid this makes the situation far more serious than we had even imagined. Perhaps you could consider canceling any public appointments until we've worked out what's going on."

"I appreciate your concern, Bentley, but I simply can't do that. I'm the prime minister; I have responsibilities. I'll increase security for us both and trust that you will resolve this situation as soon as possible."

"I understand," said Sir Bentley, shaking the prime minister's hand. "Thank you."

CHAPTER THIRTEEN

Wednesday, November 28

Chris sat down at his desk in the classroom and waited nervously for Ms. Lamb to arrive. Rex had been winding him up all morning, and the other children hadn't argued in his defense, suggesting they might not think Rex's ideas for his punishment so far-fetched. He looked down sheepishly as the door opened and Ms. Lamb stormed in, her heels making loud clacking sounds on the hard floor.

"Today," she began, looking at everybody except Chris, "we will continue our lesson on telepathy. We will be learning to extract memories and then writing them up as reports. When you begin working for us, you will need to pass the information you find to the authorities, so it's essential that you are able to communicate exactly what you have seen with as much detail as possible. You," she said, pointing to Sebastian, "hand out these forms."

Sebastian stood up and walked over to Ms. Lamb, who handed him the papers and some pens. He handed one of each to all of them.

Chris looked down at the printed sheet.

"On here, you must fill out the relevant information. Name, date, time," said Ms. Lamb, running her finger across the top of the sheet. "In which street and building you found the information, and in the large box below, a detailed description of exactly what you saw. Understood?"

The children nodded.

"Now all we need is somebody's mind to access. Let's have . . . you," she said. Chris looked up and saw that Ms. Lamb was pointing at him.

"Come now, don't be shy. You certainly weren't yesterday. As you clearly have no need for any training, the others can test their Ability on you."

"I . . . um . . . would prefer not to."

"Unfortunately for you, it's not an option. Get up here . . . *now*."

Chris stood up slowly and walked over to the front of the class. The rest of the pupils looked at him with a mixture of sympathy and relief that it wasn't them.

"Your task today is to find out what this boy's most embarrassing memory is."

Chris looked over at Ms. Lamb, horrified.

"But—I—"

"Stop talking, boy. Now, to access that memory you must walk up Emotions Street which is . . . here," she said, pointing to a long road on the left-hand side of the diagram on the wall. "Find the building marked 'Embarrassment'—a red building, of course—and look on the ground floor for the largest and most prominent filing cabinet. Open that up, remove the largest folder, and make a mental note of everything you see. When you have finished, withdraw back to Reception and out; then write a detailed description of the memory. And if any of you decide not to do this, I will choose one of you to take this boy's place instead. Begin."

Chris looked over at Philip, who gave an apologetic shrug. He looked at the door and considered making a run for it before suddenly coming up with a better plan.

Chris closed his eyes and started singing to himself, louder and louder.

Ring a ring of roses, a pocket full of posies, a-tishoo, a-tishoo, we all fall down. Ring a ring of roses, a pocket full of posies, a-tishoo, a-tishoo, we all fall down. Ring a ring—"

All of a sudden, a loud knock to his left disturbed him from his thoughts. He opened his eyes and saw the door open and Sir Bentley walk in.

"Pardon the interruption, Ms. Lamb."

Ms. Lamb looked annoyed but said nothing.

"I have a rather urgent matter to discuss with the children. Do you mind?"

"Of course not," said Ms. Lamb. "Sit down, boy; we'll continue this later," she whispered to Chris, who rushed back to his seat in relief.

"There has been a rather significant turn of events in the last twenty-four hours. Although we wouldn't normally ask pupils to begin work before the New Year, I'm afraid we are going to have to speed things up. Ms. Lamb,

I will need to take two pupils with me now. Perhaps you could tell me who would be most able to take on a Mind Access job so early in training."

Ms. Lamb thought for a moment, her lips pursed.

"I recommend you take that boy," she said finally, looking over at Rex.

"Yes, ha!" said Rex, standing up.

"I need two, Ms. Lamb. Is there anybody else who is particularly strong in this area?"

Ms. Lamb shifted uncomfortably and grimaced.

"I suppose you'd better take that one," she said at last, pointing at Chris.

Chris stood up and smiled at Rex, who gave him a thumbs-up.

"Excellent, thank you, Ms. Lamb. Christopher, Rex, follow me. The rest of you, enjoy your lesson. I'll see you all later."

Chris practically skipped down the hall behind Sir Bentley, who led them out past the Dome and into his office in the staff quarters.

"Take a seat, both of you," said Sir Bentley, sitting down slowly in the leather chair behind his desk.

Chris and Rex sat down and listened carefully as Sir Bentley explained the situation as simply as he could, beginning with Cecil Humphries and Richard Baxter and finally leading to the conclusion that the person responsible had to have something to do with Myers Holt.

"And so," he continued, "I need you both to interview two people, Lady Magenta and Clarissa Teller, today and find out if they know anything." Sir Bentley slid two photographs across the table.

Chris looked surprised. “Clarissa Teller, the writer?”

“Yes, do you know her books?”

“Of course, everybody knows them! You know her, Rex, right?”

Rex nodded. “Yeah, and I hate to read. They’re the only books without pictures that I’ve actually finished.”

“Wonderful, I’m sure she’ll appreciate meeting some fans of hers. Now, back to business. You’ll be using your Ability to access their minds. Listen carefully. I want you to go to Calendar Street, go into the first building on the street, which houses all memories for this year, and find the filing cabinet for yesterday. Check it to see what they were doing at midday exactly—that’s the time that the Ability was being used on Richard Baxter. Then I want you to go down People Street and find the building marked ‘Old Acquaintances.’ There you should find a drawer for Richard Baxter. The drawers are labeled alphabetically, so it shouldn’t be too difficult. The folder at the front will contain the most recent encounter that Clarissa and Lady Magenta have had with Baxter. If they aren’t involved with what happened yesterday, you should find that their last memories of Baxter are from some time ago. As far as we know, neither Clarissa nor Lady Magenta stayed in contact with him since leaving Myers Holt. Any questions?”

“So,” said Rex, leaning forward, “we are basically working for the prime minister.”

Sir Bentley nodded.

“The prime minster needs me, Rex King, to help him?” asked Rex, checking.

“Yes, Rex, that is correct.”

Rex grinned. "Wow! Chris, we'll be famous! This has got to get us a medal or something."

"Now, now, let's not get carried away," said Sir Bentley. "You haven't actually done anything yet, and let me remind you, all your work here must be carried out in the strictest confidence. Let's go."

Rex stood up and saluted. "Let's save the world," he said. Chris laughed, and Sir Bentley smiled.

"Come on, Superman, we have work to do."

"Where are we going?" asked Chris, as they stood up.

"To a small island in the Outer Hebrides to meet Clarissa Teller," said Sir Bentley, leading them out of the room.

"Aren't they up near Scotland?" asked Chris, confused.

"That is correct, Christopher. We'll be getting there by helicopter."

"Helicopter?" shouted Rex.

"Yes, helicopter," confirmed Sir Bentley.

"Wow!" said Chris, as Rex gave him a high five.

"Do you think they'll let me fly it for a bit?" asked Rex.

Sir Bentley was about to respond, but then something occurred to him, and he stopped dead.

"What's wrong, sir?" asked Rex.

"Boys, I don't want any . . . messing around on the flight."

"Yes, sir," said Chris and Rex, still smiling.

"I mean it. You don't realize quite how powerful your Ability is yet, and you certainly haven't learned to control it. If you start thinking about the helicopter doing stunts or crashing into the sea or anything like that, there's a good chance that you might actually make it happen."

Chris's and Rex's eyes widened in horror as they realized the full implication of what Sir Bentley was saying.

Sir Bentley saw the looks on the boys' faces and smiled. "Don't worry; I'm sure it will be fine," he said, stepping into the elevator.

"Are you okay, Rex?" asked Chris, as the elevator began to rise.

Rex shook his head, looking a little pale. "I'm just thinking about something my dad once told me."

"What?" asked Chris.

"He told me that if you want to make someone think about an elephant, then all you have to do is tell them *not* to think about an elephant."

Chris thought about this for a second, confused, and then his eyes widened.

"Oh," he said, and suddenly all that Chris could think about was helicopters crashing.

By the time the car pulled up at the heliport in Battersea, all thought of helicopters crashing was long forgotten, replaced with the excitement of the journey they were about to take.

"Stay right where you are," instructed Ron, as John pulled into a parking space next to one of the three other unmarked cars that had escorted them. Ron, who was on a permanently heightened state of vigilance following recent events, jumped out and crouched down. Chris watched the top of Ron's head move slowly around the car, and then the head disappeared. Seconds later Ron jumped up and ran across the tarmac, past a fleet of waiting helicopters to the other side of the heliport, where he scanned his surroundings, his eyes darting about for any lurking dangers. Chris looked over at John, who, although completely still and staring straight ahead, seemed also to be on high alert.

The door next to Sir Bentley opened, and Chris and Rex jumped. They looked over to see Ron, who was motioning for them to step out of the car.

"Coast is clear," he said, leading them quickly over to the first helicopter. John followed behind them, walking slowly, his head scanning the landscape from left to right and back again.

Chris climbed up the steps into the helicopter. He greeted the two waiting pilots and fastened his seat belt.

Ron closed the door and ran over to the helicopter next to them as the rotors started spinning. Chris looked out and watched as the helicopter began to rise slowly, then dip forward and suddenly speed up, soaring upward over the river and across London. Chris looked behind him and saw three helicopters following them—he jabbed Rex in the shoulder to show him.

"WE'RE INCREASING SECURITY," explained Sir Bentley, shouting over the noise of the helicopter.

"WHAT DO YOU CALL A SHEEP WITH NO LEGS?" shouted Rex, looking terrified.

Chris and Sir Bentley both looked at him in surprise.

"I NEED TO STOP THINKING BAD THOUGHTS!" explained Rex, clearly panicking as he pointed up to the rotors above them. A look of alarm suddenly appeared on both Chris's and Sir Bentley's faces as they realized what Rex was talking about.

"WHAT DO YOU CALL A SHEEP WITH NO LEGS?" repeated Rex.

"I DON'T KNOW, WHAT DO YOU CA—" replied Chris.

"A CLOUD," shouted Rex, without laughing. "WHAT DOES A TREE DO WHEN HE'S READY TO GO HOME? HE LEAVES. WHAT WAS WRONG WITH SANTA'S LITTLE HELPER? HE HAD LOW ELF-ESTEEM. . . ."

Chris watched Rex, more fascinated than concerned, as Rex proceeded to recite the entire contents of *The Definitive Joke Compendium*, which he had committed to memory the night before.

"WHAT DID THE ZERO SAY TO THE EIGHT? NICE BELT. WHY DID THE BABY STRAWBERRY CRY? BECAUSE ITS PARENTS WERE IN A JAM. DOCTOR, DOCTOR . . ."

Chris was about to punch Rex in the arm to shut him up, but then, realizing the alternative might be crashing into the fields below, decided to do his best to ignore him. Sir Bentley, obviously thinking the same thing, took out a newspaper and began to read. Chris pressed his face up against the window and, blocking out the sound of Rex's voice, watched, amazed, as the helicopter took them on a journey past the countryside, villages, and towns.

Finally, after more than an hour of listening to Rex's nonstop barrage of jokes, they began their descent toward a tiny island, with only a small white cottage on it.

"At last," said Rex, breathing a huge sigh of relief as the helicopter touched down near the building. Moments later, the three other helicopters that had followed them landed and from them emerged Ron and John and ten other bodyguards, all of them surly and alert. John motioned to Sir Bentley to wait as the rest of the team circled the cottage.

"All clear," called John.

Sir Bentley turned to Chris and Rex. "Follow me," he said, as the door opened and the cold air swept in.

Chris climbed down last and followed Sir Bentley and Rex toward the cottage, but before they could reach the front door, a woman in a cream woolen sweater, jeans, and Wellington boots emerged from the cottage.

"Sir!" she said, smiling. She kissed Sir Bentley on both cheeks.

"Thank you so much for agreeing to this," said Sir Bentley.

"For my old teacher how could I refuse? I just can't believe everything that's happened recently—I'll do anything I can to help," she said, then looked over at the boys. "Hello! I'm Clarissa."

"This is Rex and Christopher," said Sir Bentley. "They're our new Myers Holt pupils that I told you about, and great fans of yours."

Chris and Rex both stared up at her, awestruck.

Clarissa laughed. "It's always lovely to meet fans. And Myers Holt pupils too! It just doesn't seem that long ago. . . . Was I really that young?" she asked, turning to Sir Bentley, and he nodded, smiling.

"It's freezing out here," she said. "Come inside and I'll make us all a hot cup of cocoa."

Chris was surprised to see that the cottage was even

smaller than it appeared from the outside, perhaps because all the walls and every surface were stacked high with books, one on top of the other. On the far end was a wood burner that was pumping heat into the room. A couple of worn sofas covered in thick blankets dominated the space, and in the corner was a tiny kitchen that consisted only of a fridge, an old stove, and a sink.

Sir Bentley sat down on one of the sofas, and Chris sat opposite him, sinking down into the soft cushions next to Rex.

"How are you, Clarissa?" asked Sir Bentley, as Clarissa walked over with a tray of steaming mugs.

"Really well, thank you. Working hard, keeping warm. I'm just finishing my next novel."

"What's it called?" asked Chris.

"Ahh, that's a secret," she said, smiling, then leaned over and whispered to them, "*The Rat Catcher's Revenge* . . . but don't tell anyone."

"What's it about?" asked Chris.

"Well . . . that you'll just have to wait and see," she said, "though knowing what you boys are capable of, you could probably find out for yourselves!"

Chris and Rex considered this for a moment before Sir Bentley gave them a stern glance.

"Uh-hum, no you won't," said Sir Bentley. "We're here on business only, please; no messing around."

Chris and Rex looked disappointed but nodded.

"I just can't believe about Cecil and Richard," said Clarissa, taking a seat next to Sir Bentley, holding the mug of chocolate with both hands. "It's just awful."

"I know, I know," said Sir Bentley sadly. "I think we all hoped we'd never hear anything of this again after . . . what happened."

"You know, not a day goes by when I don't think about Danny or Anna," said Clarissa softly.

"And me, Clarissa, and me," agreed Sir Bentley.

For a moment nobody spoke. Chris and Rex sat awkwardly, not knowing what to say, until Clarissa sat up suddenly, shaking herself from her thoughts.

"Right, well, you boys don't need to see me getting all morose. Why don't we get straight down to work?"

Chris and Rex nodded, relieved that the tension had been broken.

"What do you need me to do?"

"Nothing at all," said Sir Bentley. "The boys are going to use their Ability to see if there's anything that could help us. I can't imagine for a moment that you'd have anything to do with this whole mess, but we have to be thorough. I hope you understand."

"Of course; I don't mind at all. I have nothing to hide."

"Boys? You know what to do," said Sir Bentley, and Chris and Rex pushed themselves forward and sat up straight on the edge of the sofa. Chris suddenly felt very nervous.

"It's okay—remember, I did this myself when I was your age," said Clarissa, reassuring them, "and I promise not to block you!"

Chris smiled awkwardly, suddenly very aware that he was about to enter the mind of his favorite writer, and looked at Rex, who nodded back at him.

Clarissa sat back on the sofa and took a sip from her mug. "Well, off you go."

Chris stared at Clarissa's face, and within seconds he was standing in a large room. He paused to get his bearings and saw images of himself and Rex floating around his head. He walked over to the double doors ahead of him, the sound of his footsteps echoing about him, and stepped out onto the empty road. Chris surveyed the landscape and saw rows and rows of colored buildings reaching out into the distance and, to his right, an enormous, deep-turquoise skyscraper that towered over him. He craned his head, looking up at the top of it, curious to work out what it could be, but it was in the opposite direction of where he was supposed to be going, and he thought better of it.

He turned left and sped forward, until he reached the turn that marked the beginning of Calendar Street. Chris ran straight through the open door of the first building on his left and stopped to look around. Unlike the room he had entered in Ms. Lamb's mind, this room was bright and airy, and the filing cabinets looked brand-new, their gleaming white exteriors bouncing the sunlight that was streaming in from the windows about the place.

Directly in front of him was a small filing cabinet with a single drawer that was open. Suddenly he heard a whooshing sound, and a green folder flew in from outside, passed his shoulder, and landed inside the drawer, which then closed abruptly. He looked over at the cabinet and saw the fresh white sticker that had the word TODAY written on it and next to it a slightly larger cabinet, which, as Chris expected, was labeled YESTERDAY. He walked over to it and leaned down to open the bottom drawer. Inside, the hanging files were labeled with times. Chris pulled out the file marked MIDDAY and opened it. A bright image floated up from between the green files and hovered in front of him as the sound of jazz music filled the space around him. Chris watched Clarissa standing next to her stove, spreading butter on a slice of toast. She leaned over, took an apple from a fruit bowl in front of her, placed it on the plate, then carried it over to the small desk he had seen earlier by the fireplace. She sat down, took a bite of the apple, picked up the pen that had been left on the yellow writing pad in front of her, and began to write. Leaning over the floating image, Chris looked down and watched the words form beneath him.

Jack looked up at Aurelia, his hand still resting on the dragon's chest. "He's dead," he said gently.

Chris stepped back and watched as Clarissa put her pen down and picked up the piece of toast.

Wow, thought Chris, realizing that he was the first person to read something from Clarissa Teller's latest book. He wanted to stay and read more but reminded himself that he was here to work. He closed the folder, and with that the image of Clarissa Teller at her desk vanished. He placed the folder carefully back at the front of the drawer, closed it and stepped out on to Calendar Street. He turned and headed quickly in the direction of People Street toward a small cluster of buildings in the distance, each one a different shade of purple. He slowed down as he neared the front entrance to the first and looked up at the sign.

FAMILY

He walked on past the next one marked BRIEF ENCOUNTERS, and stopped at the door of the violet building next to it: OLD ACQUAINTANCES. The door opened in front of him, and he entered a dark and musty room, lined with rows of old filing cabinets covered in a thick layer of dust. He walked up to the first one and brushed the dust and cobwebs from the front of it to read the label.

AA-AD

Chris suddenly realized that he didn't know if he should be searching under first or last names. He opened up the drawer and saw that the first folder was labeled AARON BLESSING.

First names, then, thought Chris, walking along the filing cabinets and peering at the labels until he came to the one marked RI-RO. He opened it up and found the folder that he was looking for. He pulled out Richard Baxter's file and let it fall open, but instead of a single image appearing as it had before, a group of scenes flew up in the air, each one behind the other, forming a line that led far down the corridor of cabinets. Chris looked confused and walked around the tunnel of moving colors, which swirled round in a blur. Chris raised his hand to touch it, and the tunnel suddenly broke into two. He walked into the space between them and looked at the one end, which was now a perfectly clear image of a young boy laughing hysterically as he helped a smiling girl Chris recognized as a young Clarissa to her feet. Chris stepped back, and the two tunnels came together again as one. Walking over to the end of the tunnel, he turned to see the final image in the line. This time Clarissa was a young adult, and she was walking down a busy shopping street. The sound of traffic and people bustling to and fro filled the room. Chris watched Clarissa walking quickly and recognized the adult Richard Baxter immediately from the photograph Sir Bentley had shown them, emerging out of a crowd of people with a purposeful stride. He walked straight into Clarissa and knocked her backward.

"Careful!" Chris heard Clarissa say. "Richard?"

The young man turned his head, and a look of recognition spread across his face.

"Clarissa! Wow! How are you?"

"Yeah, really good. Oh, my goodness, it's been, what, ten years? How are you?"

"I'm a real estate agent—getting a bit bored of it, to be honest; think I'm ready to go it alone. What about you?"

"I'm a waitress back home in Bournemouth."

"What are you doing here in London?"

"Actually, I'm going to meet an agent; they're interested in my book," said Clarissa, holding up the folder in her hands.

"That's great—so I'm going to see your name in print?"

Clarissa blushed. "Maybe . . . fingers crossed. Look, I'd better be going; I don't want to be late. It was great seeing you."

"And you," said Richard. "Good luck with your meeting. Just keep telling yourself, 'I'm a winner, I'm a winner.'"

Clarissa laughed. "I'll try that. Take care, Richard," she said, and with that the image froze.

So that was the last time they saw each other, thought Chris, closing the folder and placing it back in the drawer. He walked back over to the front door and opened it. He was about to step out into the road when a small black dot appeared in the distance. Chris quickly stepped back into the room and peered round the door, watching the black dot speed forward, growing larger until it became a figure running toward him. Chris froze, unsure what to do next. He watched as the figure ran up the street in his direction. It wasn't until it crossed the junction of People Street and Arts Avenue that he saw the figure was Rex. Unlike Rex in real life, however, this Rex wasn't out of breath.

"Hey, wow! I didn't realize we'd be able to see each other in here!" said Rex, as Chris stepped out of the doorway to greet him. "Are you going in?"

"No," said Chris, "I already looked. She hasn't seen Richard Baxter in years. Where have you been?"

Rex looked annoyed. "All right, Mystic Mike, no need to show off. I reckon I should see for myself, even if you've already done it. I'll see you on the outside."

Chris nodded. "Yeah, I think Sir Bentley wants us both to do it, to be sure. I'll see you back in the cottage."

Rex walked past him, toward the line of filing cabinets, and Chris walked back out, turned down the street, and ran off. He reached the junction of Arts Avenue and decided to take a detour, curious to see what the skyscraper was. Walking slowly, he noticed that all the buildings on this road were much taller than the others. He stopped at the double doors that marked the entrance to the tower and looked up to see the word LITERATURE emblazoned in gold letters above the doorway.

Ahh, that makes sense, thought Chris, thinking back to the piles of books in the cottage. The doors opened, and for a moment he considered entering and finding out more about *The Rat Catcher's Revenge*, but he couldn't bring himself to do it and, instead, turned away and walked off back toward Reception.

"That was quick," said Clarissa, as the blinding light faded and he was brought back into the room. Next to him, Rex had a blank expression on his face and was still staring intently at Clarissa.

Chris looked over at Sir Bentley, who raised his eyebrows in question.

Chris shook his head. "Nothing—the last time she—I mean you," he said, looking at Clarissa, "saw Richard Baxter was in the street years ago, when you were a waitress."

"Really?" asked Clarissa, looking confused.

"Umm, yeah, I think so. You were in London to meet an agent."

Clarissa thought about this, and then her eyes widened. "Oh, my goodness, yes! I remember, we bumped into each other on Oxford Street." She looked at Chris and smiled. "Amazing," she said.

Chris smiled proudly. "And yesterday at midday you were sitting at your desk, writing."

Sir Bentley gave a sigh of relief. "Well, thank goodness," he said. "I couldn't have imagined you having anything to do with this."

"Did you read what I wrote?" Clarissa asked Chris, teasing him.

Chris looked embarrassed. "I only saw a sentence, that was it. And I won't say anything, I promise."

Clarissa smiled. "That's okay—I would have done the same myself, I'm sure."

"What have I missed?" said Rex, suddenly waking up from his trance.

"Welcome back, Rex. Chris was just telling us what he saw."

"Waitress, going to a meeting, writing yesterday lunchtime?" asked Rex, despondent.

Sir Bentley nodded. "Yes, well done."

"Guess you didn't need me. Psychic Sam already did all the work."

"You did well," said Sir Bentley, reassuring him. "We needed you both to make sure the details were correct."

Rex shrugged, annoyed.

"Clarissa, we're going to have to go," said Sir Bentley, placing the mug back on top of one of the stacks of books on the coffee table. "Are you sure you won't come with us? You'll be much safer on the mainland—we don't know what we're up against."

Clarissa shook her head. "Thank you, but you know I only leave the island for the Antarctic Ball, and that's only because I'm patron to the Children's Welfare Charity. If it wasn't for that, I'd be quite happy to never leave. I'll take my chances here."

"Very well," said Sir Bentley. "I know how stubborn you are, so I won't try to change your mind, but please be vigilant. If you see anything suspicious at all, no matter how small, call me immediately and I'll get people over to you straight away. And I'm going to send a team over to install cameras, which we'll keep an eye on."

"Very well, thank you," said Clarissa, showing them all to the front door. "It's been lovely to meet you both," she said, turning to Chris and Rex, "and please, take care of yourselves."

"I won't let anything happen to them," said Sir Bentley, guiding the boys out in front of him. "I learned my lesson a long time ago."

An hour and a half later, the helicopter carrying the boys and Sir Bentley landed gently back on the tarmac of the Battersea heliport. Sir Bentley stepped out and down the stairs that had been wheeled up to the door. The boys followed him into the waiting car.

"Hungry?"

The boys nodded eagerly.

"Good, me too," said Sir Bentley. "Napoli, John."

"Yes, sir," said John, starting up the engine.

The line of cars pulled up outside an unassuming white-fronted restaurant in a small cobbled plaza, and Chris, Rex, and Sir Bentley waited as Ron jumped out, followed by a group of guards from the car behind them, and went inside to make inquiries. After a couple of minutes Ron reappeared and, after a quick scan of the street, motioned that the coast was clear. Chris and Rex stepped out of the car and followed Sir Bentley in to find a short, white-haired man in a chef's suit waiting for them.

"Signor Bentley, welcome!" he said in a strong Italian accent. "We have your room ready for you at the back."

"Thank you, Giovanni," said Sir Bentley, motioning for

the boys to follow him toward the back of the restaurant.

They entered the room and took a seat at a long table covered in a red-and-white-checked tablecloth. Giovanni handed each of them a menu.

"I recommend the Giovanni special," he said to the boys. "Best pizza outside of Italy."

The boys nodded eagerly, their mouths watering at the thought.

"Excellent work, boys," said Sir Bentley, as Giovanni left the room. "You did very well with Clarissa. After we've eaten, we'll go to Lady Magenta's, and then you can head back to Myers Holt and relax."

"Does she live near here?" asked Chris.

"Not far, just off Park Lane. I'll warn you now, she's a rather—how shall I put it?—eccentric woman. Quite different from Clarissa."

"Eccentric?" asked Rex.

"Yes, you'll see what I mean. She's also rather less agreeable to us turning up. Lady Magenta is known for her dinner parties, and apparently we're interrupting her preparations for one she's hosting tomorrow night."

"Was she a pupil at Myers Holt too?" asked Chris.

"No, a teacher. And a very good one, though not too popular with the students, I'll admit. . . . Ahhh, Giovanni!"

"I hope you're hungry!" said Giovanni, carrying in the three most enormous pizzas the boys had ever seen.

After lunch, stuffed full of pizza and cheesecake, they drove to Lady Magenta's home in the prestigious neighborhood of Mayfair. Sir Bentley stopped the boys on the steps of the grand apartment building and gave Rex a warning look.

"No comedy this time, please, Rex. You both need to be on your best behavior."

"Moi?" said Rex, pretending to look insulted. "I don't know what you mean."

"Hmmm," said Sir Bentley, tutting gently. He led them through the revolving door, across the foyer, and into the elevator.

The doors of the elevator opened out onto the penthouse floor, and Chris walked into the marble entrance hall behind the line of security guards led by Ron and John. The men divided themselves into two groups, flanking the doorway, and Sir Bentley stepped forward between them and pressed the doorbell. A few moments later a butler, distinguished-looking and in full uniform, opened the door and tipped his head in greeting.

"Lady Magenta is expecting you; please follow me," said the butler, leading them across a corridor and into an enormous room, bigger than the whole of Chris's house.

"I wish I brought my sunglasses," whispered Rex to Chris, as they both looked round at the gold curtains, gold wallpaper, and grand oil paintings that hung in ornate gold frames. Gold urns, filled with flowers and cascading ivy, stood between the heavy gold curtains that covered the floor-to-ceiling windows, and hanging from the center ceiling was a gold (in keeping with the theme) chandelier, bigger than a car and lit with hundreds of lights that danced over the marble floor.

At the far end of the room was a long dining table, covered in swaths of fabric, and two figures standing on either side of a tall, thronelike chair, their backs to the arriving guests.

"This looks cheap," said a clipped voice coming from the other side of the chair. A piece of dark blue fabric was thrown onto the floor. "This is unbearably tacky," continued the voice, and another piece of fabric was discarded. "And this . . . monstrosity of a dress . . . I wouldn't even wipe my floors with it," said the voice, throwing the fabric at the sheepish-looking woman on the right.

"I'm terribly sorry, ma'am," said the lady. "If you give us five minutes, I'll bring in some other samples we have."

"You've wasted enough of my time as it is," said the voice. "Get out."

"But—" said the woman.

"I said, get out!"

A hand appeared from the other side of the chair, shooing the woman away. The woman, looking as if she was about to cry, knelt down and gathered the dresses from the floor as her companion scooped up the ones on the table. They turned and rushed out with their heads down.

The butler turned to Sir Bentley and motioned for him to stay where he was. He approached the throne slowly.

"Lady Magenta?"

"What is it, Alfred?" said the voice, irritated.

"Sir Bentley and guests are here to see you as arranged."

"I've changed my mind; I'm far too busy. Tell them I'm out. Make something up—a charity function or something," she said.

"They're standing behind you," whispered Alfred, leaning over.

"For goodness' sake, Alfred," she said, showing no signs of embarrassment. The chair was pushed backward and from it emerged a tiny woman with an elaborate red beehive that added some two feet to her petite frame. The hair had been pinned so tightly that it looked like she was standing in a wind tunnel, her skin taut and her eyes pulled back so far that they looked like two cat's eyes.

"Arabella, how are you?" said Sir Bentley, stepping forward.

"Busy, Bentley, terribly busy. I'm afraid I'm going to have to cancel our meeting today—I still have nothing to wear for tomorrow's dinner."

"This won't take long," said Sir Bentley firmly.

"I don't think you understand," she said. "The Duke of Belfry will be attending, and everything must be perfect. We can do this another time. Alfred, call Dior and ask them to come round immediately with some options for my dress tomorrow." Lady Magenta walked over to an armchair and took a seat beside a pot of tea. She poured herself a cup without offering one to anybody else, and took a sip.

"Yes, ma'am," said Alfred, hurrying out of the room.

"Arabella, I don't think you understand the gravity of the situation," said Sir Bentley.

"No, Bentley, I don't think *you* understand the gravity of *my* situation. I have less than twenty-four hours before I host one of the most talked-about social functions of the year, and I have nothing to wear."

"Perhaps I didn't make it clear enough when we spoke," said Sir Bentley, a note of irritation creeping into his voice.

"Your life may be in danger, not to mention Clarissa's, my own, and the prime minister's."

"I'm sure you're exaggerating," said Lady Magenta calmly, taking another sip of her tea. "And besides," she said, looking up, "I don't think I need to remind you that I am well versed with all the techniques of the Ability. I could block a thousand little brats trying to use it on me at the same time. They wouldn't get far." She looked over at Chris and Rex for the first time and gave them what might have been a frown, though her face, pulled back as far as it was, barely moved.

Chris, however, didn't react, his face blank as he stared intently at the woman.

Sir Bentley sighed. "I can see we're getting nowhere. Perhaps we can visit at another time that's more convenient."

"Perhaps," said Lady Magenta dismissively. "Call Clara and she'll see if I can fit you in."

"Very well. Good day, Arabella. Come on, boys," said Sir Bentley, leading Chris and Rex out of the room. He pressed the button for the elevator.

"Honestly, that woman is infuriating," said Sir Bentley, mostly to himself. "It's enough to make me wonder whether she could have something to do with this whole mess."

"She doesn't have anything to do with it," said Chris.

"I just can't understand why—what did you say?" said Sir Bentley in surprise, looking round at Chris.

"She didn't have anything to do with it. I used the Ability when you were talking to her and checked. She hasn't seen Cecil Humphries or Richard Baxter in years.

And she was at a racecourse having lunch with a group of ladies yesterday."

Sir Bentley looked at Chris with a stern expression on his face. For a moment Chris thought he might be in terrible trouble, until Sir Bentley started chuckling.

"Quite unorthodox, Christopher . . . but brilliant. Well done," he said, patting Chris on the head. Rex looked annoyed that he hadn't thought of doing this himself.

"I wonder how she didn't notice," said Sir Bentley. "Your Ability must be incredibly strong—if she had heard the whisper of ringing in her ears, she would have blocked you immediately. Very impressive, young man."

Chris smiled, proud of himself.

"This doesn't, however, bring us any closer to solving the mystery of who is organizing these attacks," said Sir Bentley, suddenly looking serious. "I'm afraid we still have work to do—what work, however, I'm still not sure. I have men watching everybody we think is at risk, but until something new presents itself, it seems like we're back to square one."

From the window of a hotel room opposite, Dulcia watched Sir Bentley leave the building with Chris and Rex and get into the car that was waiting for them. She was fuming.

"So, he thinks he can use the Ability to help him," she said, having heard the entire conversation from Mortimer and Ernest, who were standing dutifully at her side, using their Ability to listen in on Sir Bentley. "We'll have to speed up our plans; I can't risk Bentley Jones finding out anything. Our surveillance is over, boys; pack your bags. Tomorrow you will take care of Lady Magenta. There's nothing we can do about the others; we'll have to wait until the Antarctic Ball—it's the only time that we know the rest of them will be in public. Hopefully, there'll be enough distractions for us to carry out our work and get out before they notice us. In the meantime we're going to have to tread with care. Don't you dare ruin this for me."

"Yes, mother," said Mortimer and Ernest in unison.

CHAPTER FOURTEEN

Thursday, November 29

At eleven o'clock the next morning, while Chris was sitting in his think tank being guided round a castle by Cassandra on an elaborate treasure hunt set in medieval times, Mortimer was walking into Astell's of Knightsbridge, a boutique hairdressing salon in South West London. Inside the immaculate white surroundings, the buzz of mindless chatter filled the room as women, seated in two long rows of white leather chairs, discussed their forthcoming holidays and the latest celebrity gossip. Mortimer walked up to the gleaming, curved counter and took a sweet from the glass bowl.

"Yes?" said the receptionist, giving Mortimer a disapproving scowl.

"I'd like my hair cut, please," said Mortimer.

"We're not a children's hairdresser," said the woman dismissively, picking up the ringing phone. "Astell's of Knightsbridge, how can I—"

Mortimer leaned over the counter and hung up the phone.

The woman glanced up at Mortimer with a look of astonishment. "What are you—"

Mortimer placed four fifty-pound bills on the counter.

"This should cover it," he said. "Now, where do you want me to sit?"

The woman opened her mouth but was lost for words.

"Over there?" said Mortimer, pointing to an empty chair at the back of the room.

The woman thought for a moment, then nodded, taking the money from the counter.

"Good. I'll have a lemonade," said Mortimer, walking away. The receptionist watched as he took his seat and picked up a magazine in front of him.

Moments later, after a huddled whisper among staff, which Mortimer watched from the corner of his eye, a young woman dressed in a starched white uniform approached him.

"Hi, welcome to Astell's of Knightsbridge," said the woman, slightly apprehensively. "How can we help you today."

"I want my hair cut," said Mortimer to the reflection of the woman in the mirror in front of him.

"Do you have anything special in mind?" asked the woman, following her well-rehearsed script.

Mortimer shrugged. "No, whatever you think . . . just

take your time," he said, looking over at the clock on the wall.

"Errmm, well, there's not really too much to do," said the woman, running her hands through Mortimer's hair. "How about a trim, some highlights, and a side parting?" she asked.

"Yeah, fine, whatever," said Mortimer, distracted, turning to watch as the front door opened and Lady Arabella Magenta and her enormous red beehive entered the salon.

"Lady Magenta, how *are* you?" said the receptionist loudly, with an enthusiasm that had been completely absent when she had greeted Mortimer.

"Yes, very well, thank you," said Lady Magenta, as a team of staff suddenly dropped what they were doing and rushed over to attend to their best customer. One of the staff took the enormous fur coat that Lady Magenta was wearing from her shoulders as another fetched the special fennel tea that they kept in the back room especially for her and put the kettle on to boil.

"Your favorite seat is ready for you," said one of the women, as another hairdresser hurriedly shooed a customer out of the chair behind Mortimer. The surprised customer, her hair wet and only cut halfway around, was dragged over to the back of the room, where she was sat on a plastic chair in the corner to wait.

Lady Magenta took her seat and gave clipped orders to the senior stylist, who was smiling and nodding frantically at everything she was told to do.

". . . and don't you dare leave a strand out of place. Understand?"

"Yes, of course," said the stylist, gently removing the first of a hundred clips that kept Lady Magenta's hair in place.

Mortimer watched attentively and paid no attention to his own hairdresser, until she eventually gave up trying to make small talk and attended to him in silence. Meanwhile Mortimer kept his eyes on Lady Magenta carefully as her enormous hair was flattened and each strand meticulously painted with a red dye before being wrapped in a mass of silver foils. Finally the last strand was twisted and folded into the foil, and a large dryer was wheeled over and lowered over Lady Magenta's head. Mortimer watched the woman flip the switch, and through the noise of the salon he made out the whirring of the machine as it came to life. His eyes went blank and he stared intently, completely oblivious to everything else happening around him.

Lady Magenta felt the heat of the dryer intensify, and she settled back into her seat, as far as the enormous contraption on her head would allow her to go. The sound around her had been completely replaced by the loud humming of the machine on her head, and she took advantage of the relative peace to run through her checklist for the evening's event.

Nails, she thought to herself, looking down at her hands, *fabulous.*

Dress . . . divine—thank heavens for Dior. Shoes . . . perfectly matched. Two million pounds' worth of diamond necklace en route from De Beers. Marvelous. I look twenty-five, she thought, rather optimistically. She looked up and studied her face in the mirror in front of her and marveled at its silky smoothness, worth every moment of the painful acid that had peeled away her top layer of skin earlier in the week. She smiled widely at the mirror, examining the gleaming veneers that had been fitted on her teeth, which made them sparkle so white that they probably shone in the dark.

As she examined herself closely, marveling at her ability to have evaded looking her real age, she suddenly froze. Just under her left eye she noticed a dark spot, one that she could have sworn hadn't been there earlier that day. She leaned forward as much as she could, dragging the dryer closer to the mirror, and saw, to her horror, that the spot was in fact a large brown mole. Lady Magenta gasped. She raised her hand up to her face to try to wipe it off, desperately hoping it was just a bit of dirt, but found that it was firmly attached to her face and, that even worse, there seemed to be *hairs* growing out of it, which appeared to be getting longer by the second. In a panic she started to pull them out, but the more she yanked at them, the faster they seemed to grow, and then, just as suddenly as that mole had appeared, another dark spot appeared above her top lip . . . and then another.

Lady Magenta stared at her reflection in the mirror, and her mouth dropped open in horror. As she did so, she felt something in her mouth. She spat it out into her hand in disgust and looked down. It was gleaming white. She looked back up and opened wide, and as she did so, the rest of the veneers on her teeth fell to the floor, revealing a row of dark-yellow, withered stumps that seemed to hang precariously from their roots. Lady Magenta slammed her mouth closed and puckered her lips tight to try to hold them in place. She put her hand up to her face and looked around for help, but nobody seemed to have noticed what was happening to her. She was about to scream but was momentarily distracted by a pulling sensation, as if somebody were tugging at her face. She watched as the tight skin pulled away and drooped down into folds of baggy wrinkles, her eyes sunk deeper, and dark rings appeared around them. In a panic she pulled the dryer away from her hair and screamed.

"Aaargggh. Help Me!" she yelled, as she watched the curlers in her hair drop out, one by one, with her hair attached.

"Lady Magenta! What's wrong?"

"My hair! My face! WHAT'S HAPPENING TO ME?" she screamed.

"But . . . I can't see anything . . . ," said the stylist, confused, putting a hand on Lady Magenta's shoulder to reassure her.

The last thing that Lady Magenta saw, before she passed out, was the image that was to remain in her mind for the rest of her life—the lined, withered face of a hideous old lady with a bald head.

Mortimer watched the staff gather around the collapsed body of Lady Magenta—who looked exactly as she had on entering the salon, only paler—and stood up quickly, his hair still wet. He ripped off the black apron from his neck and rushed out just as two large men Mortimer recognized as part of the team of bodyguards that had accompanied Sir Bentley the evening before rushed in.

They stopped in their tracks as they saw Mortimer and immediately matched the face to the photograph of the boy that Sir Bentley had instructed them to look out for.

"You!" said one of the men, reaching out to grab Mortimer, but a sudden loud ringing in his ears shook him and he froze. Mortimer stared at the two men in turn and blanked out the surroundings around him.

"You are ready for sleep," he said slowly. "You are so tired."

The men both paused and stared at Mortimer vacantly, suddenly oblivious to the screams of the staff and the wailing of the approaching ambulance.

A minute later Mortimer slipped out of the salon and ran down the road as fast as he could, leaving behind him an unconscious old lady surrounded by a team of panicked staff and two large men curled up on the floor, snoring gently.

CHAPTER FIFTEEN

Friday, November 30

"This is absolutely disgraceful. How could this have happened?" asked the prime minister, pacing his office with a vexed expression on his face. Sir Bentley sat on the edge of the armchair and watched his former pupil pace the room.

"I don't know what to say, Prime Minister; we had some of our best men watching her and she herself said that she would be able to block anybody that tried to use the Ability on her."

"Yes, I remember a few detentions from pupils attempting to do that—I don't understand how they managed to get past her block."

"Well, we think the noise of the hairdryer must have masked the sound of the ringing. It seems whoever did this understands the Ability very well."

The prime minister nodded solemnly. "I see . . . well, that makes sense. But what about security? What do they have to say?"

Sir Bentley shifted uncomfortably. "I'm afraid that they don't remember a thing. They were—ahem—asleep when we arrived."

"Asleep? What kind of buffoons are we employing?"

"Whoever did this used their Ability on them, too. The last thing they remember is stepping into the salon."

"And the staff?"

"Well, they all describe the same boy who was responsible for Cecil Humphries. Pale, black hair, about twelve years old."

"And where is he now?"

Sir Bentley thought for a moment, trying to think of the best way to explain, and then shrugged, defeated. "I'm afraid we have no idea. By the time we got down there, he was long gone."

The prime minister sighed and rubbed his forehead in thought. "Right, well there's nothing to be done. So what do we do next?"

Sir Bentley stood up. "Prime Minister—Edward—we are now sure that your life is in danger. Any doubts we had before have been completely removed after yesterday's incident. It's too late to do anything for Arabella, Cecil, or Richard, but we can still do something to protect you."

"What do you suggest?"

Sir Bentley looked the prime minister in the eyes. "Cancel the Antarctic Ball."

The prime minister looked shocked.

"Cancel the Antarctic Ball? Impossible!"

"I'm deadly serious, Edward. Think about it—you'll be surrounded by five hundred children. It's the only time that Clarissa Teller makes a public appearance in the year, and as head of security I'm always there also. It's the perfect place to attack the three of us, and it's less than a month away. If anybody is going to attack us, that will be the place they will do it. You must cancel the ball."

The prime minister considered Sir Bentley's words but he was clearly skeptical. "If this boy, whoever he is, is going to attack us, then he will find a way. If the last few weeks have taught us anything, it is that the boy and whoever he is working for are resourceful."

"That's true, but we could orchestrate a carefully managed situation to catch him. Perhaps arrange a visit to a small school for you and set a trap. And it will give the children at Myers Holt more time to learn the techniques. They're talented, but this is too soon."

"I understand what you're saying but I simply can't do it. The Antarctic Ball has taken place every Christmas for the last two hundred sixteen years. Children have received the invitations; heads of state are flying in; everything is already in place. It's simply too late to do anything now."

"Well, then, perhaps *you* should consider not going."

The prime minister shook his head. "Again, impossible. The prime minister has given the opening speech at every single Antarctic Ball in its history—can you imagine the uproar? Churchill managed to attend with bombs raining down in London during the war; Andrew Bonar Law was wheeled in from his hospital bed for the opening ceremony. I don't think the possibility of a twelve-year-old boy attacking me is a good enough excuse."

"Very well," said Sir Bentley, "I understand. I'll make arrangements. We'll increase security—I'll brief all the staff personally. If that boy is there, we'll catch him before he even sets foot in the palace."

"And the Myers Holt children?"

"We'll bring them—we have to—they're our best defense if anything goes wrong. We'll spend the next two weeks training them intensively."

"Good. I have faith in you, Bentley."

"I hope it's well placed. I'll get to work immediately. I'm on my way to Myers Holt now to brief the children—we have a lot of work to do in the next three weeks. In the meantime, cancel all your public appearances."

"Fine. I'll arrange that."

"And keep your wits about you—we have no idea what we're dealing with."

"Will do," said the prime minister, shaking Sir Bentley's hand. "Take care of yourself."

"And you, Edward."

Chris closed the last page of the exam booklet in front of him and looked up at the clock—there were still twenty minutes to go, and he had already checked his answers three times. He heard a soft squeal come from behind him and turned to see Lexi glaring at Rex. She picked up the scrunched-up ball of paper that had landed on her desk and threw it back at him, hitting him square in the eyes.

"Ow!" said Rex, louder than intended.

Miss Sonata looked up from her desk.

"Have you all finished?" she asked, realizing that everybody had put their pens down.

"Affirmative, Miss Sonata. We concluded our examination before the appointed time," said Sebastian in his thick Spanish accent.

"Uh, thank you, Sebastian," said Miss Sonata, looking at him strangely.

"He read the entire *Oxford English Dictionary* last night," explained Daisy.

"Oh! I see, well, good for you, Sebastian."

"Much obliged, Miss Sonata. I would like also to say that you look resplendent today," said Sebastian.

Rex pretended to gag. "Shut your north and south—did you look that up?" asked Rex, rolling his eyes. Sebastian looked confused.

"Rex, there's no need to be rude!" said Miss Sonata, collecting their papers. "Thank you, Sebastian; that's very sweet."

"North and south—mouth, in Cockney rhyming slang," explained Chris. "You know, like apples and pairs—stairs. Whistle and flute—suit. It's from the East End of London."

Sebastian didn't look any more enlightened.

"I'm just pointing out that reading the dictionary isn't going to get him far with the ladies," said Rex.

"And you're the expert, are you?" asked Lexi, rolling her eyes.

"Not talking to you, Frizzo," replied Rex.

"Yeah, a real charmer," said Lexi, turning her back to him.

"Now, now, children, let's try not to argue for once," said Miss Sonata, before Rex could respond. "I'm going to send these off to be marked, and hopefully you'll all have your second A level of the week. Well done, everybody."

Chris couldn't believe how easy it was to do exams now that he was learning how to use his Ability. He had barely scraped a pass in his science test two months ago, and now here he was, sitting his Chemistry A level after only one day of reading the books on the syllabus—and he was pretty certain that he had got everything right. He looked over at Philip, who gave him a thumbs-up sign.

"How did you do?" he asked Chris.

"Pretty good, I think. I reckon physics on Monday will be harder."

"I don't think so. I'll help you tonight if you want. You just have to make sure you look at all the equations—they'll make sense when you try working them out. Come on, let's go get something to eat—I'm starving."

Chris collected up his pens and pencils, put them back in his bag, and followed Philip out of the room, behind Sebastian, Daisy, and Lexi and Rex, who were still squabbling.

"Christopher, can I have a moment?" called Miss Sonata, as Chris was about to leave.

"I'll join you in a moment," said Chris to Philip, who nodded and walked off.

"I just wanted to have a quick chat to see how you're doing."

"Oh, right . . . fine. Actually, really good."

"That's great. I, well, I just wanted to check—we haven't really had a chance to speak recently."

Chris reddened. "I'm okay now, really."

"I'm sure you are; you're a strong boy. I thought you might like to know that your mother's doing really well. We're taking good care of her—I'm making sure of that personally."

"Thank you," said Chris, genuinely grateful.

"Have you spoken to her?" asked Miss Sonata.

"Just once, the second night I was here. She called to say she was sorry."

"Good. Well, that's all. I'm really proud of how well you're doing—Sir Bentley's very impressed with you too."

"Really?" asked Chris.

"Yes, we all are."

"I don't think Ms. Lamb is," said Chris. "She hates me."

"Well," said Miss Sonata, choosing her words carefully, "Ms. Lamb doesn't always see eye to eye with everybody—but her bark is worse than her bite, if you pardon the expression."

Chris thought the expression was actually very appropriate.

"She's spent the last few years training spies and wasn't too pleased to be assigned to a school, but she'll come round. Anyway," continued Miss Sonata, "if there's anything you ever want to talk about—I'm here. Now you'd better get a move on; you don't want to go into your next lesson on an empty stomach."

"Okay, thanks," said Chris, picking up his bag and walking toward the door. He stopped and turned to Miss Sonata. "Miss Sonata?"

"Yes, Christopher?"

"Are you going to see my mum today?"

Miss Sonata put her pen down and looked up at Chris. "No, but I'll be talking to her later. Do you want me to pass on a message?"

"Erm, yeah. Can you tell her that I'm all right . . . and that I miss her."

Miss Sonata smiled gently. "Of course, but you know, you could call her yourself."

"I know, but I'd prefer if you said it."

"I understand. I'll call her in a bit."

"Thank you," said Chris, rushing out the door to catch up with his new friends.

"I'm just saying, hands are pretty useless when you have the Ability," said Lexi, her sandwich hovering at her mouth. She leaned forward, hands behind her back, and took a bite.

"Hmmph, see!" she said, with her mouth full.

The others all looked impressed and put their hands behind their backs also. Chris looked at the glass of apple juice in front of him and willed it to rise. It lifted off gently and glided toward his mouth, then tipped forward suddenly and sent a gush of juice forward, causing Chris to splutter.

"It's not that easy!" he said, laughing. The others all laughed with him and everybody except for Daisy tried to copy him, all with exactly the same messy results.

"Why do you not make attempts at this, Daisy?" asked Sebastian.

Daisy looked down at her dress and shook her head.

"Can't ruin her favorite pink dress, or she won't have anything to wear tomorrow," Rex said, looking over at the éclair in front of him. The plate shook, and the éclair rose quickly. Rex opened his mouth and closed his eyes in anticipation.

"Hey, Rex?" said Lexi.

"Yes," said Rex, opening his eyes, the éclair still rising toward his mouth.

"You should learn some manners," she said, and looked over at the éclair, which suddenly flew forward and crashed into Rex's surprised face, covering him in a thick layer of cream.

"You . . . what are you doing! I was looking forward to that," said Rex angrily, wiping off the cream and licking it off his fingers.

"She's doing you a favor," said Philip. "Being overweight increases your chances of heart disease. Fact."

"Are you calling me fat?" said Rex, glaring at Philip.

"No, I said 'fact.'"

"Not that bit," said Rex, irritated. "The bit before, about being overweight."

"Well, unless all your clothes shrank in the wash," said Philip unapologetically.

"Right . . . ," said Rex, looking over at the water jug.

"Watch out!" said Chris, pushing Philip off his seat as the jug rose upward and tipped out its contents, most of which fell on Sebastian.

"My hair!" cried Sebastian, his usually perfectly quiffed hair dripping wet and flat on his face. He looked over at the fruit bowl at the far end of the table, and a line of oranges rose up in the air and then fired off in the direction of Rex.

"Ow! Ow! Ow!" cried Rex, as each piece of fruit smacked him on the side of the head.

"Stop that right now!" said a voice, and the remaining fruit dropped suddenly back on the table and rolled off onto the floor. They all looked up and saw Sir Bentley standing in the doorway, surveying the mess.

"Get up off the floor, Philip, and wipe your face, Rex; we have work to do. You have five minutes to clean up this mess and meet me on the hill."

Anticipating trouble, the children all put their grievances to one side and quickly tidied the room using their Ability.

"Sorry," said Rex, turning to Philip.

"And I'm sorry I called you fat," said Philip, wiping the water from his face.

"Are you okay, Daisy?" asked Chris, watching Daisy picking bits of éclair from her dress.

"I'm fine," she said quietly. "It's just that my mum will kill me if I ruin my clothes. We can't really afford to buy much with so many of us at home."

"Oh," said Chris, surprised. "I know what you mean."

Daisy looked at Chris's designer jeans and sweater, then down at his brand-new sneakers.

"They were a present," said Chris, suddenly feeling very self-conscious. "They're the first new clothes I've had in years."

Daisy looked confused. "Oh . . . but when Rex called you

rich boy . . ." She saw the embarrassed look on Chris's face and realized why he might not have corrected him. She didn't finish her sentence. "Let's go catch up with the others," she said, grabbing his arm and pulling him out of the room.

Sir Bentley chose not to say anything about the lunch incident, other than to ask them if they had tidied up after themselves. He led them up to the bench under the tree at the top of the hill, and the children all sat down on the grass in front of him.

"I'm afraid we have had some bad news," he said. "Lady Arabella Magenta was attacked using the Ability yesterday. She collapsed and is now in hospital—and I don't think she'll be making a recovery."

Chris turned to Rex, who looked just as shocked by the news as he did.

"As you all know," continued Sir Bentley, "we had a strong suspicion that whoever was carrying out these attacks had something to do with Myers Holt. We are now absolutely certain that's the case—in the last couple of months we have had three ex–Myers Holt pupils and staff members attacked. What we don't know, however, is why this is happening or who is behind it, but we do know that everybody involved in the final mission at Myers Holt thirty years ago is in danger."

"That means you're on the firing line, right?" asked Rex.

"Well, yes, though I'd rather you didn't put it like that. But I'm not the only one who is probably going to be targeted—the author Clarissa Teller was a pupil here at that time, as I'm sure Christopher and Rex explained."

Sebastian, Daisy, Philip, and Lexi nodded.

"Good. So I imagine they must also have told you that the prime minister, Edward Banks, was a pupil here at the same time, which makes this an extremely sensitive and urgent investigation. Do you understand?"

"Yes, Sir Bentley," they all replied.

"Now, I have been working day and night to try to anticipate where the next attack could happen. We have tight security in place for myself and the prime minister, and even Clarissa Teller has agreed to have some men stationed on her small island—just in case. So far we haven't come across anything suspicious, but we're certain now that another attack is imminent, and the only opportunity that we can think of where an attacker would be able to get near to any of us—in fact, all of us—is at the Antarctic Ball in a couple of weeks."

"The Antarctic Ball?" said Daisy. "In Hyde Park?"

"Yes, Daisy, that's right," replied Sir Bentley, "the most famous children's ball in the world. More than five hundred children will be there, as well as myself, Clarissa Teller, the prime minister, and over twenty heads of state. It is enormous, spectacular, and the perfect opportunity for a child to mill about unnoticed in close proximity to the prime minister. I could be wrong, but my instinct and years of experience tell me that this is where the attacks are most likely to take place. Clarissa Teller leaves her island only once a year—specifically to attend the ball. As you may know, she donates all the proceeds from the sales of her books to a number of children's charities, so she will be attending, along with a number of other very generous patrons of similar organizations. I am always there; as head of security I am in charge of making sure that everybody—particularly royalty, the prime minister, and other visiting dignitaries—are kept safe. That leaves the prime minister himself, who as everybody knows, starts off the proceedings each year. He will—"

"Is there really a palace made of ice?" interrupted Daisy.

"Of course, and it's rather wonderful; I'm sure you'll be very impressed," said Sir Bentley. "But as I was saying—"

"And that they freeze the lake so you can skate on it?" asked Lexi.

"Yes, that's also true. Now, if I can—"

"What about flying monkeys—are there any flying monkeys?"

"No, Rex, no flying monkeys. Now, I'm happy to answer any questions about the Antarctic Ball in just a moment, but first I need to finish what I was saying. Understood?"

They all nodded their heads.

"Good. So, we have decided to continue with the ball—it's too late to cancel it now—and I am going to make sure that if the boy who attacked Cecil Humphries, Lady Magenta, and probably Richard Baxter turns up, he will be caught and we can find out who is behind all of this."

"What are his physical characteristics?" asked Sebastian.

"He's asking what the boy looks like," explained Philip.

Sebastian turned to Philip, annoyed. "I peruse the dictionary so that I no require the translation furthermore," he said.

"I'd give up if I were you, Shakespeare—stick to Spanish," said Rex.

"Lárgate, idiota."

"Get lost yourself, Pedro—or did you forget that we all took our Spanish A level?"

Sir Bentley sighed. "Boys, stop. This is important, and I need you all to be serious. We'll have stationed more than two hundred guards at the palace for the evening—that's not including all the people watching the security cameras we're having hidden around the place. But—and this is where you all come in—we need to make sure that if anybody does use their Ability in there, they can be stopped. So—"

"We're going to the ball?" asked Daisy, thrilled.

"Yes, Daisy, you're all going to the Antarctic Ball."

"Yay!" cheered the children, turning to one another in excited chatter.

"But!" interrupted Sir Bentley. "You'll be working."

"But we'll be eating dinner there?"

"Yes—"

"Yay!" cheered the children once more. Sir Bentley looked exhausted.

"Children, please. Calm down. You'll be attending, but you will also be working. I know you're all excited, but this is a very serious thing we're asking you to do. If—and I sincerely hope it doesn't come to it—that boy or anybody else comes in trying to use the Ability, you are going to have to stop it. There are lives in danger, and I don't want any of you to come to any harm, but I can't lie—it could be dangerous."

"How dangerous?" asked Chris.

"Well, hopefully not very. We're going to spend the next

three weeks training you intensively. You will still do your exercise with Mr. Green, but after that we're going to stop all your normal studies with Miss Sonata and focus entirely on using your Ability, so Ms. Lamb will be taking all your lessons outside of your think tanks. I'm afraid there'll also be some lessons on the weekends to make sure we remain on schedule."

The children all groaned.

"We will catch up on your academic studies after Christmas," continued Sir Bentley, as if he hadn't heard them. "It won't take long, but in the meantime we need to make sure you're ready to tackle anything that may happen at the ball. Before we do so, I just want to make sure that you all understand the seriousness of what I'm asking you to do."

The children nodded.

"And I want you to know that you are under no obligation to come. If you would prefer to stay here, we will completely understand. So . . . is there anybody who would prefer not to attend?"

The children all shook their heads vigorously.

"You all want to come—bearing in mind that you will be working?"

"Yes!" said the children emphatically.

"Are we going to go in one of the glass carriages?" asked Daisy, wide-eyed.

Sir Bentley thought for a moment.

"Well . . . you have to get there early before the rest of the guests arrive, so we were going to take you in cars."

"Ohhhh," groaned the children.

"But maybe we can arrange for you to arrive there early

in one of the carriages—I'm sure it shouldn't be too difficult to organize."

"Yay!" they all cheered.

Sir Bentley smiled. "I'm glad you're all so excited, but please remember, you will be *working*."

The children all nodded solemnly.

"That's better. Your invitations will arrive in the next few days, and we'll get you fitted for your tuxedos and dresses soon."

"Yay!"

"One more thing," said Sir Bentley, looking like he couldn't wait to leave, "you are all to stay here at Myers Holt until the day of the ball. I know that some of you had planned to go home on some weekends, but I'm afraid that will have to be cancelled—we just can't risk letting you out of our sight. Understood?"

"But . . . ," said Chris, suddenly serious, "I have to do something on Sunday the sixteenth."

"I'm afraid you'll just have to call and cancel, Christopher—reschedule it for January."

"But—"

"No buts, Christopher; you have to stay here. I need to make sure you're safe at all times. Understood?"

Chris nodded. He wondered how Frank would feel when he broke his promise and didn't turn up at the pawnbroker's.

"I'm off to bed; you staying up?" asked Philip, peering round Chris's open cabin door. Chris looked up from his desk and nodded.

"I can't find anything in the manual that says that we can move objects from far away."

"You can't," said Philip. "Give up. You'll just have to make it up to him in the New Year."

"But I promised him," said Chris, looking concerned. "I can't let him down."

"You heard what Sir Bentley said; you'll just have to explain that you're busy."

"I can't—he needs the shop tidied up before Christmas. Maybe I'll just sneak out for a couple of hours that Sunday—I'm sure nobody will notice. Will you cover for me?"

"Okay, but for the record I don't think it's a good idea."

"I know . . . but you'll do it?"

"Yeah, I'll do it."

"Okay, thanks," said Chris, closing up the manual and putting it back on the shelf. "Guess I'll go to bed too then."

"All right, see you tomorrow. We've got Ms. Lamb first thing."

"Urgh. Don't remind me," said Chris, climbing up the ladder to his bed. "I'll have nightmares."

The next morning Chris walked into the classroom to find Ms. Lamb standing by her desk with an enormous German shepherd at her side. As if this weren't disconcerting enough, the moment the dog laid eyes on Chris, it began to growl softly. Chris sidestepped to his desk and took his seat.

Ms. Lamb turned to the dog. "Children, this is Hermes."

Hermes sat back on his hind legs and lifted his front paw.

"Aaah, he's so sweet," said Daisy, cooing.

"No, he's not; he could rip your head off in one bite," said Rex darkly, from the back of the room.

Daisy's eyes widened in fear, and she turned to Ms. Lamb for reassurance, but Ms. Lamb just nodded.

"The boy is right. And I won't have anybody treating him like a plaything, understood?"

Hermes bared his fangs and growled, as if on cue. Suddenly he didn't seem quite so adorable.

"Today's lesson is in suggestion, though it's a rather misleading name, given that you won't be suggesting anything—you're *commanding* somebody to do exactly what you want. By the end of the week I'll expect all of you to be able to transmit messages to a human being quickly and efficiently. The Antarctic Ball is three weeks away, and there's a possibility that one of you will have to do this—so I expect you to listen carefully."

Chris sat up straight and tried to focus on Ms. Lamb instead of the dog, which was difficult, as it seemed to be eyeing him up personally for its lunch.

"Implanting thoughts is the most difficult thing to do with the Ability—unlike telepathy, where you're effectively visiting somebody else's mind and having a look around, suggestion involves changing the mind's environment with whatever you want that person to think or do."

The image of Ms. Lamb disco-dancing suddenly popped into Chris's head, and he smiled to himself.

"To start you off," continued Ms. Lamb, "we'll be practicing on Hermes. Dogs are particularly sensitive to the Ability and won't fight it in the same way that humans will.

We'll begin by getting Hermes to sit. So, exactly like you do with telepathy, I want you to enter his Reception area, where current thoughts are. When you're there, I want you to shout, 'Sit!'—not out loud, obviously, but in your mind. Concentrate on making it a strong enough command that it replaces any sounds and images that are already in the dog's current thoughts. Right, let's not waste any time. You—begin."

Ms. Lamb looked over at Chris, who was not at all surprised to be picked first. He leaned forward nervously in the direction of Hermes and tried to ignore the menacing look that the dog was giving him. He stared the dog in the eyes and tried to clear his mind. A moment later he was standing in a vast room, surrounded by images of himself and the other pupils sitting at their desks. All he could hear was the loud pounding of the dog's heartbeat. Chris looked around and shuddered—in the corner of the dog's Reception he could make out the image of himself on the floor of the classroom, being attacked by Hermes. He tried to focus on the word "sit," but all he could seem to think about was how difficult that was to do with Ms. Lamb staring at him. A minute passed, and Hermes hadn't so much as flinched.

"Are you even trying, boy?" asked Ms. Lamb, finally.

Chris's concentration was broken, and he was suddenly back in the room.

"Yes," said Chris, trying not to sound as annoyed as he felt.

"Well, whatever you're doing, it's useless—not that I'm surprised. What did you do?"

Chris shrugged nervously. "Umm, I went into his Reception and thought of the word 'sit.'"

"That's not an answer. What exactly did you think of?"

"I . . . um . . . thought of the word 'sit' in black letters."

Ms. Lamb gave a scornful snort. "The last time I checked, dogs weren't able to read. Pathetic. You have to fill Reception with an image of the dog doing what you want him to do—that's the only way that he'll understand. Try again."

Chris tried to shake off his nerves and stared at the dog once more. This time when he entered the dog's Reception, he imagined Hermes sitting. He heard a low growl but tried to ignore it and instead focused on the image even harder. He looked around the large space, and the image of the dog sitting appeared, faintly at first, then clearer, and eventually large enough that all the other sounds and images around him disappeared. He heard a soft whimper. Chris quickly blinked and looked to see that Hermes was sitting dutifully, though the expression on his face still suggested he'd quite like to rip Chris to pieces.

Ms. Lamb made no comment. Instead she turned to Daisy. "Your turn."

Daisy looked terrified, as she always did when she was asked to do anything by Ms. Lamb. She stood up slowly and focused on Hermes. Hermes lowered his head, and his eyes narrowed. He growled.

Daisy's bottom lip wobbled, and she looked as if she was about to burst into tears. She stood up and faced the dog. Hermes growled louder.

"Any second now he's going to attack her," said Rex,

sounding like he would rather enjoy the spectacle.

Daisy heard him and paused. She turned to look at Rex, and he grinned. "What?" he said, the picture of innocence. She turned to face Ms. Lamb.

"Can I go last?" she asked nervously.

"Of course not," barked Ms. Lamb. "Get on with it."

Daisy turned, trembling, and stared at the dog. Finally, after a few minutes of silence, the dog let out a long, low moan and sat back on his hind legs.

Over the course of the next hour, the children took it in turns to make Hermes sit, play dead, walk around the room, and hide under the table. Finally Ms. Lamb called Hermes back to her side.

"Not terribly impressive, but we'll move on nonetheless," she said. She handed the dog a biscuit, which he wolfed down in one gulp, and instructed the children to follow her out to the Dome where Mr. Green had set up an obstacle course for Hermes made up of ramps, hoops, and cones.

". . . finally, Hermes must jump through these two hoops, run back over to you, and sit down next to you," said Ms. Lamb, having walked them around the course. "Right, girl in pink—you can start."

Chris thought he saw a smile briefly flash across Ms. Lamb's face as Daisy approached and the dog growled. Daisy took a step back.

"I don't think he wants to do it," said Daisy.

"Of course he doesn't want to do it—otherwise you wouldn't have to suggest anything to him. It doesn't hurt him, he enjoys the treats afterward, and as long as you don't break your concentration, I'm sure he won't turn against you."

"Turn against me?" asked Daisy, taking another step back.

Ms. Lamb sighed. "I really can't be bothered with your whining. Get on with it."

Chris leaned over and whispered in Daisy's ear.

"I'll stop the dog if he goes for you—don't worry."

Daisy smiled gratefully and stepped out to the line of chalk on the path that marked the start of the course.

Ahead of her, Ms. Lamb leaned over in her teetering turquoise high-heeled boots and unclipped the dog from his leash. Before she had even had a chance to stand up again, the dog leaped forward in the direction of Daisy, who screamed.

"Your Ability!" shouted Chris as Ms. Lamb remained still, watching the dog as it sped toward Daisy.

Daisy shook herself out of her shock and leaned forward, staring directly at Hermes. The dog seemed to take no notice of her, and for a moment Chris thought he might need to intervene—even if it did mean he got into trouble for it—but, just as the dog prepared to jump at Daisy, Hermes froze. They all watched as Hermes let out a small whimper and sat down at Daisy's feet. Daisy looked round at Chris and the others and smiled, at which point Hermes immediately snarled and leaped back to his feet. Daisy spun her head round and ordered the dog back down in her mind and Hermes returned to his sitting position.

"As you can see—if you break your focus, the suggestion

will fade," said Ms. Lamb, with what seemed like a slight note of disappointment that Daisy had reacted as quickly as she had. "It all depends on how strong the suggestion is, and the best way to enforce it is to repeat it, preferably three times, to fully cement it in that person's—or, in this case, dog's—mind."

Daisy completed the course in two minutes and fifty-four seconds, with a five-second penalty for patting the dog at the end ("He's not a teddy bear," said Ms. Lamb, irritated). Sebastian and Rex followed, both managing to complete the course without incurring any penalties, while they all watched in silence.

"You," said Ms. Lamb, pointing at Chris, "and don't mess it up."

Chris stepped forward to the starting line and turned to Hermes.

"Get on with it!" barked Ms. Lamb. Chris felt himself tense up—he had barely looked at the dog.

Chris focused on the dog's mind, and almost immediately he found himself in the dog's Reception, which was full of the sounds of the Dome—he could even hear the heartbeats of himself and the others. The room was filled with one image only: Ms. Lamb standing in her tight, shiny, purple suit on the path ahead. Chris shuddered and focused on replacing it with the first suggestion . . . to run up a yellow ramp.

"For goodness' sake! Hurry up!" shouted Ms. Lamb, breaking Chris's concentration. Chris breathed out, angrily; he had been trying for less than ten seconds—the others had spent far longer at the start of the course. He tried again, but no sooner had he placed the image of the dog running up to the ramp in his mind then Ms. Lamb shouted at him again.

"You're wasting our time!"

Chris felt his face go red in anger. He closed his eyes and counted to ten to try to calm himself, but all he could think about was how satisfying it would be to set Hermes on Ms. Lamb. No sooner had he let the thought enter his mind than he heard the other pupils behind him gasp.

Chris opened his eyes and watched, in horror, as the dog lurched forward onto Ms. Lamb, knocking her to the ground, his jaw open, fangs bared.

"AAAAARGH!" screamed Ms. Lamb as Hermes sunk his fangs into her ankle.

"Somebody stop him!" shouted Daisy, but Chris and all the other pupils were frozen in shock watching the attack as it became increasingly frenzied.

The louder Ms. Lamb screamed, the more violently the dog shook his head, her ankle wedged firmly in his mouth, and then suddenly John appeared, running toward them, followed by Ron. John's giant hands grabbed Hermes by the jaw and wrenched open his mouth. Ms. Lamb's leg fell to the ground, surrounded by a pool of blood and shredded turquoise leather, and John fell backward as he wrestled with the furious dog.

"It's all right, boy, it's all right," said John in a low voice over and over, until Hermes began to calm. Finally the dog stopped struggling and whimpered. John stayed holding on to him as Ron attended to the hysterical Ms. Lamb by ripping his trousers off and wrapping them round her leg, creating a tight tourniquet.

Chris looked over at the carnage he had created—the blood, Ron in his boxer shorts, John lying on the ground with his arms wrapped round the whimpering dog—and his heart sank.

"What's going on?" shouted a voice from the other side of the hill. The children looked over to see Mr. Green running toward them.

"It's all under control," said Ron, as Mr. Green approached.

"Go straight to the Map Room, all of you!" instructed Mr. Green, looking over at Chris and his fellow pupils.

"Is she going to be okay?" asked Chris, genuinely concerned.

"I'm going to be in better shape than you will be once I've finished with you, boy!" screeched Ms. Lamb. Mr. Green looked over at Chris and nodded for him to get out. Philip grabbed his arm and pulled him away toward the exit.

Back in the Map Room, Chris paced the floor nervously.

"I'm in trouble now," said Chris.

"That's the understatement of the year," said Rex, "but still, if it makes you feel any better, at least you entertained us."

"Glad I could help," said Chris miserably.

"What were you thinking?" asked Lexi.

"I think we know *exactly* what he was thinking," said Rex.

Chris sat down on the edge of the sofa and put his head in his hands. "They're going to throw me out for sure. . . . I can't believe I did that."

"She deserved it, Chris," said Philip. "That woman is a witch. Back in the Middle Ages they'd have burned her at the stake."

"Philip!" said Daisy.

Philip shrugged his shoulders unapologetically. "What? It's true—that woman is pure evil. Did you see the way she was trying to wind Chris up? She's lucky she got away with just one shoe missing. I don't know why you're sticking up for her anyway, Daisy—you could tell she wanted that dog to rip you apart."

Daisy considered this for a moment, then nodded. "It's true. And those boots are hideous—you should have got the dog to take the other one too."

"Daisy! I'm proud of you!" said Rex, putting his arm around her. "I never knew you had it in you!"

"It doesn't mean I want Chris thrown out of here, though," said Daisy, looking over at Chris, who still had his head in his hands. Chris looked up.

"Do you really think they'll throw me out?" he asked. Nobody answered.

Chris took a deep breath and, suddenly overcome with the need to be by himself, he walked out of the room. For the next few minutes he paced up and down the corridor, his head spinning, until an opening door interrupted him and Ron and John stepped in from the Dome.

If Chris hadn't felt as terrible as he did, he would have probably laughed at the sight of Ron in his sunglasses and boxer shorts, but as it was, Chris didn't even break a smile.

"That was quite a stunt you pulled there," said Ron.

"I—I'm so sorry," said Chris, his head bowed in remorse.

"Sorry? You've got nothing to feel sorry for," said John.

Chris looked up in surprise.

"What?"

"I said, you've got nothing to feel sorry for. Come here—I want to show you something," said John, reaching into his jacket pocket and pulling out his wallet.

Chris walked over as John opened up the wallet and handed it to him. Curious, Chris took it, only to find himself looking at a photograph of a small white poodle with a red collar curled up on a sofa.

Chris didn't know what he was supposed to say. "Er, is he your dog?" he asked.

"She," corrected John. "Her name's Fifi. Beauty, isn't she?"

Chris nodded and looked at Ron, who just cocked his head as if to say, *I've got nothing to do with this.*

"My point is," said John, taking the wallet back, "I love that dog. She's my best friend. Mind you, I love all dogs. See, dogs, they're just not like humans, are they, Ron?"

"No, John, they're not," agreed Ron.

"They're loyal, they don't talk back, and they trust you. What that teacher of yours did today is the single most despicable act I've seen in all my years of service—and I've seen some despicable acts, Chris, let me tell you."

Chris, who didn't really know what John was talking about, remained silent.

"That dog . . . what's his name?"

"Hermes," said Chris.

"Hermes. Well, do you think little Hermes would have agreed to have people experiment on his brain if he'd been able to talk?"

"I suppose not," said Chris, not having thought of that before.

"No, exactly. He would have said, "No, Mummy, please don't let them use me like that. I just want to play fetch with you, Mummy."

Ron peered over his sunglasses at John as if he couldn't quite believe what he was hearing.

"That teacher got exactly what she deserved. You did a good thing today, son; just remember that. No matter what happens, you know you can walk out of here with your head held high."

John patted Chris on the shoulder. "Take care of yourself," he said, and then turned to Ron. "Come on—I want to see how that dog's doing."

Chris watched as Ron's pale white legs disappeared around the corner, and his shoulders dropped. He knew that John was just trying to comfort him, but all he could think about were the words "no matter what happens." He knew exactly what John meant, and—dignity intact or not—he simply wasn't ready to leave Myers Holt. He sighed deeply and put his head in his hands. *What's going to happen now?* he thought miserably.

Chris didn't have to wait long to find out. An hour later, while Chris was eating his lunch in silence while the others discussed the morning's events, Sir Bentley walked into the room.

"Christopher, come with me, please," he said. Chris stood up.

"Good luck," whispered Philip as Chris passed him.

. . .

"What on earth did you think you were doing?" asked Sir Bentley, back in his office. "This is extremely serious. Ms. Lamb is understandably furious—she's in hospital right now getting stitches to her leg."

Chris sat in the chair opposite Sir Bentley's desk and bowed his head.

"I don't know what happened—I just . . . I just thought about it, and the next thing the dog was attacking her. I didn't mean it to actually happen."

Sir Bentley sighed. "This was exactly what we discussed when you first joined, Christopher. With great power comes great responsibility. You have an extraordinary talent, Christopher, nobody would deny that, but today you let yourself down."

Chris nodded. "I know—I'm really sorry, I really am. . . . Are you going to expel me?" asked Chris, looking up at Sir Bentley.

Sir Bentley sighed. "I don't know what I should do. Ms. Lamb certainly doesn't think you should be allowed to remain here—she made that quite clear—and I can't have members of staff being attacked, regardless of how talented you are. . . ."

Chris braced himself.

"But," continued Sir Bentley, "I believe you when you say it was an accident."

"It really was," interrupted Chris.

"Yes, I suppose it was. Nevertheless, I can't ignore what happened. I think, at the very least, you owe Ms. Lamb an apology. A written one. And I need your assurance that nothing like this will happen again."

"I promise," said Chris.

"I really mean it, Christopher; you're going to have to learn to control your Ability, and you're going to have to learn to control it soon. Do you understand?"

"Yes," said Chris.

"Good. Go back to your room now and write that letter. That's all for now—off you go."

Chris stood up. "Thank you."

"Don't thank me, Christopher; just make sure nothing like this happens again."

"Yes, sir," said Chris.

"You can give me the letter this afternoon—I'll be taking the lesson."

Chris left the room, feeling hugely relieved.

While his classmates ran around the Dome with Mr. Green shouting at them, Chris sat at his desk and attempted to compose the letter to Ms. Lamb, but no matter how hard he tried, he found it impossible to apologize sincerely to somebody he disliked so intensely.

An hour passed, and Chris still had nothing to show for his efforts but a wastebasket full of crumpled-up paper. The door opened, and Chris turned to see Philip, grinning.

"Hey! He's here!"

Chris heard the footsteps of the others running up the corridor. Lexi peered over Philip's shoulder.

"What happened?" she asked. "Did you get into trouble?"

Chris nodded. "Yeah, but at least I didn't get expelled.

I've just got to write a letter to Ms. Lamb and say I'm sorry."

"Oh, yay!" said Daisy, running into the room and giving Chris an enormous hug.

"That's it? You lucky dope!" said Rex.

"Not really," said Chris, still red with embarrassment from Daisy's hug. "I've been trying to write this letter for ages. Here's what I've written so far—what do you think?" Chris picked up the piece of paper in front of him. "'Dear Ms. Lamb, I'm very sorry. Yours sincerely, Chris.'"

"Oh, no, this is inadequate!" said Sebastian, walking up to Chris. "I suggest you provide her with poetry; she will be melted with your sentiment."

Chris raised an eyebrow. "I'm not writing her a poem. I mean, I'm sorry about her leg and everything, but I don't think I need to go that far."

"I don't know, I think Pedro's onto a winner," said Rex, grinning. "I'll help you. How about, 'Violets are red, roses are blue, I hope your leg rots and the other one too.'"

Lexi laughed.

"Rex! He'll definitely get expelled if he writes that!" said Daisy, looking horrified.

"It's okay, Daisy—I'm not desperate enough to take Rex's advice yet," said Chris, looking back down at the piece of paper in his hands. He sighed. "Then again, I might have no choice. . . ."

"I assist you," said Sebastian. "I have been perusing much poetry in recent times."

Chris shrugged. "Okay, I'm desperate. What have you got?"

• • •

That afternoon, after a game of soccer in the garden, the children filed into the classroom for Sir Bentley's lesson. Chris went up to the teacher's desk and handed the letter to Sir Bentley, who opened it up and started to read it as Chris stood by his side, looking mortified.

"Dear Ms. Lamb, I am very sorry I hurt your leg. To show you how sorry I am, I wrote you a poem."

Sir Bentley looked up at Chris and raised his eyebrows before looking back down and reading the poem out loud.

> *"'O how I regret the pain you suffered, the hurt that I caused you.*
> *The sorrow for my actions flows, like the ocean, from me to you.*
> *Be this the start of pastures new, a Spring to follow Winter.*
> *I hope you'll soon be fully healed and running like a sprinter.'"*

Sebastian smiled and raised both thumbs up to Chris, as Sir Bentley continued to read on.

"'I hope that you get well soon. I promise that from now on I will work harder and not get into trouble again. Yours sincerely, Christopher.'"

Sir Bentley looked up. "I hope you mean it."

"I really do, sir," said Chris.

"Very well. It's clear you put some effort into it. I'll pass this on to Ms. Lamb. Now, sit down—I want to have a word with all of you."

Chris took his seat and listened as Sir Bentley gave them a stern lecture, not dissimilar from the one he had been given earlier that day, about taking care when using the Ability.

". . . and that's all I want to say about that. Let's forget all the nonsense of this morning and get on with your training—we have work to do. Today's lesson is, perhaps, the most important one in preparing you for the Antarctic Ball—assuming you need to use your Ability at all there."

Sir Bentley walked over to the mind map painted on the wall.

"This, as you all know, is the map of a person's mind. As you've learned, you can retrieve information from it and place suggestions in the person's current thoughts to make them do or think whatever you want. It was believed, for a very long time, that that was the extent of what you could do to somebody's mind. Some countries experimented with trying to kill people using the Ability, but with no success at all. It seemed that the moment that somebody tries to suggest a person do something that could kill them, the person's survival instinct kicks in automatically and provides a complete block. That, as far as we know, is still the case, although not much research has been done about the Ability in a very long time. However, we did find out that while a person couldn't be killed using the Ability, they could be damaged for life—such as what happened to Cecil Humphries."

"Please can you define 'damaged'?" asked Sebastian.

"I mean you can manipulate the mind so that you fill Reception with whatever you want and then destroy the rest of the information in the mind. The person's brain is tricked into believing that it's still functioning, because their Reception is still filled with thoughts, while the rest of the person's thoughts and memories are completely destroyed."

"Wow!" said Rex. "That's amazing!"

"Amazing, yes," said Sir Bentley, "but also terrifying. The powers that you have can damage a person for life. That's exactly what happened to Humphries, Richard Baxter, and Lady Magenta. And it's completely irreversible. Their Receptions were filled with whatever each one of them was most terrified of—which means whoever did it accessed their Fears and Phobias and used the information to leave them in a permanent state of terror. It's an extremely complex technique—one which we call Inferno."

"Why Inferno?" asked Chris.

"Because to destroy the rest of the person's mind—once you have filled their Reception area with whatever current thought you want—you then visit every building of the mind and set fire to it until the whole mind has been effectively burned down."

"Are we going to learn how to do that?" asked Rex enthusiastically.

"No, Rex, you're not."

"Ohhh," said Rex, disappointed.

"But you are going to learn how to stop it from happening. Unfortunately, this won't be a practical lesson—there's no way that we can replicate the effect to let you practice—so I will teach you how to do it, and you'll have to listen carefully. If you do ever have to use what you're learning today, then it will be while somebody is already using Inferno, and you will have minutes, maybe even seconds, to stop them."

Sir Bentley spent the next hour guiding them round the map, teaching them how to stop the process of Inferno by attacking the person who was using the Ability and replacing their current thought with suggestions to stop what they were doing. He also explained how to stop the process in the mind of the person being attacked (if it wasn't possible to see who was carrying out the attack) by meeting the attacker in the victim's mind and forcibly removing them from where they were, using a complicated system of blocks and suggestion. It was a long lesson, in which Sir Bentley loaded them with information as they all listened attentively. At the end he handed them each a set of printed sheets with diagrams and step-by-step instructions for all of the scenarios he had discussed.

"Commit these to memory," said Sir Bentley, as the children leafed through the pages. "You never know—this information may save somebody's life."

· CHAPTER SIXTEEN ·

Friday, December 14

As London entered the coldest December on record and snow and gale-force winds caused havoc above ground, the children of Myers Holt picnicked daily under the blue skies and gentle heat of their man-made environment. Their lockdown had made little difference to the children, who ran free around the garden and swam in the warm waters of the pool at every opportunity they had.

Chris had never enjoyed school as much as he was enjoying his time at Myers Holt, and he didn't let himself dwell on what would happen when the year was over—he felt confident that by then everything would be different. Occasionally his mind would also wander back to his old life, but it was a good feeling—although there had been only a few brief phone calls with his mother, he was sure that she would be doing better now that the bills were being taken care of. He felt relaxed and confident for the first time in his life, and even Ms. Lamb's return—a bloody bandage wrapped tightly above a brand-new pair of identical turquoise boots—couldn't dampen his happiness at finally finding himself in a place where he was worry-free and surrounded by a group of people that he could actually call friends. It was the first time in his life that he was able to say that, and in spite of all their differences, he couldn't have wished for a better group to be a part of.

Daisy's initial homesickness had disappeared, and although Rex still had the ability to reduce her to tears with one of his comments, Chris admired the way that she wouldn't have a bad word said about him, or anybody else, for that matter. Sebastian's English, although still stilted despite his vast vocabulary, had greatly improved, and he had become quite a fan of Shakespeare, quoting sonnets at the girls, which caused Daisy to blush furiously and Lexi to hit him round the head with a book. This was to the great amusement of Rex, who preferred to try to impress the girls by using his Ability to trip them up, levitate books out of their reach, and lock them in their bedroom when they were running late for classes. Yet, as annoying as Rex could be, he was also able to reduce them all to hysterical laughter with one of his uncannily accurate impressions of their teachers or—their favorite—of John and Ron: As Ron, Rex would jump out when they least expected it, doing ninja impressions, and as John, he would sing country songs about Fifi the poodle and pretend to cry. It was for this ability to keep them all smiling that they had developed a soft spot for him—though none of them would ever have admitted it.

Chris, for the first time since his mother had taken the phone call about his father seven years earlier, felt truly happy.

The two weeks after Sir Bentley's talk with them were filled with lessons and information about every possible eventuality that they might face at the Antarctic Ball. Some of the lessons had been practical and better than any computer game that Chris could have imagined. In their think tanks they had navigated their way around a strangely deserted London, battling enemies hidden in dark alleyways and abandoned buildings, rescuing people hidden within burning buildings, and taking control of speeding vehicles leaving crime scenes. Their lessons with Ms. Lamb were far less action-filled, but with the exception of Ms. Lamb herself were just as interesting, as they all learned how to navigate one another's minds. The fact that they had to use themselves to practice on was unsettling at first, but their increasing confidence in using blocks was reassurance enough that nobody would be finding out anything they shouldn't be, and they all were soon comfortable enough letting their fellow pupils run around their minds in races to find specific pieces of information while their heads exploded with the sound of the ringing in their ears.

It was during one of these lessons that Ms. Lamb finally revealed to them their particular strengths. Philip and Daisy were Data Gatherers and would be used for any task that required them to remote-view. Lexi and Sebastian were, to no surprise of any of them, Suggesters—their strength was in controlling people and objects.

"And the other two," said Ms. Lamb, not looking at either Rex or Chris, "are Mind Accessers—if the situation arises, you will be the two who will enter people's minds to extract information or to block Inferno."

Ms. Lamb spoke dismissively, as if this were a footnote barely worth mentioning, but they all knew that this was the most difficult of all the roles, and Chris couldn't help but feel thrilled at Ms. Lamb's obvious discomfort at having to acknowledge this out loud. Rex and Chris turned and grinned at each other.

"You should all be afraid—very, very afraid," said Rex as they all walked out of the classroom. "I am Rex the Mind Accesser, and now everyone will have to do exactly what I want—ha, at last! Philip, I suggest you go to your room and get me one of those chocolate bars that your mum sent you."

"And I suggest you stop talking, Rex," said Philip, smiling.

"You're just jealous of my amazing powers. What did Ms. Lamb say you were, Einstein? Oh, yeah, that's right—a geek," said Rex.

Philip was about to respond with a quote about how geeks rule the world, when they were interrupted by John, who was waiting for them, with Ron, in the Dome.

"We need your help. Can you all come with us—it won't take long," said John.

Curiously, they all followed John and Ron, who led

them round the back of the hill to the playing field by the swimming pool.

"We need you to settle a bet," explained John, leading them over to a large crate filled with small, colorful plastic balls.

"What kind of bet?" asked Chris.

"Do you want to explain, Ron?"

Ron nodded and folded his arms. "The scenario is as follows. We're at war. We're leading a team of men across open terrain, when—*pow!*"

They all jumped.

"*We're under attack!* Suddenly we're being fired at from all sides; our men are falling all around us; we need to get to safety to mount a counterattack. There's an unoccupied building up in the distance. We need to get there before we get hit. Question is, who would get there first—me or John?

"Me, of course," said Ron, not waiting for an answer.

"And that's where I disagree, Ron," said John.

"Disagree all you like, John; it won't make you right."

"So what do we have to do?" asked Rex, eager to get started.

"Well, John reckons that using live ammunition is a bit risky in here. Probably because he knows he's going to lose."

"Just get on with it, Ron," said John.

"We need one of you to time us. The rest of you will use that mind-power thing that you've got—"

"The Ability?" asked Daisy.

"Right, your Ability, to make those plastic balls hit us as hard as you can while we cross the pitch to get to the flag over there," continued Ron. He pointed to a stand with a red flag at the far end of the grass. "The first person to reach the flag wins. So will you take part in our little bet?"

"Yes!" they all replied immediately.

"Excellent," said Ron. "Remember, hit us as hard as you can."

Daisy, who had volunteered to be in charge of the stop-watch, stood at one end of the pitch. The rest of them lined up along the edge of the pitch, piles of plastic balls at their feet.

Ron and John made their way over to the goal line at the other end from the flag.

"I'll go first," said Ron. "Person to reach the target in the shortest time wins, agreed?"

"Agreed," said John, and the two men shook hands.

"Ready?" asked Ron, turning to Daisy. Daisy nodded.

"Three . . . two . . . one . . . go!" she shouted.

Ron ran off to the left and threw himself on the ground, landing catlike on all fours, and then rolled three times before ducking down behind a large bin that was being pelted by the balls that Sebastian was firing off from his position at the other end of the pitch. Ron's eyes darted about, and then he suddenly jumped up and ran, zigzagging his way across to the right side of the field. He turned his head and saw that a ball coming from Lexi's pile was within inches of hitting his leg. Drawing from his years of martial-arts training, Ron jumped up, pulling his knees into his chest, and then, having avoided the ball, fell to the ground with a roll. He leaped up, ran a few yards, and then did a backflip to avoid another hit.

As Ron made his way from one obstacle to the next, Chris, who was last in the line, got ready to attack. He looked down at the pile of balls and concentrated his mind on them. Immediately the balls all rose up from the ground and arranged themselves in a neat line, hovering gently. Chris waited, watching the balls, until Ron appeared from behind an obstacle next to him. Beside him, Philip was firing balls furiously at Ron—who managed to avoid every one—and then the last ball disappeared and Chris took over.

Chris, with a determined look on his face, began his onslaught, firing the balls one by one with as much force as he could let his mind imagine.

"Come on, Chris—get him!" shouted Rex.

The balls flew fast and furious, smashing into the obstacles, but not one managed to hit Ron, who was ducking, diving, rolling, and leaping from one side of the pitch to the other. Finally there was only one ball left. Chris waited as Ron ran toward the flag and then released the ball, watching as it flew in a straight line. Ron turned his head just in time and jumped over it, then flew forward onto the ground, arms outstretched, fingers touching the base of the flag.

"Forty-eight seconds!" called Daisy.

Ron jumped up and smiled. He ran over to John, who had watched the entire episode with his arms folded and no expression on his face.

"You can give up now, if you want to save yourself the humiliation," said Ron.

"I'll give it a go," said John. "Just to check, the winner

is the quickest person to get to the flag from here—is that right, Ron?"

"That's right, John."

John turned to face the flag and waited as Chris, Rex, Lexi, Philip, and Sebastian retrieved all the balls using their Ability. Once the balls were all hovering in the air, John turned to Daisy and nodded his head.

"Three . . . two . . . one . . . go!" shouted Daisy.

Chris watched from the corner of his eye as John began to walk in a straight line toward the flag. Sebastian fired off the first ball, but John didn't even look round to see where it was heading. Instead John maintained a steady stride and continued walking straight ahead, not even flinching as the ball smacked into his shoulder.

Watching from the sidelines, Ron's face dropped as the barrage of balls flew in John's direction and then bounced off his gigantic frame until he became just a blurred mass of colorful dots moving slowly and steadily without a break in pace or direction. Moments later John reached the other side, and as the last ball hit him, he calmly placed his hand on the flag.

"Sixteen seconds!" called Daisy.

John turned around and smiled as Ron ran over to him, bright red and fuming.

"You *cheated*," said Ron, furious.

"I don't think you'll find that to be true, Ron," said John calmly. "You were very specific—winner is the first person to reach the flag. You didn't mention the balls."

"I didn't need to mention the balls; it was obvious," protested Ron.

"That's precisely the kind of thinking that gets people killed, Ron," said John.

Ron looked as if he were about to explode with frustration. He clenched his teeth and, without saying anything to anybody, stormed off.

"Thanks for all your help," said John, turning to face the pupils.

"No problem!" said Rex. "That was *amazing*! Let us know if you come up with any other bets."

"Will do," said John, giving a small salute. "Right, Ron, so what you making me for dinner tonight? Remember, it's got to be three courses," he called out as Ron disappeared around the hill.

John waved and walked off to catch up with Ron, leaving Chris and the others laughing.

CHAPTER SEVENTEEN

Sunday, December 16

That Sunday, while most other children were enjoying their day off school, the pupils of Myers Holt were working hard in Ms. Lamb's lesson after an exhausting hour in the Dome running an obstacle course that Mr. Green had set up for them. As Ms. Lamb tapped her desk with a ruler to keep time, they all recited, in unison, the order of the buildings on the mind map, but, though this was something they did every day, Chris kept losing track. It didn't go unnoticed.

"Wake up, boy!" shouted Ms. Lamb, slamming her hand hard down on Chris's desk.

Chris jumped.

"Oh, uh, sorry," said Chris, desperately trying to remember where they were.

"What room is next?" said Ms. Lamb, glaring down at him.

"I . . . uh . . . ," hesitated Chris. He looked around for help.

Surprise, mouthed Philip.

"Oh, yeah, the next building is Surprise and Confusion," said Chris, turning back to Ms. Lamb.

Ms. Lamb didn't look impressed.

"And what street is that on?"

"Emotions Avenue," said Chris. Ms. Lamb walked away from his desk.

"After Surprise and Confusion we come to the building housing the memories of what?"

"Jealousy," said the children in unison.

"Very well, continue from there," said Ms. Lamb. She started tapping her desk with the ruler and counted the children in: "Three . . . two . . . one."

"Embarrassment . . . Pain . . . Happiness . . . Excitement and Joy . . . Fears and Phobias . . ."

"Turn left!"

"People Street . . . Family . . . Brief Encounters . . . Old Acquaintances . . . Famous People . . . Strangers . . ."

As he recited the names of the buildings, Chris's mind began to wander once more toward thoughts of Frank at the pawnbroker's, waiting for him to turn up, and how angry he would be at having placed his trust in him. Chris had been determined to keep his promise, but as the day had neared, his resolve had begun to wane, and the reality of sneaking out was unnerving to him.

In the Map Room, after lunch, he confessed his uncertainty to Philip, who was quick to agree with him.

"You could get thrown out of here if you get caught. It's not worth it," whispered Philip.

"What are you two whispering about?" said Lexi, looking over from the sofa.

"Nothing," said Chris abruptly.

"All right, keep your hair on—not interested anyway," said Lexi, turning back to the television.

"I just feel bad—I promised him I'd be there. He lent me money," whispered Chris.

"What did you borrow money from him for?" asked Philip.

Chris had forgotten that, apart from Daisy, they all believed he was rich. "It's a long story," said Chris. "The thing is, I never break a promise—" Chris suddenly heard a ringing in his ears. As quickly as he could, he began to recite "London Bridge Is Falling Down" in his head. The ringing stopped immediately.

"What promise did you break?" asked Lexi. Chris and Philip looked around at her, and she smiled mischievously. "No point in having the Ability if you're not going to use it. You'll have to stop me quicker than that. So, what's the promise?"

"What promise?" asked Sebastian, walking over from the pool table.

Chris hesitated, but before he had a chance to think of an answer, Philip jumped in.

"He promised his mum he'd eat five pieces of fruit every day, but he forgot to do it yesterday," explained Philip.

Chris looked at Philip and gave him a *what are you talking about?* look. Philip shrugged.

"Best I could do," said Philip under his breath.

"We won't tell if you don't, mummy's boy," said Rex, from across the room.

"Right, yeah, thanks," said Chris.

"No, no!" said Sebastian, walking over to them. "A man is only as good as his word. And you never must break promises to your mother—she gave you life. I go procure *ten* pieces of fruit for you now; then you will make up your promise." Sebastian walked out of the room.

"It doesn't matter if you didn't mean to break the promise," said Daisy kindly, looking up from the book she was reading. "Just start again today."

Chris thought for a moment. "No, Sebastian's right. I gave my word. I've got to do it."

"All right, if you're sure," said Philip.

"This should be fun to watch," said Rex as Sebastian walked back into the room with two bunches of bananas.

That evening, after a dinner that Chris barely touched—his stomach still full of bananas—Chris told the rest of the group that he was too tired to join them in the Map Room for their film night and that he was going to bed. He went into his bedroom, grabbed a pile of clothes from his wardrobe, climbed up to his bed, and then stuffed them all under his duvet, arranging them carefully so that it looked like he was under the covers, asleep. He tiptoed down the hallway—unnecessarily, given that the Map Room door was closed and the loud soundtrack of explosions and cars screeching from Rex's chosen film filled the air. Chris opened the door into the entrance hall and walked past the elevator down another hallway until he reached the first door. He knocked loudly.

"Come in!" said John's voice.

Chris turned the handle, but as he did so, he felt himself become suddenly very nervous. It was one thing sneaking out, he thought, but it was another thing entirely to have to lie to Ron and John to do it. He was about to change his mind, and then, convincing himself that it was just a small lie that was needed to do something good, he entered Ron and John's quarters for the first time.

Inside, he found that John and Ron were in the middle of a game of cards. The room was small and sparsely furnished. In one corner, next to a closed door, was a filing cabinet with a television showing an old black-and-white war film, and next to it were two lockers—one decorated with certificates and the other plastered with hundreds of pictures of a white poodle. Chris was pretty sure he could work out who each locker belonged to. Looking up, Chris saw a row of screens that were linked to the security cameras. Chris quickly scanned them and noted the two he was most concerned about—the one showing the entrance foyer and the other showing a dark picture of the street outside.

"Everything all right, Chris?" said John, putting the cards he was holding down on the small wooden table.

"I think so," said Chris, hoping they wouldn't notice his face turning red. "It's just . . ."

"What?" asked Ron, jumping up.

"I heard a strange noise coming from the Dome. I think there might be someone in there."

Chris was grateful not to have to say anything more as Ron jumped up from the table and pulled a truncheon out from the utility belt he was wearing. "Probably a break-in, John, let's go."

"Don't get excited, Ron; it's probably just a pipe," said John, who nevertheless stood up. "Go back to the Map Room with the others and don't worry about anything," he said to Chris. "We'll have a look. I'm sure it's nothing."

"Thanks," said Chris, feeling terrible. *At least,* he thought, *they'll probably never find out.*

He followed Ron and John out of their room and watched as they sped off toward the Dome; then, as soon as they disappeared from view, Chris quickly ran over to the elevator and pressed the button. The doors opened, and Chris entered the kitchen. He pressed his thumb to the handle of the kettle, and the doors closed behind him.

Knowing that he probably didn't have very long before Ron and John returned to their room, Chris stepped out of the elevator when the doors opened at street level and ran over to the front door. He opened it and stepped out. Immediately he was hit by the piercing cold of the winter air and drew in a sharp breath. He looked down at his bare arms and realized how inappropriately he was dressed, but he knew it was too late to go back down for a jacket. Unsure if it would work, Chris closed his eyes and imagined himself getting warmer, and almost immediately he felt his temperature rise as if the harsh wind had transformed into warm rays of sun hitting his skin. He looked around to check that the coast was clear, then ran down the steps and along the pavement in the direction of Oxford Street.

• • •

"Going to the beach?" asked the taxi driver, looking at Chris in the rearview mirror.

"Um, no, I forgot my jacket."

"And scarf and hat—it's freezing out tonight; you'll catch a cold. Anyway, where you off to?"

"King Street, Hammersmith," said Chris.

"King Street it is," said the taxi driver, pulling away.

Ten minutes later and the taxi ground to a halt behind a seemingly endless line of cars, their brake lights a vibrant red against the black night.

"Traffic's terrible since they closed off Hyde Park," explained the driver. "Every year it's the same—you think they'd do something about it."

"Why is it so bad?" asked Chris.

"The Antarctic Ball—they close off all the roads around the park so that nobody can see what they're doing. Tried to take a cheeky shortcut across yesterday, but the police were having none of it—though I did manage to see a line of trucks unloading blocks of ice as big as this taxi. Unbelievable."

"Wow," said Chris, trying to imagine a block of ice that big.

"Always my dream to go to it," said the taxi driver wistfully.

"I'm going this year," said Chris.

"You're what?" said the taxi driver, turning round in his seat to look at him. "Lucky you! I'd have cut my right hand off to get an invitation to that when I was a boy—still would, for that matter. There's more chance of winning the lottery though—bet you didn't know that."

"No," said Chris, amazed. "I think it's going to be really good."

"Best night of your life, I'd bet."

The driver turned back to his driving as the line of cars began to move slowly forward, and Chris leaned up against the window and watched his breath mist up the window. He had never really thought of himself as lucky or unlucky, having always felt that it was up to him to make his own luck in life, but the driver's words stuck with him, and he spent the rest of the journey thinking about the incredibly fortunate series of events that had unfolded for him recently through no doing of his own. It was true, he thought; he really must be a very lucky person.

"Here we are," said the taxi driver, breaking Chris from his thoughts. "That'll be sixteen pounds forty."

Chris suddenly froze. In all his preparations for sneaking out of school, he hadn't once stopped to think about bringing some money. Now, here he was, in the middle of London at night, and there was nobody he could call. He put his hand in the pocket of his jeans in case a twenty-pound note had miraculously appeared there, but of course it hadn't. Chris's mind raced—he truly had no idea what to do, and for once he didn't think that being honest was going to be the best option.

The driver watched him in his mirror with increasing suspicion as Chris pretended to fumble in his pocket. "You've got the money, right, son? I don't want any messing about."

Chris didn't say anything, desperately trying to think of what to do.

The driver turned around and glared at Chris. "You've got five seconds to pay me, or I'm calling the police. Five . . . four . . ."

There was only one option that Chris could think of at that moment. He pushed aside the feeling of guilt that was beginning to form and looked up at the driver.

"Oh yeah, here it is," said Chris quietly, looking straight into the man's eyes. He let his eyes glaze over, and within a couple of seconds he found himself standing in the Reception of the driver.

"You have twenty-five pounds in your hand," said Chris, repeating the sentence three times, watching the image of the money suddenly appear before him, small at first but growing rapidly, until it was all that filled the man's mind.

The driver looked down at his empty hand and smiled.

"Blimey, thank you!" he said. "Happy Christmas and have a good time at the ball."

"Thanks," said Chris, full of guilt. He stepped out of the taxi as quickly as possible and watched the man drive away, and vowed that after this night he would never do anything like that again.

Looking around at the familiar surroundings, Chris realized how little thought he had given to his old life since he had arrived at Myers Holt. It made him feel even more unsettled than he was already feeling, and he crossed the road quickly, eager to get the job done.

Although all the shops were closed, the street was still full of people hunched over and rushing to their destinations in order to escape the bitter cold. A few of them looked up and gave him a strange look. For a moment Chris wondered if they knew that he was here to break into the building in front of him, and then he realized that they were probably staring at him because he was a twelve-year-old boy standing in the street at night in a T-shirt. He pretended to look at his watch, as if he were waiting for someone, hoping that nobody would ask him any questions—which, fortunately, nobody did.

Finally, after he had loitered impatiently for over ten minutes, the section of street he was on cleared, and he quickly looked over at the door and willed the lock to open. He heard a loud click, and, looking around him one last time to check the coast was clear, he pushed the door open and hurried inside.

Chris switched the light on and looked around at the piles of boxes, televisions, radios, and other equipment stacked up against all four walls. The cabinets were stuffed full of jewelry that looked lackluster behind the dirty glass cabinets. Chris sighed at the enormity of the task ahead of him, knowing that he had to be back at Myers Holt as soon as possible—even using his Ability, this was going to take a long time. He stepped into the middle of the room and looked over at the wall to his left. Focusing on a large set of speakers, he watched them lift up from the shelf they were sitting on and glide over to the back wall.

Two hours later, after watching the entire contents of the shop fly about him and rearrange themselves in their new positions, Chris stopped and wiped his brow. He looked at the counter and watched the dust cloth rise and fly over to the final cabinet, which now contained neat rows of jewelry, ordered by type and price. The dust cloth slammed into the glass and began to rub against it furiously, until all the dirt was gone and it sparkled with the reflection of the diamonds contained within.

Chris walked over to the back of the shop and put away all the cleaning equipment. He picked up the pad of paper, now positioned neatly on the counter by the till, and the pen from the polished pen holder beside it.

Dear Frank,
I'm sorry I didn't come earlier today, but I didn't forget my promise to you. I hope you're happy with the job I did.
Have a good Christmas,
Chris
P.S. Sorry about breaking in.

Chris jumped out of the taxi a block away from Myers Holt and waved to the smiling taxi driver, trying to ignore how guilty he felt for having had to use the Ability on him. Chris took a moment to look up at the front of the Myers Holt building. Having seen the screens in Ron and John's room, he knew that he could avoid detection if he just stayed close to the railing and approached the door from the left, which was exactly what he did. He looked at the lock on the door and, blurring his eyes, willed it to unlock. He heard a click and then carefully opened the door. He ran into the elevator, which was already at ground level, and descended. Now he just had to hope that John and Ron were distracted enough not to notice him arriving, or—even better—asleep.

Chris tapped his fingers nervously on the kitchen counter as the room shook gently and came to a stop. Chris walked up to the doors and watched them open, willing this last bit to be over.

"Where have you been?"

Chris jumped. There, standing directly in front of him, were Sir Bentley, Ron, and John. And not one of them looked pleased to see him.

"I asked you, where have you been?" asked Sir Bentley and though he didn't raise his voice, Chris could hear the anger in his question.

Chris hesitated, but he couldn't think of a believable excuse that would get him out of the trouble he was in. He decided to tell the truth.

"I made a promise to do some work at a shop—the man had already paid me to do it."

"You were under strict instructions not to leave Myers Holt."

"I—uh—I know . . . it's just that I made a promise," said Chris, realizing how ridiculous this sounded. Sir Bentley looked at him with a look of suspicion and anger that Chris had not seen before.

"Come with me, Christopher," said Sir Bentley, leading Chris toward his office. "Ron, John, you know what to do."

Ron and John nodded and walked off in the opposite direction.

Inside Sir Bentley's office, Chris took the same seat he had taken after Hermes had attacked Ms. Lamb. He suddenly realized, with a sinking feeling, that this was probably a step too far, and he cursed himself for having risked his place at Myers Holt over a small promise he had made to a man he would probably never see again. He also realized he was shaking.

"Put this round you," said Sir Bentley, handing Chris the tartan blanket that was draped over the worn leather sofa by the fireplace. Chris wrapped it round his shoulders and smiled gratefully. Sir Bentley didn't return the smile. Instead he took out a pad of paper and a pen from the drawer in his desk and looked up at Chris.

"Now . . . very precisely, I want you to tell me exactly what you did tonight."

Chris began his confession, leaving out the part where Philip had agreed to cover for him. Sir Bentley didn't speak except to clarify details every so often, and as Chris spoke, he wrote everything down.

"So, this is everything?" asked Sir Bentley, once Chris had finished speaking.

Chris nodded.

"And this is the complete truth?"

"Yes. Of course," said Chris, surprised at the question.

"Christopher . . . if you are working for somebody else . . . if you are in any way involved with what happened to Cecil Humphries and the others, then I think it's best you say now—because we *will* find out."

Chris took a moment to process what Sir Bentley was suggesting, and his eyes widened in shock.

"You think that I—what?—no! I don't know anything about what happened to them!"

"I hope not, Christopher . . . I really hope not," said Sir

Bentley, standing up. He walked over to the door of his office, opened it, and called out down the hallway. "You can come in now."

Chris looked around, not knowing what to expect. A wave of nausea hit him, and he took a deep breath.

"Come in," said Sir Bentley, stepping out of the way.

Lexi and Rex walked in in their pajamas, followed by Ron and John.

They looked over at Chris, who looked back at them in surprise.

"Not a good idea," whispered Rex. "You're in big trouble."

Chris nodded but didn't say anything.

"Christopher," said Sir Bentley, walking back round behind his desk, "I suggest that you don't resist this. If you use a block, then I will take that as an admission of guilt. Rex and Lexi—you are going to use your Ability to find out precisely what Chris was doing tonight between the hours of eight forty-five p.m.—the time he activated the elevator—and eleven ten p.m. You may not speak at all while you do this, and when you have finished, Ron and John will lead you into separate rooms to write up a report. I will check them and see if all three accounts—both of yours and Christopher's—match. For your sake, Christopher, and ours, I hope that they do. Do you all understand?"

Chris, Lexi, and Rex all nodded.

"Very well, you may begin."

Chris sat back and tried to relax as the ringing in his ears began.

. . .

After what seemed like hours but was in fact just twenty minutes, Sir Bentley walked back into the office alone. Chris watched as he laid the pile of papers he was carrying down on his desk.

"The reports all matched, Christopher."

Chris breathed a sigh of relief.

"That's not to say you're not still in trouble, though I'm glad my worst fears weren't realized. We have a duty of care for you, and what you did tonight was beyond foolish. It was dangerous. You may feel that you can take care of yourself now that you know about your Ability, but the fact remains that you are only twelve years old, and the streets of London are not a safe place for you to be roaming about unescorted at night. Do you understand?"

"Yes, sir," said Chris. "I'm really, really sorry. I know I shouldn't have done it; I just wanted to keep my promise."

"And your integrity is one of the qualities we most admire about you, but you took it too far tonight and put your safety at risk. Do you want to tell me what was so important about helping this man tidy up his shop?"

Chris knew that if he had any chance of staying at Myers Holt, he would have to be completely honest, and so, for the first time in his life, he spoke about everything that had happened since his father had died. Sir Bentley listened as Chris poured out the details of the last seven years—the way it had changed his mother, the difficulties at his old school, the responsibilities he had at home, and the trouble he had in paying the bills every month.

"He wouldn't take the medal, but he offered me money

in exchange for getting the shop ready for Christmas. Nobody had ever trusted me like that, and I didn't want to let him down," said Chris finally. He felt completely drained and at the brink of tears.

There was a long pause. Finally, Sir Bentley sighed.

"I knew you'd been through a lot, Christopher, but I had no idea your situation was as bad as it was. You should have spoken to someone about this sooner and asked for help."

"I didn't want them to take me into care and leave Mum on her own."

"I understand, but that's always the last option, Christopher. There are many more ways you could have been helped—you didn't have to go through all of that on your own. You are going to have to learn to trust people more."

Chris nodded.

"Well . . . I suppose this all makes a lot more sense, but it doesn't change the fact that what you did tonight was foolhardy. If you had spoken to me, we might have been able to work out something. Aside from that—did you really think we wouldn't find out?"

Chris chose not to answer this—it was obvious he hadn't thought his plans through.

"Apart from the cameras, you activated the elevator with your thumbprint, which goes on record. You were never going to get away with it."

"I know—I didn't think."

"No, you didn't. Not only did you choose to disobey rules, but you also chose not to use your common sense, and that concerns me greatly. In a week's time you are all going to be put in a position of great trust and possibly considerable danger, and the last thing we need is a maverick making up his own rules and possibly putting the lives of a lot of people at risk. So, I've made my decision: You'll come to the ball, but you'll stay with me the entire time. Do you understand?"

Chris couldn't believe his luck. "Yes, thank you."

"I don't want you out of my sight for one second. If we need you, then I will be with you to make sure you follow instructions to the letter."

"Yes, sir."

"Good. Now, we come to the matter of you stealing."

"Stealing?"

"Yes, the money that you didn't pay the taxi drivers."

"Oh," said Chris quietly.

"Just because they weren't aware of what you were doing doesn't make it any less of a crime. I have to say that I'm absolutely disgusted that you would use your Ability in that way. It's particularly surprising to me given that you stole from people in your attempt to pay back somebody else. I am greatly disappointed."

Chris hung his head in shame. "I know I shouldn't have done it—I felt really bad. It's just . . . well . . . I didn't have any money, and I only remembered when I got to the shop," said Chris, knowing that it wasn't going to be an acceptable explanation.

"That's no excuse at all. There is never a good reason to steal, and you are the last person I thought I'd have to explain that to. You will have to make amends. I expect that you remember the registration plates of the two taxis?"

Chris nodded, the image of both taxis suddenly clear in his mind.

"Good. After Christmas, when you come back, you will be earning the money back by helping Maura. Then we will find the drivers, and you will return the money and apologize. Is that a fair punishment?"

"Yes, sir," said Chris.

"And finally, and I mean this, if you ever pull a stunt like that again, you will be out of here. This is your last warning. Do you understand?"

"Yes, sir," repeated Chris.

"Good. Now . . . it's late. Go to bed."

Chris walked out of the room and found Ron and John standing in the hallway.

"I'm so sorry," said Chris, looking up at them both.

"Do you have any idea what kind of danger you put yourself in?" asked Ron.

"I know," said Chris, his head bowed.

"No, I don't think you do," continued Ron, clearly furious. "What you did tonight was a breach of security. You know what I think should happen to someone who deliberately breaches security . . . I'll tell you what I think should happen. I think that person should be lined up against the wall and—"

"All right, Ron, that's enough. You can see the boy's upset."

Chris, tears welling up, looked away and wiped his eyes with the back of his hand.

"Well, John, he should have thought of that before he decided to break the rules."

"We've all made mistakes, Ron, or do I need to remind you about a certain night in Hong Kong?"

Ron snapped his head round, alarmed. "That wasn't a mistake, John; it was a misunderstanding," he said, nevertheless suddenly looking a lot less annoyed.

John, satisfied, turned back to Chris and put his hand on his shoulder. "You've learned your lesson, and that, as far as we're concerned, is that. I know you were trying to do the honorable thing, son, but I don't think I need to tell you that you went about it in the wrong way."

Chris nodded, grateful for the words of comfort.

"Go back to your room now and get some sleep," said John. "Tomorrow's a new day."

Chris walked back into his bedroom to find Philip sitting up in his bed, waiting for him.

"Are you okay?" asked Philip.

"Yeah. You were right—I shouldn't have gone."

"But you're staying, right—you didn't get expelled?"

"No," said Chris, climbing up to his bed, "but it's my last chance."

"Phew. We all thought you might not come back. Everyone's going to be really happy."

"Really?"

"Yeah, of course. We're a team, aren't we?"

Chris smiled. "I guess we are," he said, laying his head on the pillow. He closed his eyes and fell into a deep sleep.

CHAPTER EIGHTEEN

Friday, December 21

Though they were over an hour away from each other and their motives were poles apart, the pupils of Myers Holt and the Genever brothers at Darkwhisper Manor were following an almost identical schedule of preparation in the week running up to the Antarctic Ball. Both sets of children had received their gilded invitations, been fitted for their white tuxedos (and sparkling white ball gowns for the girls), and had undergone intensive training in the Ability—with particular emphasis on understanding Inferno. But while Mortimer and Ernest Genever were focused and somber in mood, Chris and the rest of the Myers Holt pupils were counting down the days with giddy excitement, much to the displeasure of Ms. Lamb.

"Can you all stop this racket immediately and get back

to your desks!" barked Ms. Lamb, having walked in to find them all huddled about Philip's desk, talking loudly about what they thought the ice palace at the ball would look like.

The children all ran back to their desks and took their seats.

"You all seem to be under the impression that we're going for a jolly day out tomorrow. Let me tell you now—you are all very much mistaken. Forget the palace, the dinner, the ice cream—"

"Ice cream?" said Rex, delighted. They all grinned.

"For goodness' sake, you're all behaving like children—grow up! The only reason that any one of you good-for-nothings is invited to this ball is that you are expected to work and to protect the lives of the very important people who will be there. I have here the security schedule for tomorrow, and I want you to listen very carefully. You," she said, pointing at Chris, "as we all know, can't be trusted, so you'll be stationed with Sir Bentley for the evening. Don't take your eyes off him for one moment."

Ms. Lamb walked over to the wall and pulled down the screen. She picked up the remote control on her desk, and the projector in the ceiling whirred into life. A photograph appeared of Clarissa Teller.

"This is Clarissa Teller, the author. Some of you may know her already. A number of generous patrons to children's charities are invited to the ball each year. Miss Teller donates the entire proceeds of her writing to a number of charities, making her the most high-profile of this group of people, and as such she will be seated at the top table. You," she said, pointing to Lexi, "will be watching her for the evening." Ms. Lamb pressed a button, and the photograph switched to one of the prime minister.

"This, as you all know, is Prime Minister Edward Banks. We consider him to be the prime target at tomorrow's event. You and you," she said, pointing to Philip and Daisy, "are in charge of watching him and anybody near him. He will likely be surrounded by people, so you will have to keep your wits about you—if you have any."

"Finally, you two," she said, looking over at Sebastian and Rex, "will be standing at the entrance with the security guards, checking everybody who enters. If this boy appears"—Ms. Lamb pressed a button, and a blown-up photograph appeared of Mortimer Genever, sitting cross-legged in front of the stage where Cecil Humphries had given his talk—"you must immediately detain him by using suggestion to have him lie flat on the ground. Once he has been handcuffed, you must use your Ability to escort him outside to the waiting police van and remain with him until you arrive at the prison, where a special cell has been prepared with a lining of lead so that his Ability is rendered useless. At that point your services will no longer be required, and you will be escorted back to the group. While he is under your care, as you have already learned, you must fill his Reception with a clear block. What block have we all agreed to use?"

"'Twinkle, Twinkle,'" answered Rex.

"Precisely. That way he can't use his Ability while in transit. Now, I want you all to commit this photograph to memory. The boy may come in another way, so you must all be able to identify him immediately if he appears."

Chris looked up at the picture of the pale boy with slicked black hair. He was surprised at how young he looked, even though he knew they were both the same age. It was hard to believe that this was the boy who had managed to willfully destroy three lives in as many months.

The picture disappeared, and Ms. Lamb pulled up the screen.

"Your success or failure tomorrow will reflect directly on my teaching, so I expect you all to take this seriously and study every piece of information tonight that you have been given in your time here. I don't want any mistakes. That's all. Now get out, all of you."

The day of the Antarctic Ball had finally arrived, and at three in the afternoon, after some halfhearted studying and a picnic in the Dome, the children were all led upstairs by Maura into two large rooms aboveground that had been transformed into dressing rooms for the day, one for the girls and the other for the boys. Chris and the rest of the boys walked in to find a large team of people waiting for them. Chris was led over to one of the four large chairs that had been placed in a row in front of a line of full-length standing mirrors and took a seat as the man behind him began to cut his hair. The radio blasted, and the boys chatted excitedly among themselves as they waited for their tuxedos to be steam-pressed.

"I could get used to this," said Rex, as a woman did up his bow tie. Only Philip, who wore a bow tie every day, was able to do his up by himself.

"Do we get to keep these tuxedos?" asked Philip.

"Yes, they've been made especially for you," said the man, taking out a pair of polished white leather shoes.

"Fantastic!" said Philip. "I was thinking I needed something more formal for dinner in the evenings."

"More formal than a three-piece suit?" asked Rex.

"That's daywear, my friend. Dress to—"

"Impress," said Rex, Sebastian, and Chris at the same time.

"You're learning," said Philip, smiling.

The boys thanked the team and walked out into the hallway to wait for the girls. Finally, after what seemed like a very long time, the door to their room opened, and Daisy and Lexi stepped out. The girls were dressed in similar, but not identical, white dresses, with a full satin skirt and long sleeves that had been painstakingly adorned with hundreds of crystals, which sparkled under the hallway lights. Daisy's hair had been curled, and her blond ringlets were pushed back off her face by a diamond tiara, on loan for the evening from a jeweler in Soho. Lexi's hair, normally a wild mass of dark hair, had been straightened, slicked back, and pinned up behind a tiara also on loan from the same jeweler.

"Ooh la la," said Sebastian.

"Isn't it beautiful?" asked Daisy, holding her tiara in place as she spun around.

"You actually look like a girl," said Rex, looking at Lexi.

"Shut up, Rex," said Lexi, blushing.

"Well, well . . . what have we got here?"

The children all turned to see Sir Bentley come in through the front door, dressed in a white tuxedo.

"You look just like James Bond, sir," said Lexi.

"Thank you, and you both look very beautiful," he said to the girls.

"What about us?" asked Rex.

"You look very beautiful too, Rex," said Sir Bentley, smiling.

They all laughed.

"Really boys, you all look very dashing—like young James Bonds. Now . . . we have our cars waiting outside."

"I thought we were going in the carriages," said Daisy, looking disappointed.

"We are, but they collect people from different places in London. Our ones will meet us at Marble Arch at five, so we'd better get a move on—remember, we have to be at the palace before any of the other guests arrive. Do you have your invitations?"

The children all held up their cream-and-gold cards.

"Excellent. Let's go," said Sir Bentley, leading them out into the dark winter night.

The area around Marble Arch was closed off to traffic, and crowds of excited children, all dressed in white tuxedos and dresses, filled the pavements as they waited to be allowed in. John pulled up as close to the security barrier as he could and dropped them off, then drove away as arranged to park the car at the ice palace. Sir Bentley led the way as they pushed through to the front, much to the annoyance of the waiting guests.

"Sorry," said Chris repeatedly.

The others were also apologizing as the crowd grew

more irate. Well, except for Rex, who was very much enjoying the moment.

"Very important people coming through!" shouted Rex, barging his way past.

Finally they reached the entrance, and Sir Bentley flashed a badge and gave a whispered explanation to the security man at the door. The man nodded and opened the door.

"Invitation, please," said the man. Chris handed him his invitation and in turn watched as the handheld machine scanned the small gold bar code printed on the bottom left of the card. The machine flashed green, and the man waved Chris through.

"Enjoy your evening," he said, as Chris stepped out onto the ring road surrounding a spotlit Marble Arch. Chris looked around in awe. He felt as if he had traveled back in time—the only transport was a long line of at least a hundred ornate glass carriages, each led by a white horse and a driver in a white top hat and suit.

"Can you see the carriages 'Vanguard' and 'Albemarle'?" asked Sir Bentley, looking at the ticket the security guard had given him.

"They are yonder!" said Sebastian, spotting the gold lettering on the side of the two carriages at the front of the line. They all ran toward them.

"Children, stop!" said Sir Bentley. He walked up to them. "You have to remember to stay with me until we get to the ball, and then you *must* stay in your assigned places. Please don't forget that you are working tonight."

The children all nodded obediently and walked alongside Sir Bentley.

"Chris and Rex, you can both accompany me in the first carriage. The rest of you can follow us in the other."

Daisy, Lexi, Philip, and Sebastian ran off toward their carriage.

"Good evening," said the driver, who was dressed all in white and holding the reins to a beautiful white mare, which stood still and majestic, waiting for his orders.

"And good evening to you," said Sir Bentley. "We're scheduled to be leaving a bit early—I hope that was explained."

"Yes, sir," said the driver. "We're ready to go when you are."

Sir Bentley thanked the man and walked over to the glass door of the carriage, turning the gold handle and opening it up to let Chris and Rex in. The boys clambered in and sat in the white and gold leather seat at the back, and Sir Bentley sat opposite them, closing the door behind him.

"And off we go," said Sir Bentley, as the horses sprang to life and the two carriages, sparkling under the streetlights, set off down the road. Chris and Rex jumped up and down on the seat in excitement, not noticing the note of trepidation in Sir Bentley's voice.

The carriages proceeded slowly down Park Lane, which had been cleared of traffic, and behind the barriers that had been erected at the side of the road a growing mass of curious people stopped and pointed in awe at their two-carriage procession, two crystal balls gliding along under the moonlight. A small part of Chris was aware that he should be on the lookout for the boy in the photograph, but except for cursory glances amongst the gathering crowds, he spent the ride laughing and chatting with Rex, who for once had nothing but positive things to say.

"They think we're famous!" said Rex, waving to the crowds and enjoying the celebrity.

The crowds cheered and cameras flashed as the children grinned.

"I think we're here," said Chris, as the carriages took a turn right and stopped at the Queen Elizabeth Gate, which was heavily guarded by what seemed like a hundred police officers. Beside them, less than ten feet from where the carriages stood as they waited for security clearance, the final group of bystanders was jostling forward, trying to get a look at their carriages and perhaps even a glimpse of the palace.

Rex leaned over to Chris's side of the carriage and looked out of the window.

"They're practically green with envy!" said Rex, holding up his invitation as a tease to a group of boys on the curb beside them.

"I can't see the palace," said Chris, as the carriages were waved through by the line of police.

"It's just round the corner; you'll see it in a moment," said Sir Bentley.

Sure enough, a few minutes later the carriages made their way round the black wall of oak trees that had been blocking their view, and the Serpentine Lake appeared before them, a gleaming blanket of solid ice that had been lit from beneath, as if the moon had been laid down on the ground at the foot of the ice palace standing behind it.

Both boys gasped.

Although they had spent the last few weeks discussing and imagining what the palace would look like, nothing had quite prepared them for the size or magnificence of the scene before them. The enormous palace, supported by crystal-clear carved columns, was made entirely of ice, which sparkled under the cool white light of a hundred spotlights; leading up to it was a path overlooked by two lines of trees carved out of ice, white lanterns hanging from their branches.

"It's amazing!" said Chris, leaning forward out of his seat, his face pressed up against the side of the carriage.

"It must be as big as Big Ben," said Rex.

"Almost," said Sir Bentley, "and made of more than five thousand blocks of ice, each one taller than me. Look"—he pointed to the top of the palace wall—"up there you can see that the ice has been carved out—each section depicts a scene from the voyages of James Cook."

The boys looked up and marveled at the scenes of ships, icebergs, and animals.

"And if you think that's incredible, wait until you see inside," said Sir Bentley as the carriage came to a stop.

"Good evening, Sir Bentley," said the waiting footman, opening the door for them.

"Good evening," said Sir Bentley, stepping out onto the red carpet that ran up to the arched entrance of the palace.

"Good evening, boys. Welcome to the Antarctic Ball," said the footman as the boys jumped down.

"Hi!" said Chris and Rex, waving to their carriage driver

and hurrying past the footman to catch up with Sir Bentley. Behind them the other children jumped out of their carriage and ran over to them, but before they had a chance to say anything to one another, Sir Bentley stopped them.

"I know you are all terribly excited, but I have a lot to discuss with you before the other guests arrive. I don't suppose you'll listen to a word I say until you've had a chance to look around, so I'm going to give you five minutes—and I mean five—and then I want you to meet me back here and we can get started."

Sir Bentley had barely finished his sentence before the children ran off through the archway and into the great hall of the palace.

"Wow!" said Lexi as they all stopped dead in their tracks.

Chris, standing next to her, looked up, awestruck. For a moment nobody said a word. Directly in front of them, in the center of the vast room, was a circular wall of ice from which rose a life-size ice whale, which spouted water high up into the vaulted ceiling of the palace and back down into the black rippling waters contained below.

"I can't work out how it doesn't fall over," said Philip, walking up to the fountain and looking up for wires. "It just doesn't make sense," he said.

"It's magic," said Daisy.

"No such thing as magic," said Philip, now peering intently into the water.

"Of course there is," said Daisy, and while Philip didn't look satisfied with this answer, he let her lead him away to join the rest of them, who were standing at one end of a table of ice that ran far into the distance, along the back wall, and back round the other side. Each setting was laid with crystal plates, glasses, silver cutlery, and a carefully folded white cloth napkin on which lay a place card with the name of the guest handwritten in gold ink.

"I wonder where we're sitting," said Lexi, reading the names as she walked along the table.

"We don't have time," said Chris. "We have to be back in three minutes—it'll take forever to find our names in here. Let's look around more."

They all nodded in agreement and spent the next few minutes running around and trying to take in everything—the ice statues of the animals of the Antarctic; the carved replica of James Cook's ship, the *Endeavour*, atop an ice plinth behind the top table; the tunnel onto the iced lake outside, lined with ice skates for the children to help themselves to; and their favorite—through an archway toward the back of the palace—the ice cream room, filled with iced vats of every flavor ice cream surrounded by hundreds of glass bowls filled with toppings.

Out of time and having explored only half of the palace, the children rushed back to Sir Bentley, who was surrounded by guards in white uniforms and police officers.

"Ah, here they are," said Sir Bentley, motioning for the children to join him next to Ron and John and a group of other guards that Chris didn't recognize.

"This is Christopher, Rex, Lexi, Philip, Sebastian, and Daisy," said Sir Bentley. "They will be stationed at the entrance until the people they are escorting arrive—except for Christopher, who will be accompanying me, and Sebastian and Rex, who will stay with security at the entrance for the entire evening with Ron and John."

Ron and John both nodded their heads in unison.

"I'm not going to go into any more detail, but these six children have been briefed to look out for the boy in the photograph that you have all been given. They have full security clearance, and if they report anything suspicious to you, I expect you all to act immediately, without question. Is everybody clear on that?"

All the guards except Ron and John nodded, though Chris could see from the way they were looking at him that some of them were skeptical about following instructions from a group of twelve-year-olds.

"Good," said Sir Bentley. "The carriages will begin arriving in five minutes. The VIP guests, including the prime minister and other heads of state, will arrive at the same time as the invited children, so you must all keep your wits about you at all times. Right—everybody to their posts, and let's make sure that everything runs smoothly tonight."

"Yes, sir," they all said, dispersing in every direction.

Chris and the other pupils followed Ron and John over to the security desk at the entrance and waited. As the minutes ticked by, a growing sense of unease came over them all, as they were suddenly aware that, at any time, all their training could be called into use.

From behind them the sound of the orchestra started to play, filling the room with classical music, and up ahead, from beyond the lake, Chris saw the procession of glass carriages come into view.

"I'm scared," whispered Daisy.

"It's all right; I'm sure nothing's going to happen," said Chris, though he felt just as nervous as Daisy looked.

The nerves eased off as the guests began to arrive and the room started to fill with excited chatter. The orchestra played as the waiting staff walked round with silver trays of colorful hors d'oeuvres and drinks. Excited children ran around the palace, cones filled with scoop upon scoop of every flavor ice cream, stopping only to stare in wonder at the fantastic statues of ice, while the pupils of Myers Holt could only watch in envy.

Clarissa Teller was the first familiar face that came through the entrance. She greeted Chris and Rex warmly, hugging them both, and was introduced to Lexi, who led her off to give her a tour of the palace. Soon after, to great excitement from the guests that had already arrived, the prime minister and his wife walked in. He smiled as he walked past security and straight over to Sir Bentley.

"How are you, sir?" asked the prime minister.

"Very well, Edward, very well."

"Any developments?" asked the prime minister.

"None. But we have everything well taken care of. Just enjoy your evening—we'll do the rest."

"Excellent. So where are my two chaperones, Philip and Daisy?" asked the prime minister.

Philip and Daisy stepped forward, looking starstruck and slightly nervous.

"Ah, wonderful! I've heard I'm in good hands with you two—is that right?"

"Yes, sir," said Philip.

"Good. Well, come with me; we have lots of people to meet."

Philip and Daisy waved to Chris, Rex, and Sebastian and hurried off behind the prime minister, who was already by the fountain, shaking hands with the prime minister of Canada.

After a while, and following a quick word with Rex and Sebastian about staying vigilant, Sir Bentley motioned for Chris to follow him away from the entrance. Chris did as told without a word and stood dutifully at Sir Bentley's side as he walked around greeting guests. Every so often, Chris looked over at Rex and Sebastian, who were staring intently at each child standing in line at the entrance. He was keenly aware that at any moment they might need help.

CHAPTER NINETEEN

Ernest stood in line, tugging at his bow tie uncomfortably, his nerves growing as he neared the wall of security blocking the entrance to the ball. Behind him, some fifty feet away, was his mother, standing alone, and following in a carriage behind was his brother, Mortimer. Ernest fought the urge not to look back at them for reassurance.

"We'll do best if we split up," his mother had said that morning, giving Ernest strict instructions to ignore them when they arrived at the ball. "It would be impossible to avoid notice if identical twin brothers walked in together."

"Yes, Mother," Ernest had said, and at the time he had felt thrilled that his mother had trusted him to work on his own.

The group of four girls in front of him skipped forward

and were waved through after having their invitations scanned, leaving Ernest to approach the desk on his own, head bowed low.

"Welcome to the Antarctic Ball," said the security guard, taking the invitation from him without looking up. He scanned the bar code, and there was a loud beep. Ernest held his breath. The light went green.

"Enjoy your evening," said the guard, holding out the invitation. Ernest reached out and took hold of it, but just as he was about to take it out of the guard's hand, the man looked up and a look of recognition flashed across his face.

Ernest quickly looked the man in the eyes and tried to enter his Reception, but his heart was pounding, and he struggled to keep focused.

"You!" the man shouted before Ernest had a chance to pull himself together, and within seconds he was being flung down on the ground and his hands were being pulled back behind him and secured with handcuffs. Ernest looked up in horror as the biggest man he had ever seen walked over to him and lifted him up horizontally, placing him under his enormous arm as if he were just a rather large book.

Ernest heard gasps from onlookers as he struggled to get away, but the guard didn't flinch, and his arm stayed firmly locked, pinning Ernest's arms to his side. Though unable to move, Ernest did manage to twist his head round enough to see two boys, both dressed in white tuxedos and one of whom he recognized from their surveillance at Lady Magenta's house, running over toward him.

He looked behind him, out into the night, and saw his mother standing in line, watching him calmly. Panicking and realizing that there was no way he was going to be able to escape without help, Ernest tried to send her a message, but instead he heard her thoughts, as clearly as if she were whispering them into his ear.

"Good. He's out of the way, as planned. Now the other can get on with his work; then I'll be rid of both of them."

Ernest felt as if he'd been punched in the stomach. He suddenly realized that the last few years had meant nothing to his mother, and that he and Mortimer were no more than pawns in her plan, to be dispensed with like unwanted rubbish once she'd done what she had set out to do. He tried to scream to warn Mortimer, but no sound left his mouth as the familiar sound of ringing in his ears washed over him and rendered him speechless. He looked up at the boys and recognized their blank stares. At that moment he knew they were standing in his mind, and there was nothing he could do about it.

"I'll bring him round," said the gruff voice of the guard carrying him. Ernest looked up helplessly as he was lifted to his feet and dragged out toward a side exit, surrounded by policemen and guards. Guests stared at him as he passed them, and although he could see their mouths moving and the orchestra behind them, all Ernest could hear in his mind was the sound of "Twinkle, Twinkle, Little Star" being sung loudly by the voices of the two boys trailing behind him, blocking any chance he had of using his Ability to get away.

The giant guard carried Ernest out into the cold night

air toward a waiting police van with its lights flashing blue. He heard the faint sound of the men talking and watched the police van doors open.

"Take him to the cell at Waterloo and don't take your eyes off him for a moment," said a skinny guard in sunglasses. "He may be a child, but he's extremely dangerous."

"We've got it all under control, Ron; this is a police matter now. You two go back to the others and we'll take it from here," said a policeman, climbing into the van. Ernest felt himself being lifted up into the van, and then the giant man laid him down on the metal floor. Turning his head, he saw the two boys taking a seat at the back of the van and watched as the doors closed. The floor of the van rumbled as the engine started up.

Fifteen minutes later the van doors opened, and Ernest was lifted back onto his feet and down into the police parking lot.

"You boys are all done here now," said a faint voice that seemed to come from an older man in police uniform in front of him. "One of my men will take you back to the ball."

Ernest saw that the two boys had heard what the man said, but they remained still and staring at him.

"I said, you boys are dismissed. We'll take the boy up to the cell."

Ernest felt the sound of "Twinkle, Twinkle" fade as the boys turned to face the man.

"We have to stay here until he's locked up," said one of the boys, "just in case."

"Just in case what?" said the man, clearly annoyed. "I think between five men we can handle a twelve-year-old boy. Arthur, take these boys back to Hyde Park."

"Yes, sir. Come with me, lads."

"No! We can't—"

Ernest, his mind suddenly clear and his thoughts on his brother, realized that this might be his only opportunity. He looked over at two of the largest men and, focusing his mind, sent them flying back suddenly into the rest of the group. The two boys fell to the ground beneath the mass of bodies, and Ernest turned and ran over to the driver's side of the van. He looked at the ignition and used his Ability to make it move forward. Spinning the van around, Ernest felt the change of gears in the van, and he sped off past the gates as the men struggled to their feet and tried to run after him.

• CHAPTER TWENTY •

Meanwhile, back at the ball, Sir Bentley was congratulating his security team.

"Absolutely fantastic news! I'll leave after dinner to interview the boy. Christopher, I think it would be useful if you came along with me."

"Yes, sir."

"In the meantime, you can all relax and enjoy yourselves. Dinner starts after the speeches in twenty minutes. I'm going to go and have a word with the prime minister and tell him that everything has been taken care of."

Chris, Philip, Daisy, and Lexi ran off toward the tunnel to grab some skates and hurried out onto the lake of ice outside to join the hundreds of children gliding around, until the sound of a single trumpet called them to dinner and they joined the line to get back in.

"How do we know where to sit?" asked Daisy. "Do we have to check each place?"

"There's a table plan next to the polar bear statue—on the wall—it's carved into the ice. I saw it earlier," said Philip, as they walked back into the main hall.

The guests were all seated in order of their carriage number, which made it easy for them to find their names, once they had managed to jostle their way past the crowds to the wall. Carriages two and three were sat at the right side of the room, with the exception of Sir Bentley, who sat at the top table alongside Clarissa Teller and another woman they didn't recognize—a first-time attendee to the ball called Dulcia Genever, who had in the last year, for reasons unknown, matched Clarissa Teller's substantial donations to various children's charities around the country. Her generosity had earned her a coveted seat at the top table alongside other dignitaries and donors. It had also earned her the trust of the organizers of the ball, who were about to find out just how misplaced their trust had been.

Chris took his seat and poured himself a glass of water from the crystal jug in front of him. He looked around in wonder at his surroundings, taking everything in.

Finally the seven hundred plus guests were seated, and the orchestra stopped playing. Everybody hushed and watched as a man dressed in a white suit and elaborate white feathered hat walked over to the podium at the side of the room and rang a small gold bell three times. The sound, amplified through the microphone, bounced around the walls.

"Esteemed guests, ladies and gentlemen, boys and girls, welcome to the Antarctic Ball. Without further ado, I would like to welcome to the podium your host for this evening, the prime minister of the United Kingdom, Edward Banks."

The entire room applauded as the prime minister thanked the master of ceremonies and stepped up to the podium.

"Good evening to you all, and welcome. Two hundred seventeen years ago, this ball was established in order to give children from all walks of life and around the United Kingdom a chance to learn about the great achievements of the British explorer James Cook and find out more about the places he discovered. Nowadays, thanks to the power of radio, television, and other media, our knowledge of the world is far greater, and while we still honor the achievements of James Cook every year, we also use this event as an opportunity to acknowledge the generosity of people who choose to donate . . ."

The prime minister stopped and raised his hands to his ears. Chris froze and watched, his heart in his mouth, as the prime minister looked up at Sir Bentley, his eyes wide with horror, and began to sing:

"Old King Cole was a merry old soul and a merry old soul was he. Old King Cole was a merry old soul and a merry old soul was he. *Old King* . . ."

All the guests turned to each other in confusion. Chris saw the paramedics at the other side of the hall scramble to grab their bags. They ran over to the prime minister, who was now shouting at the top of his voice.

"Someone's using their Ability," said Daisy, in a horrified whisper. "What should we do?"

Chris looked over at Daisy and saw the terror in her face.

"The block's not working!" he said, as the prime minister's voice began to fade.

"Do something, Chris!"

And then, with a jolt of clarity, Chris suddenly realized what he had to do. Any nerves or fear he had felt disappeared instantly, replaced with a complete sense of calm and focus. He looked around as the rest of the audience watched silently while the prime minister struggled to regain his composure.

Chris turned to Lexi.

"Put a block in the prime minister's head! Do it now!" instructed Chris, as he pushed his chair back and stood up, scanning the face of each child seated in turn. Seeing nothing, he began to walk around the tables as quickly as he could without bringing any attention to himself. And then, suddenly, he spotted a lone figure in a dark alcove behind the orchestra. Chris stopped dead in his tracks and ducked. He squinted, and the figure started to come into focus. It was him—the boy from the photograph—standing completely still and staring in the direction of the prime minister, who was now clutching at his throat as he leaned on the podium for support.

Chris didn't stop to think about how the boy they had only just arrested had managed to reappear. He stood slowly and stared directly at the boy. For a moment nothing happened, and then suddenly the boy jerked his head round. Chris's eyes narrowed with concentration, and before the boy had a chance to react, he was thrown violently up in the air and slammed against the wall behind him. The shocked silence of the crowd, who had until that moment been entirely focused on the prime minister, was broken as everybody turned to see the boy landing on the floor with a heavy thud. Chris jumped over the table, knocking glasses and plates to the ground, and, ignoring the screams of panic around him, he ran over to the boy, who was lifting himself up slowly.

"Watch out!" screamed Lexi, as the boy leaned forward, staring at Chris. It was too late. Chris felt himself lifted off the ground and flying back in the air, landing painfully on the hard ground. He lifted his head and saw the boy turn to run. Chris let his eyes glaze over and stared at the boy, who rose up into the air once more and soared backward, landing at the foot of the fountain.

Sir Bentley was already up on his feet and about to make his way over, when the woman next to him grabbed his arm.

"Excuse me!" said Sir Bentley, wrenching his arm away.

"Don't you know who I am, Sir Bentley?"

Sir Bentley stopped. He looked down at the woman who had been sitting silently next to him and struggled to place the vaguely familiar face.

"I need to go," said Sir Bentley, unnerved by the woman's calm tone of voice. She stared up at him and lifted her hands to her eyes. When she moved her hands back, her eyes had changed from a deep black to a brilliant emerald, and Sir Bentley took a sharp breath. Sir Bentley had only seen eyes like that on one person—a young girl, more than thirty years earlier—and suddenly everything that was happening and all the events leading up to it started to make sense.

"That's right," said Dulcia, seeing the recognition sweep across Sir Bentley's face. "Anna Willows."

"Anna? I—I don't understand. . . . I thought you were—"

"Dead?" interrupted Dulcia. "You shouldn't have given up on me so easily, but I suppose my life wasn't as valuable as yours."

Sir Bentley looked horrified. "That's not the case at all. We came back for you. We found your jacket washed up on the shore, covered in blood."

Dulcia's eyes narrowed, and she stood up to face Sir Bentley.

"And that's it? A jacket with some blood and you gave up all hope. You just went back to your happy lives and left me to rot in a cellar for the rest of my childhood."

"I don't know what to say, Anna. We saw you going over the cliff—we didn't think anybody could have survived that."

"And yet I did survive, didn't I?"

Sir Bentley put his hand on Dulcia's arm. "I'm so sorry, Anna. Please, stop all this and we can talk—there's no need for anybody else to get hurt."

"It's a bit late for talking now, I think," said Dulcia, her voice so calm it sounded almost robotic.

Sir Bentley opened his mouth to speak, but a glint of silver caught his eye. He looked down at Dulcia's hands and saw that she was holding a knife. He watched as she drew her arm back.

"Stop!" shouted Sir Bentley, but it was too late for reasoning. Dulcia lunged forward just as Sir Bentley threw himself backward. He crashed into the seat behind him and fell to the floor. Everybody around him jumped up, screaming in terror, as Dulcia walked calmly over to exact the revenge she had been planning for so many years.

"NOOOOO!" screamed Daisy as Dulcia raised the knife up with both hands. Dulcia jerked her head round, knife poised, and saw the girl stop suddenly, her eyes completely blank.

Dulcia knew immediately what the girl was doing. Realizing that she only had seconds to do what was needed, she gripped tighter on the knife and tried to force it down, but it was too late. She felt the full force of the Ability focused on her hands, and the next thing she knew, the knife flew out from her grasp and landed on the floor behind her.

Dulcia scrambled backward to grab the knife just as John and Ron appeared, running. Seeing the pair fast approaching, Dulcia grabbed the handle of the knife; then, with crazed eyes and a look of pure determination, Dulcia threw herself forward toward Sir Bentley, who was in the process of getting up. Ron, seeing what was about to happen, jumped up in the air, ninja-like, and spun, his legs kicking out and hitting Sir Bentley with such force as to send him flying to the side and out of harm's way. Meanwhile John, who lacked the grace but none of the power of Ron, hurled himself forward in Dulcia's direction and slammed straight into her. With the full force of John's weight on top of her, Dulcia fell backward and hit her head on the floor, which knocked her immediately unconscious.

Ron, seeing John lying across Dulcia, leaped over Sir Bentley and ran over as he removed the handcuffs from his belt.

"Ready to secure the target, John."

Ron looked down at the back of John's head, waiting for John to move, but John didn't respond.

"John?"

Ron heard a low moan. He knelt down and pushed John, his legs scrambling against the floor with the effort. Finally, Ron took a deep breath and gave a final push. John's body rolled over.

"John?"

Ron stepped over the unconscious body of Dulcia and looked down at John, who slowly opened his eyes.

"Ron?"

"You all right, John?"

John lifted his head up and looked down. Ron, following his gaze, saw the handle of the knife sticking out from John's stomach.

"Somebody call an ambulance!" shouted Ron.

"It's all right, Ron, calm down," said John quietly. "It's only a scratch."

John reached down, and then, as the growing group of people gathered around him watched with horrified gasps, he slowly pulled the knife out.

A woman behind John fainted as he placed the bloodied knife on the ground next to him. Slowly he lifted himself to his feet; then, his hands pressed firmly against the wound to stem the flow of blood, John shuffled away, leaning against Ron for support.

Two policemen pushed their way through the crowd; then, having secured handcuffs to Dulcia, they carried her out to the waiting police van.

Sir Bentley, placing a comforting arm around Daisy, watched them carry Dulcia away. He looked around to see where the rest of the pupils were. It was only then that he saw the fight that was in progress on the other side of the room, and he began to run.

"SOMEBODY STOP THAT BOY!" shouted Sir Bentley, watching as the pale boy, who now stood by the fountain, threw Christopher up in the air like a rag doll.

Chris looked down at the ground far below him as the boy turned and began to run and the force of the boy's Ability, which had lifted him up, disappeared. A sense of defeat washed over him as he watched the muted chaos far below him. Chris closed his eyes and braced himself as he began to fall and then, suddenly, a familiar sound of ringing filled his head.

"I've got you, Chris," said a voice in his mind. Chris opened his eyes and looked down to see Philip standing below him, staring at him blankly, and his body immediately slowed. Everyone around him gasped as he landed gently on his feet.

Chris didn't have time to feel relieved. All he knew at that moment was that the boy was getting away and that it was his responsibility to stop him—he needed to prove to

Sir Bentley that his belief in him was justified. Panic swept over him as he realized that the boy was fast approaching the main doors. With all his might he willed the boy back and imagined him landing on the ground below him—but as he did so, he knew that the adrenaline had taken over him. He felt that frighteningly familiar feeling of losing control of his Ability, just as he had done when he had set the dog on Ms. Lamb, but it was too late. He watched the boy fly backward, the boy's body flailing as he fought the violent force that was lifting him up into the air. There was nothing that Chris could do but watch helplessly as the boy slammed into the enormous ice whale in the center of the fountain, then fall to the ground at his feet, unconscious.

"Watch out, Chris!" shouted Philip.

Chris heard people screaming and looked up to see the full-size whale of ice come crashing down. Chris jumped back as the three tons of ice landed on top of the unconscious boy and smashed to smithereens. The room fell silent.

Chris rushed over to the boy and knelt over him. His eyes were closed, and he was no longer breathing. Chris grabbed the boy's wrist, but he already knew that it was too late. The boy was dead. He, Christopher Lane, had killed someone, and he knew that it hadn't been necessary—if he had just managed to stay in control, the boy would have lived, and it would have been for other people to decide how he should pay for his actions. For a moment all Chris could hear was the sound of his own breathing, and then, appearing as if out of nowhere, Chris heard a voice and looked up to see another boy, identical to the one lying on the ground.

"You killed him," said Ernest Genever in a tight whisper. "You killed my brother."

Chris looked up at the boy and saw the tears in his eyes.

"I—I didn't mean to," said Chris.

"You killed my twin brother!" said Ernest, louder. He looked over at Chris, who was frozen in horror, his hand still holding the dead boy's wrist, and his eyes glazed over.

Chris heard the ringing start up in his ears and scrambled to his feet.

He turned to run but was knocked back to the ground by the group of policemen who were running toward the crying boy.

Ernest Genever wiped the tears from his eyes and looked at the men in turn, fixing them with a steely stare. As he did so, each one was thrown backward. Before they had a chance to get back to their feet, he scooped up the body of his brother in his arms and carried him out through the main archway and into the black night.

CHAPTER TWENTY-ONE

Late that night

The mood was somber in the prime minister's office on Downing Street as Sir Bentley explained the identity of the woman now locked up under tight security in Waterloo to the prime minister, Clarissa Teller, and the Myers Holt pupils.

"Anna Willows . . . I can't believe it," said Clarissa Teller, shaking her head. "That poor girl. I just don't understand—we saw her . . . we saw her fall—there's no way she could have survived."

"I'm as baffled as you are, Clarissa, but we can't alter events of the past, and you must remember, she's changed; it's not her anymore," said Sir Bentley gently. "She's where she should be now after everything that's happened."

"And the boys—do we know who they were?" asked the prime minister.

"No . . . she's refusing to talk. We'll find out soon enough from her, but the important thing is that she is behind bars now and you are safe. We are all safe."

The children all smiled except for Chris, who could only see the body of the boy he had killed.

"Christopher . . . are you okay?" asked Clarissa.

"I . . . It's just . . . That boy . . . I . . ."

Clarissa put her arm around Chris.

"You did what you had to do; you mustn't feel bad. This has been a difficult night for everybody, but it could have been so much worse."

Chris nodded but didn't look up.

The prime minister walked over to where Chris was sitting. "Clarissa's right, Christopher. Many people are safe because of you all, not least myself. I can't thank you enough."

Chris smiled and then grimaced as the stitches above his eyes were pulled.

"Poor you," said Daisy, leaning her head on Chris's shoulder.

"What about me?" asked Rex, rolling up the legs of his dirty white trousers. "I grazed my knee at the police station."

"Ah, poor Rex," said Daisy, smiling.

"Thank you!" said Rex, satisfied, and they all laughed quietly, glad to have the mood lightened. Only Chris remained silent, lost deep in thought.

"Right, children," said Sir Bentley, standing up. "I think we've kept the prime minister long enough. It's getting late."

The children all thanked the prime minister, who shook hands with each one of them. When he reached Chris, he leaned over and whispered in his ear. "Thank you . . . you saved my life tonight."

"You're welcome, sir," said Chris, his face going red. "I was only doing my job."

The next morning Chris woke with the sound of birds singing gently, welcoming the morning sun rising over the landscape of rolling hills that Chris had come to know as his bedroom. Despite the successful conclusion of the previous night, Chris had slept fitfully, his dreams filled with the image of the dead boy lying at his feet and the sound of the brother's grief-stricken cries. Sir Bentley had assured him over and over again that he had done what he had had to do, but deep down Chris knew that the boy needn't have died: He had lost control of his Ability, and somebody had paid for that mistake with his life. Everything had been so perfect, he thought, and now it turned out that it really had all been too good to be true.

"Are you awake?"

Chris turned to Philip, facing him on the opposite bunk, and nodded in answer.

"You don't look very well—are you all right?"

It was a simple question, but Chris couldn't think of what to say in response, and an awkward silence followed until, finally, Philip sat up.

"It's not your fault, Chris. We were all there last night, and we all made mistakes."

"Yeah, but my mistake killed that boy."

"No, *our* mistakes killed that boy. I could have stopped him, so could Daisy or Lexi, but we didn't—we froze. You were the only one who could even think clearly enough to do anything. If it hadn't been for you, well, you know what would've happened. You had to do what you did because no one else could."

"I don't know. Maybe. But I can't stop thinking about his brother—what do you think he did? Where do you think he went?"

Philip shrugged. "I don't know . . . but we'll find out. You heard what Sir Bentley said; they'll find out from the woman soon enough, and then they can make sure the boy is okay. He'll be fine—you just have to remember what he was trying to do."

"I never thought I'd say it, but I'm glad Sir Bentley decided to cut our holiday short last night. At least I won't have to wait that long to find out what's happened to him."

"I know, there's no rest for the wicked, as they say!"

Chris grimaced.

"Sorry, bad choice of words—you know what I mean. Come on, it's all over, we did everything that we had to do, everyone's safe, and that woman is behind bars, so let's have fun today—it is nearly Christmas after all."

Chris opened his mouth to speak, then thought better of it.

"You're right; I'll be fine. Come on, let's pack and go see the others."

Chris's somber mood had lifted by the time they entered the dining room for their early Christmas lunch—a result of a morning spent playing in the Dome with his classmates. Taking advantage of the warm weather that they were about to exchange for gale-force winds and snow aboveground, they had spent most of the time in the swimming pool, where—once they were sure the coast was clear—they had all levitated each other as high as they dared before letting themselves drop, performing spectacular dives into the sparkling blue waters below. Only Rex, who refused to take part in any voluntary exercise, had chosen not to join them. Instead he sat on the bench under the blossom tree and entertained himself by firing marbles he had borrowed from the Map Room at his levitating classmates. Fortunately for the rest of them, Rex's telekinesis abilities had only slightly improved in his time at Myers Holt, and he managed only a single, gentle hit on the side of Sebastian's head, which was success enough to leave Rex in fits of hysterical laughter for the rest of the morning.

"Simple things please simple minds," said Philip as they exited the changing rooms to find Rex still giggling to himself.

"Come on, Einstein, that was funny. Did you see that, right on the noggin—*bam!*"

"More like *plink*," said Lexi, rolling her eyes.

"Admit it, Frizzo, you're just jealous. You can only dream of having half the superpowers of Rex King."

"Hmm, I don't know about that," said Lexi, looking over at the pile of leftover marbles on the grass. Immediately they rose up into the air, then hovered for barely a moment before flying directly into Rex's open mouth.

Rex spluttered, his face red with surprise, and the marbles flew out of his mouth as the others burst out laughing.

"Now, *that's* funny," said Philip, smiling as he walked off toward the exit.

The dining hall had been decorated by Maura for their Christmas lunch in a sea of red and green streamers, baubles, and fairy lights, and the landscape surrounding them had, for the first time, been replaced by a snow-covered scene of crisp white hills and pine trees.

"Oh, it's beautiful!" said Daisy to Chris, who nodded in agreement and smiled as he looked out over the sumptuous feast that Maura had prepared for them. Chris had never seen anything like it, and he took note of everything on the table so that he could try to replicate it for his mother on Christmas Day.

"Now that's what I call lunch!" said Rex, pushing his way past Chris toward the table, where he grabbed a sausage and stuffed it whole into his mouth.

"Hands off, young man," said Maura, walking into the room with a large dish filled with steaming vegetables, which she struggled to find a space for on the table.

"Thorry," said Rex with his mouth full. Maura tutted gently, smiling, then turned her back to the children to rearrange the dishes on the table, at which point Rex grabbed another sausage and gulped it down in two bites.

"You are like a swine," said Sebastian, shaking his head.

"Sorry, Dad," said Rex, walking over to the plate of Yorkshire puddings.

"Right, we're nearly there," said Maura, rubbing her hands on her apron and looking very pleased with herself. "Why don't you all sit yourselves down; the teachers will be here in a moment."

"There's no way I'm sitting next to Ms. Lamb," said Chris, taking a seat quickly between Daisy and Philip. Suddenly panicking, the others jostled among themselves to try to avoid an empty seat next to them, until they were interrupted by Sir Bentley entering the room, followed by Mr. Green, Miss Sonata, Professor Ingleby, and a dour-faced Ms. Lamb, who took a seat as far from the children as possible, much to the relief of all of them.

"Excellent, you're all here already—my goodness, Maura, you've excelled yourself!" said Sir Bentley.

"Thank you, sir," said Maura, blushing furiously as she pulled out the chair for him at the head of the table.

Everybody standing took their seats, while Maura rushed round, serving them all drinks.

"Before we begin our lunch, I just wanted to say a few words," said Sir Bentley, standing. "It's been an incredibly busy first term at Myers Holt, and I wanted to thank you all, pupils and staff, for your tremendous hard work over the last few weeks. I know last night was difficult, but I hope you'll all keep in mind that, at the end of it all, we had a very successful outcome. Because of you, we now have the answers we needed and Dulcia Genever in custody, and none of you," he said, looking over at Chris, "should feel guilty about what you had to do."

Philip nudged Chris and gave him an *I told you so* look. Chris smiled and turned back to Sir Bentley.

"Next term will be very different and far less intense, you'll be glad to hear. You'll resume normal studies with Miss Sonata. PE will continue with Mr. Green, who I believe will be incorporating the use of the Ability in your lessons, is that right?"

Mr. Green nodded. Chris grinned as he imagined them all playing soccer forty feet in the air.

"Excellent. As for the Ability, you'll be moving on to the next chapter of your training, which Professor Ingleby has prepared for you in the think tanks—is there anything you'd like to say about that, Professor?"

The professor stood up eagerly, knocking over his glass of wine in the process.

"Drats!" he said, mopping up the table with his napkin. "That'll have to do," he said finally, giving up. "I must say, this has been a wonderful project to work on. I myself have learned so much, and I hope that next term's training will test your Ability even further. I am on the verge of completing the mind-map scenario for you all to explore on your return, and I have a few other tricks up my sleeve that I think you'll rather enjoy. I'll say no more, except bravo, all of you, and I hope you have a well-earned rest over the next few days—you'll need it!"

There was a round of applause as the professor sat back down.

"And last but not least, of course, you will continue your lessons with Ms. Lamb—is there anything you'd like to say about what you have in store for our young agents?"

Ms. Lamb looked unamused to have been asked to speak. She pushed her chair out and stood up reluctantly as Chris tried desperately not to think of any horrible thoughts that might cause a repeat of the Hermes incident.

"Yes, well," said Ms. Lamb, curling her lip at the pupils. "We'll be testing your pain limits with mild torture and hopefully carrying out Inferno on each of you. That's all."

Chris and the others looked horrified, except Rex, who burst out laughing.

Sir Bentley shot Ms. Lamb a disapproving look. "I guess some of us are not quite in the Christmas spirit today. I think what Ms. Lamb meant to say is that you'll be exploring some more advanced Mind Access techniques and moving onto level two suggestion. Is that right, Ms. Lamb?"

"Yes, I suppose we could do that too," said Ms. Lamb, taking a sip of her drink without looking up.

"Wonderful! And now I won't keep you from the fantastic feast that Maura has prepared for us a minute longer, except to say . . . merry Christmas!"

Sir Bentley raised his glass and everybody else followed. He was about to say something more when the sound of the door opening interrupted him, and the whole table turned to look, their glasses still raised.

"Sorry we're late," said John, walking in stiffly. Beside him stood Ron, with his sunglasses on and a huge smile on his face.

"John!" screamed all the children. Chris jumped up, followed by the rest of them, and ran over to John, who winced only slightly as they hugged him. He put his arms around the group and smiled.

"Merry Christmas," he said.

"Merry Christmas!" they all replied, grinning.

• • •

The drive back to Hammersmith was a long one, delayed by Christmas traffic and seasonably awful weather, which gave Chris a chance to look back over his time at Myers Holt. He had been surprised at how sad he'd felt saying good-bye to his classmates, even though he was going to see them all again in a few days' time. For the first time since his arrival, Chris had felt like an outsider—the only one of the children not to have been collected by his family. Daisy had left first, her two younger sisters clinging to her legs, a frenzied ball of pink squealing in excitement. Lexi's father had arrived with her three older brothers, who greeted Lexi with punches to her arms. Chris could tell that she was dying to use her Ability on them, but she had resisted—Sir Bentley's warning about using the Ability in the outside world was still fresh in her mind. Philip, another only child—possibly the reason that Chris got on so well with him—was collected by his parents, both professors at Oxford University. Rex had failed to contain his giggles as they'd watched Philip shake hands with his father, an identical version of his son, except taller.

It had been Chris and Sebastian's turn to laugh, however, when Rex's parents turned up, showering him with hugs and kisses as he struggled to pull away. Then, finally, Sebastian had left, collected by his parents and sister, who had been shocked to be greeted with a Shakespearian sonnet. That had left Chris, standing alone with Miss Sonata in the rain. She gave him a warm hug and waved him good-bye as he was driven away.

• • •

Chris stepped out of the car and waited as Ron—who, much to John's frustration, was not letting John do anything until he was fully recovered—took his suitcase out of the trunk. Then he shook hands warmly with both of them and watched as they got back into the car and drove away. It was only then that he looked around him, at the street he was so familiar with, and his nerves suddenly disappeared, replaced with the excitement of being back home and seeing his mother.

He ran to the front door and rang the bell. After a few minutes and still no answer, Chris fished out the spare set of keys from under the flower pot and let himself in. He looked around, amazed by the transformation. The house had been painted while he'd been away, and the light in the hallway was burning bright under a new lampshade. Brand-new carpet covered the floor and stairs, and there wasn't a mousetrap to be seen! He dropped his bag and opened the door to the living room. His heart sank. The room had also been decorated, but it wasn't immediately obvious under the layer of grime and mess that covered it. Mugs filled with mold were crammed on the table, fighting for space with old television guides, unopened letters, and junk mail. The television was on, blaring, and, in the corner under a blanket was the curled-up figure of his mother, asleep in the armchair. Chris picked up the remote control and turned the television off. He walked over to his mother, lifted the blanket over her shoulders, and leaned over to give her a kiss. His mother stirred and then opened her eyes slowly.

"Merry Christmas, Mum," said Christopher. "I'm back."

Chris's mother didn't say anything. Instead she sat up and looked around, as if she were trying to remember where she was. Slowly she turned toward him, and her face hardened. Her eyes were cold, her face blank. Chris smiled. His mother looked at him for a moment longer, her expression completely unchanged, and then she turned her head away. At that moment, all the excitement Chris had felt about returning home washed away. He couldn't understand it; he had been sure that everything would be different. They hadn't spoken much while he'd been away, but when they had, she had sounded better—or, perhaps, he now realized, that was just what he had wanted to believe. *Maybe*, he thought, *she hasn't really woken up yet, and when she does, she'll realize how happy she is to have her son home.* But then she spoke, and with that all hope of a new chapter between them completely disappeared.

"Turn the television back on and get me a cup of tea."

Chris opened his mouth to reply. He wanted to shout at her. He wanted to tell her that he needed her to look after him, to comfort him after what he had been through. He wanted to share all the good things that had happened too: everything that he had learned, meeting the prime minister, being invited to the Antarctic Ball, and, most important, that for the first time in his life he had friends. Everything was different for him, but he now knew that for her nothing had changed—her world, whether the house had been decorated or whether he was there or not, was exactly as it had been the day that he had run away. And there was nothing that he could say to change that.

Chris turned away from his mother, picked up the

remote control, and switched the television back on. Then he walked out of the room without a word.

As the sun began to set over the graveyard that lay deep within the grounds of Darkwhisper Manor, Ernest Genever shoveled the last mound of earth over the grave of his brother and leaned on the spade, tears streaming down his face.

"I'm sorry I wasn't there for you, Mortimer. I'm so sorry," he wept, kneeling down on the ground.

In his mind he saw the face of the boy who had killed Mortimer—the boy whose name he had managed to extract before escaping with his brother's body—and his face twisted with rage.

"I swear to you, Mortimer, wherever you are, that I'll get my revenge. Christopher Lane *will* die."

Ernest looked up at the sky and closed his eyes, and a wave of grief and fury washed over him. He opened his eyes and screamed, and the gravestones around him exploded with his anger, sending shards of gray stone raining down over the grave of Mortimer Genever.